LAST SHOT

LAST SHOT

HANK DACE

ISBN-13: 9781977867995
ISBN-10: 1977867995
Library of Congress Control Number: 2017916204
CreateSpace Independent Publishing Platform
North Charleston, South Carolina

*I want to thank the family and friends who have helped with the
writing of my story.
I also want to thank all of the CreateSpace team who helped put
my story into this book form—what a great job they did.
And I want to thank Adelle for all the tireless hours of proofreading
she did to make this book a readable story.
Thank you from the bottom of my heart, each and every one of you.
Hank Dace*

.

CONTENTS

PROLOGUE

I am Paul R. Ford, MD, PPSD, CRE.
This is my case study of Dwight Moore.

He likes to go by Duke and doesn't like to be called Dwight. I wrote his story down while it was fresh in my mind. My hope is that this study will help other veterans in their fight with PTSD. I am sure that would be Duke's wish: to help his fellow veterans.

Duke came to me a tormented soul; he left me still in that state. Duke had a strong mind-set and knew that the disease he had could not be cured. The strongest of all his beliefs was that the pills we dispensed to the veterans were intended to "zombilize" them so society could deal with them.

As a veteran, Duke had a simple way of looking at life, almost an Old Testament way of dealing with his hurt—a biblical, eye-for-an-eye sense of justice. Duke, in his own mind, was an American hero.

I recorded most of our sessions for my own record, and I believe I have transcribed his story with a great deal of accuracy. He becomes hard to follow at times, and you'll have to make your own analysis as to the condition of his mind. Your conclusions may differ from mine, and your conclusions will be as valid as mine.

This is his story.

Duke, a boy of seventeen, leaves home from an abusive family. His dad finds where he is living and haunts him relentlessly every day. For this reason, Duke joins the army two weeks before his eighteenth birthday. He finds there the family he never had. He goes to Officer Candidate School (OCS) and then moves on into the Special Forces. The army, knowing his past, exploited his love for God and country. He hardens with the Vietnam War, and then one day, it's over. He tries to become normal, but normal is not a way of being he has ever known. The boy, an old man in his early twenties, falls in love, bringing some normality to his life. But he has demons, PTSD—was it the army…or his childhood?

Normality quickly leaves his life as he is recruited once again into an elite force, this time not for God and country but for survival. He and his wife fight the good fight in the war on drugs, yet his past is always there to draw him deeper. Finally, at Duke's urging, his wife leaves with their boy, going into hiding out of fear. They all are sought by the very ones who made him the way he is.

PTSD is a life-consuming mental health disease for which no one has the cure. We watch Duke fight the curse of the disease. When he cannot fight it any longer, he goes to his old army doctor, asking for help.

"Doc, I've lost all integrity and compassion, not only for others but for myself. My mind will not let me sleep or, worse than that, enjoy life. It has come to be a constant fight to defend myself from the demons within."

ONE

"Good morning, sir!"

"Good morning, Lieutenant Moore. Duke."

"Good morning, Captain. Cap."

"Listen up, guys. The captain is here to brief us on this little outing we are about to partake in."

"I know you guys were well briefed by Duke. He, I am sure, has gone over the plan in detail. I will give you a brief outline again. If you have any questions, save them until the last. Plan is this: We're going upriver; the SEAL teams are going to make a place for our disembarking. They went in last night and will be waiting in the designated spot to get us on land safely. To deceive the enemy, the boat will dive into the bank every now and again, and as soon as the ship hits land, the pilot will have the engines in full reverse and back out. We will bail off on the third time in. Remember how to do it—off the boat in less than three seconds. Got that?"

"Any questions? Yes, Mike?"

"Sir, did I hear you correctly? The 'we' part? You're going ashore on this one?"

"Yes, the top brass wants me to observe and make sure the targets are marked positively on this mission. An observer is all I am. Duke is still team leader."

"Mike, any more questions? If there are no questions from the rest of the team, then let's get to it. Duke, a word with you in the corner."

"OK, you heard the man. I am still your team leader. Mike, kick them up a notch. Get these guys ready, and have them shred their docs on their way out. Finish stowing your stuff in the packs. Mike, I will catch up with you guys at the departure boat." I turned to face Cap once more. "Cap?"

"Duke, the brass is worried about this mission. No mark against you, but they are concerned. That's all I know. It's above my pay grade, and for some unknown reason, they're crazy scared. That's it, Duke. Just didn't want you to think anything bad, is all."

"Oh hell, Cap, I've known from a long way back that I am—or should I say, that me and my men—are just figures on a clipboard someplace in the Pentagon. Expendables."

Looking at my men leaving the room as I listened to Cap, I was thinking that these guys sure did make me proud to be their leader.

Mike was my number one guy, my spotter. We'd been tighter than fleas on a dog's back now for almost two years. He was a strong guy. He and Tex were built alike—six feet tall and weighing in at around 220 pounds. Both he and Tex could pick up about anything and take off running with it. That was a good thing, as Mike was required to pack a lot of extra ammo for us.

Allen was no slouch, nor were any of my team members. Hell, that was why we were here. We all passed the physical stuff when all the others trying to get into Special Forces failed. Allen was a funny guy, short curly hair, not like any you'd ever seen before—or at least I hadn't. He was only five foot eleven, and at 230 pounds, he was solid as a rock. Saw him mad one day in training with the SEAL team guy he was partnered with in California. He grabbed his partner, lifted him above his head, and threw the guy in the water from the middle of the dock. Hell, that was a good six-foot throw. His partner was fighting him like a wild seal caught in a net. Let me tell you, picking up a guy who's fighting and putting him over your head is pure brute strength, let alone throwing him six feet. Hell, the guy weighed as much as Allen if he weighed a pound.

John, well, he was my question guy. Never ready to hear that that was the way it was. He'd think it through and then back again. I called him my silent killer. Six foot one and seemed to be the weakest of the bunch till one day I heard him say, "Oh, hell!" Then he grabbed a fifty-caliber machine gun off the tank we were using for practice at the shooting range. He took off running with the fifty to a hill of sand around a hundred yards off, put it back down on the bank of sand, put the ammo belt clip back in it, and started shooting again. When he was done, I asked him if he was OK.

"Yeah. Well, the book said we needed to have two placements to surprise the enemy. We all were arguing about what that meant and just how to do that. That's when I said, 'Watch an' learn,' grabbed the fifty, and did just it."

"But, John, that is a mounted fifty, water cooled. It's too heavy to pack around like that."

"Well, hell's bells. No one told me."

Those were my guys. If it needed doing, they didn't wait to draw straws; they just got it done.

Looking back into Cap's eyes, hearing him finish his speech, I thought about who he was. He was a good-looking guy—red hair cut short in a buzz top like he was a marine or something. Hell, he was Special Forces like us. Special Forces, "grab a root an' growl." Six foot one, I reckon, and around 225. Looking him over top to bottom, I sure hoped he held up his part of the team. In Nam, a mistake meant some-one didn't bring his dog tag back by himself.

Cap was now finished with his "let's go get 'em" advice, so we headed into the ship to meet up with our team.

"Dang, Mike, you're the best. Thanks for bringing my gear down with you."

"Sure thing, old man. Don't want you to get worn out before the games get started."

We had finished our training on Coronado Island in San Diego, California. We had done all sorts of stuff with the SEALs two months ago in order to prepare for this mission.

We learned how to disembark from a ship with a full pack on—three seconds flat, and that was it. Let me tell you, those three seconds were a lifetime long. We learned how to tread water with our gear on and then board a fast-moving pontoon ship. It sure the hell was hard work, hoping you didn't drown or get run over by the boat. Looked easy in the movies to grab a moving ship's line and haul yourself on board, but let me tell you, it wasn't. No retakes here. You made it, or you drowned. We learned how to make a life preserver out of our pants while swimming under water. Now *that* was a chore. Those SEAL guys were the best, and they were more fish than men.

"Duke, where were you? Did you hear me? Which side you want?"

"What? Huh?" I was jarred back to reality. "You pick, Mike. Doesn't matter. You like the left best, so take it. I just hate getting all wet before we even get started."

"Mike, these SEAL guys, while they're good—I'll give them that, no doubt about it—I'm still having a hard time getting my head around so many eyes out there seeing what we're doing."

"Yes, I know, Duke. We need them, every last effin' one of them. Hell, I might drown with this oversized pack. And then there's Cap."

"What about him?"

"You looking after him, or should I?"

"Until we get to shore and have our gear ready and are in line for our walk, we both better look after him. He's cool, but neither of us has been around him in a firefight. I say we keep him in the middle. What do you say?"

"Sounds good to me, Duke."

"Hey, Cap, how you doing? You OK? Are you good with this going into the bush with us? Come here, and let's go over what's been bothering me. Look at the map with me one more time before destroying it."

The three of us huddled over the scrap of paper, and Mike pointed to our planned landing point.

"That's correct, Mike. We are going in some place in this area. From there, we walk about twenty miles. Now, this is where the hair on the back of my neck stands up. This point here is where we should find a village. There in the middle, the halfway point to our objective. Friendlies, they say. I don't like it, Cap, not one damn bit. No, sir, not one damn iota. Going into the village doesn't help our end game one little smidgen. What's the sense of this? The more eyes that see us, know we are out there, the higher the percentage of failure we are exposed to."

The other two were silent. I sighed and scratched my head.

"Mike, I say we walk around the village staying quiet, no more eyes and ears than necessary. What do you think, Cap? Mike?"

No response.

"Look, you guys, I know what I'm asking here: some more miles under our belt, maybe ten or twelve. But our team is strong at the terrain we're going to be exposed to. I would rather try and make up some time. Besides, we're to have a Vietnam regular help us in the marking along with you, Cap. Hell, maybe he'll know a shortcut. I just don't want a firefight with some village that is not friendly when they are supposed to be. We all know that happens more times than not, right? Look at the terrain again. Some damn big hills, so we'll have to stay low, walk around them. We just need to stay away from well-beaten trails. That's the smart move in my book. You guys in agreement with me?"

"Hell yes, Duke, hell-l-l yes!"

"Cap, you've been quiet all this time. What're you thinking?"

"You're the leader. Never been a quiet church mouse before, but you're the leader, and so far you never failed. I don't want to fail, and I

5

sure as hell don't want any fingers pointing to me as the one who said to go against your better judgment. Hell yes. And, like Mike said, hell-l-l yes! Damn straight. We're with you all the way, Duke."

"Mike, before we leave the trail near dusk, brief the men again on how to use their insight, not their compass. Remember, take a reading on your compass, spot a place on the horizon that we're walking toward, and then, when it's dark, you can always see your spot. Sun sets in the west; so does the moon. Put two hands off the right side of the moon, and you're close to west. Remember that so you're not lost. If you can find west and face it, you know where the rest of the world is supposed to be, correct? It's better to have two points of reference, but one is better than none. I don't want any lights on; even the dimmest light can be seen for a thousand yards. No looking at your compass after dark. Not a thing to give us away. No talking. We are Indians, remember that—quiet like church mice. Two points and you won't need to see your compass. Don't worry, you won't walk in a circle like most do when they're lost. Besides, we're never lost—just not where we're supposed to be at that given moment. Got it? We are never lost! Keep your reference in mind—twenty-five yards apart—and keep track of the guy behind as well as the one in front. Do we all know the signal to stop and the signal to bunch up if someone is straggling behind or whatever you think we need to stop or bunch up for? Silence is our weapon of choice. Let's use it to our full advantage."

At 0400, the big bay doors of the ship opened, and the big pumps screamed to life as they began flooding the dry bay. With the riverboat now afloat, the navy captain looked at me and motioned all aboard.

"OK, boys, let's mount up!"

Mike threw our gear on board and heaved other gear on board with the navy guys. He looked like he was in a hurry and had done this before. I knew he wasn't, but I just watched as I walked up to the helm and addressed the navy captain.

"Captain of the navy?"

"Yes?"

"Don't you guys know that there is enough metal in this world to go around so we don't have to ride in these old fiberglass laminated plywood antiques?"

"Lieutenant, let me tell you, fiberglass-reinforced plywood is the best thing in these waters. Mines don't go off as easily when they're hit by a plywood boat as they would from getting hit by a metal boat, so be happy about that. The gooks like to try their best to mine these waters every night!"

The ship's captain turned, looked at Cap, and then swung back, turning slightly away from me to address my team as well as his own crew.

"All right, everyone, listen up. I know you guys are loaded for an extended stay, but don't panic when you disembark. The crew will help you. As it stands now, we will have you jump off after the third time in. The wave from this ship will put you to shore if you don't panic and do like you were trained. In training, you were given three seconds. I have my hands full trying to keep this old tub afloat, so you'll be lucky to have two seconds. Get your army asses off my boat, because I am not going to be watching you. The best thing for you is to get your timing down in your head on the two dummy runs so you know when to disembark at the exact second it is needed."

He didn't ask if anyone had questions; he just turned back to the bridge and fired those monster engines up.

The ship was old and smelled musty, even through the fresh paint, creaky like old stairs. I could see cracked, splintered boards here and there from some firefights. Bullet holes riddled the top planking. The armor around the front gunner as well as the back had a lot of bullet dents—some so close to the muzzle coming out of it that it made you wonder how many gunners had seen their Waterloo. The top gunner's armor above the bridge was a real mess—its twin thirties' armor was so peppered up it looked like a backing plate at a shooting gallery. Lucky for that gunner, he was inside an armored turret that he crawled into from underneath a ladder by the captain. Once inside, the hatch closed with twin belts of ammo coming up from both sides of his seat.

The captain had a small slit to look out of when he wasn't peering over the top of his armor. Everywhere I looked, I could see this wooden boat had been shot from every angle. Yes, he had his hands full keeping this old tub afloat and everyone in it alive. When we hit the waves, it sounded like she was going to break in two. No, thank you. I will stay on land, where I have a better chance to shoot back and more places to hide. These boys and their boats were just moving targets in a shooting gallery. No, thank you; no, sir!

The best parts of the ship were her big inline Detroit-Allison motors. They were purring along; you could feel the horses beneath your feet. Now this was a job I could sink my teeth into: working with some real power like these engines had.

The navy captain motioned to Cap and me. We stood up and moved forward to the bridge to hear what he had to say.

"Men, got a message from the command ship. Looks like they got a message from the SEAL team. It now stands not at three but at number five, got that? Everyone pat your buddy on the back and make sure you're all ready. The river is deeper at that spot, and that might be the reason they want us to move upriver some. Don't know; don't care. They're good at what they do. That's why we do as they say."

Cap and I headed back to deliver the news to our team.

"Men, we're going in on number five. You hear me? Going in on five, not three. Hold up your hand so I know you're ready."

They all gave me five fingers, so I knew they were good with all the changes. I signaled for everyone to check their buddy's gear, a system we used before a jump, and it never left your brain, as your buddy was your lifeline to survival.

I made sure Mike's gear was good, and then Mike checked mine. As the navy captain backed the ship out for the second time, I held up three fingers; they all did the same. They knew as well as I did that this was it—we were committed.

The captain sure could make those engines scream as we skimmed down the river and then threw them into reverse before we hit the bank. He was treading water and backing out so fast; it was pure art of impeccable timing watching this navy guy do his thing. To be a part of it was just amazing!

The front gunner was shooting high into the trees, from around four or five feet above ground to near the tops at twenty or thirty feet high. If there were any snipers in there, they were dead meat. The top gunner was making a hell of a mess out of those trees as well. He was firing a navy twin thirty millimeters, and the two barrels were like one shot. As one recoiled, the other shot. Shoot, recoil; shoot, recoil. It was bang! bang! uninterrupted on full auto, a dual feed from each side with the ammo belts coming down to the main floor. It seemed like this could go on forever, as one of the navy mates was constantly hooking new belts to the old ones. Those two barrels glowed red in the early morning air.

The back gunner was watching the river behind us. He shot only once in a while, just to keep his barrel warm, I think. I never saw anything he was aiming at, but he seemed to be shooting a little high as well.

Every time the boat captain turned his wheel a slight bit toward the shore, the shells started ripping through the air, cutting the trees to shreds. I was mesmerized by the accuracy of their impeccable timing. The ship went in and out from shore, guns ripping the still-early morning air. They had the rhythm down to a fine art, like two dancers I would love watching in the movies—each one knowing his/her place and when to shift with his/her partner. I was just amazed to be a part of this work of art. How the gooks would know whether a team was dropped or not was impossible, because every time we went into shore, it was the same dance with never a missed step, never a misplaced shell. Pure art of teamwork. The navy captain told us there were two ships in front of us and one behind doing the same thing, so that no one but us and the SEAL team knew when anyone was dropped or where.

Each boat was secret to the other missions. The navy thought like I did: fewer eyes, less knowledge to be leaked if something went bad.

Did we drop a team then or not? The gooks would never have their heads up long enough to look with this much lead cutting through the trees, through the grass. Willy Petes were what the navy called their white phosphorous rounds. The twin thirties kicked out their Willy Petes with no rhyme or reason to anyone but the gunner and his mate. Then, at the precise moment when the boat was square with the bank, that's when the front gunner began his dance with the fifty caliber. Every fifth round he spit from his barrel was a tracer helping cut, burn, and make the bank of the river seem like a Fourth of July fireworks show.

Firepower, that was it. We could land a team every time, anywhere we wanted; they would never know. Who would dare look? And after we left this spot, we headed to the next, to the next; on and on we danced down the river with engines screaming. I was so proud of being part of this team. A team that fought and died, not for God and country, as they say in the funny papers, but for one another. Yes, each another. Die for me, and me for you.

If one member of the team were a split second off in the dance, we would die. We would all die. God, was I proud to be with each and every man there.

The navy captain held up one finger. The next one was our time. I was so uptight, having new blood with us on shore. Yet, like this boat crew, we had our timing down, so we never missed our step. Our dance was different yet the same—no missed cues, no misplaced shells. Dang, we were as good as it got, and that was why we were all here doing this dance together.

The head gunner, Steve, told me during the briefing that they do this routine, this dance, day in and day out. They have the steps down to such a timing that when they do drop, no one knows for sure when or where—not just gooks but other boats as well. As we sped up the river to the next spot, we could see the brush burning we left behind, the tracer rounds starting more fires than an arsonist with two full jerricans of gas.

"OK, guys, wake the fuck up. Get your knees under you, ready to launch yourself into the water. Don't panic, now, men. Wait for the wave to slap you to shore. Land on your back; the water will do the rest. Remember, the shore party is ours. Don't shoot until I give the word or you see me busting caps."

The boat made its turn toward shore, guns blazing, shooting higher now so as not to hit our own party. "OK, we're going in. Ready. Jump! Jump!"

The water was warm. I expected it to be cold, like in California where we trained. I was almost out of air when my feet hit the sand, and I was kneeling in waist-deep water. Looking around, I saw that everyone was OK—Cap and then Mike to my left. Good job, Mike, keeping him between us. Tex in front of me and Allen; John to my right. Good, we were all off that sitting duck of a ship. Where the hell was our greeting party? I motioned to spread out, and they were already doing everything by instinct now that we were all on the bank.

We lay down in the brush. There was no sign of the SEAL team. So we crawled to the first big set of trees, around twenty yards in, and the smoke from the fires was starting to clear some. Still couldn't see any sign of the SEAL team—no sign, no bodies, no markings of any kind, no foxholes, nothing. They were making me very nervous now. Where the fuck *were* those guys? I gave the hand signal to shoulder the forty-fives and open the dabs to take out our rifles. Everything was double sealed against the water. The Navy SEALs had taught us well on how to use their dabs to keep our rifles and clips dry, and with ease we had them out and ready for the firefight. Still no sign of the SEALs. I looked at Mike and then Cap. They shrugged their shoulders at me.

The captain crawled to me with a bewildered look on his face, his skin red as if he were mad—and not just his face but his whole body that was exposed was red. Or was he just scared like the rest of us? That's all I needed now was for him to panic, pull rank, and want to call the mission off or, worse yet, make my team start second-guessing me.

"What the hell, Duke?"

"What the hell, Cap?"

"You think they're dead?"

"I don't know, Cap. If they are, we're in deep shit. Let's move out and get ready for a fight."

When I motioned for the other four to fan out more than their five yards; they knew it wasn't supposed to be this way. Now, with fifteen yards apart, I didn't need to tell them we were in for a big fight. We readied our ammo and extra clips, and we took our water-sack dabs and stuffed it into our pouches. Locked and loaded, we belly crawled in a line from tree to tree. I looked at Cap, Mike, and then John. I motioned for the team to come to me at the next big termite hill. At the termite hill, we conferred and all agreed: none of us had seen a sign, let alone any of our greeting party. Not one bloomin' sign.

"Here's what I'm thinking. If the SEAL team had a fight at the third spot, that's why they sent us up ahead. We're on our own, guys. I don't want to move fast till we have some distance from the river, at least another five hundred yards, so Mike, Tex, and I will go up front. John, you grab Allen and bring up the rear. Leave Cap in the middle to keep an eye on both teams. OK, you guys, let's do this."

We needed to move out. Crawling in this shit was bad news, and our clothing was all wet. And I was one mad SOB. And couldn't they break radio enough to call the ship before we left? What the effing hell was up? The five hundred yards was a day out of our lives trying to crawl and be quiet. Finally, I came to a small clearing, and we grouped up there.

"Cap, you're in charge. What you want to do?"

"No, Duke, you're the team leader. I take my orders out here from you. I was just to be an observer, remember?"

"OK, Cap, then when I bark at these guys, you need to know as they do. I don't want anyone hurt. No offence, correct? You all carried your dog tags in. You all carry them back out. Agreed?"

We planned to change out of our wet clothes when we'd met up with the SEAL team, but for now, there was no stopping. We crawled wet. What a bitch of a deal, a surefire way to get our skin chapped.

We crawled over sticks, dead brush, thick stuff I'd never seen before—thicker than the blackberry thickets back in north Washington State. I was getting about fed up with this shit when I heard some movement in front of us.

I made a signal to Mike to pass on back: "We got company. Don't know who yet, but be ready." I crawled over to a damn big termite hill, biggest I ever saw—must have been ten feet in diameter and six high—when someone said, "Mate," from the other side. My response code was *asshole*, but he didn't sound like an American, and I didn't respond. Again I heard it: "Mate." I knew it was English, but it was spoken with a gook accent.

"Asshole."

"Good. I come your spot. Keep cool. No move. No shoot me, mate."

I pulled a grenade. Had the pin out. Shaking scared. Hate this shit. Caught a glimpse of Mike. He was locked, loaded, veins in his neck bulging, finger on the trigger, and aiming in front of me, ready to shoot if he thought I was in danger. Hell, he must be scared, to have his finger on the trigger, ready to go. He had never tensed up this tight in all the years and missions I had known him.

A gook crawled around the side of the termite hill, grinning with all his dirty, yellow, tobacco-stained teeth, when he saw me with a forty-five in one hand and a grenade in the other.

He started speaking English with that gook accent so fast that it was hard for me to tell what the hell he was saying. I knew he was scared now, as the sweat was beading on his splotchy, peeling, light brown, sunburned forehead and face.

"Hold on there, asshole. This is correct password. I no enemy. Just me. I here to help guide you to safe spot. Your mates are behind you. They had a big firefight last night, but no one shot. Hit us hard. They are still there to hold down the area so you won't have any more danger. Hi, asshole. Name is Charlie. Not funny, yes? Your general called me that last year. He couldn't say my real name, so he called me Charlie. OK. You put gun down now."

"Not till I see some papers from you, OK?"

"I Colonel Charlie. Yes, I have papers for you, GI. They call you captain, yes?"

"Yes. You call me that; that's fine. OK, your papers are in order."

Mike crawled up beside me as I struggled to put the pin back in the grenade.

"Give me that thing before we all get blown to kingdom come."

"The SEAL team is hung up. We're on our own," I told him, watching him put the pin in with ease.

"So it seems, Duke. So it seems."

"Looks like Colonel Charlie here is our tour guide."

He gave Mike that big, dirty, toothy grin with a sense of relief as Mike hung the grenade back on my suspenders. Mike smiled back, the veins in his neck ready to pop still. Must be like me: hates this close-quarters dagger shit. And then they nodded at each other. I whispered to Mike to tell Cap that Charlie thought I was Cap.

"Tell Cap let's play Charlie's game. Hope Cap is cool with that. If not, bring him forward, and he can take point."

"Colonel Charlie, I'll call you Colonel C from here on out, yes? Where is our first stop to unload this gear? I can tell you smoke. You need to hide your smokes and lighter in this termite hill. No smoking on my team. You got that, Colonel C?"

"Yes. I hide smokes but keep lighter. It's OK, yes? First stop about a day's walk from here—not far, you will see. Yes, keep lighter? Yes? It is OK, yes? I have for long time. My dad's lighter. I get from him when he died. Yes? OK?"

"Yeah, sure, it's OK. But I tell you, take it out of your pocket and act like you're going to use it, and I'll shoot you in the ear. Yes, you OK with that, yes, OK?"

Mike brought in the rest of the guys. He had already told them that Colonel Charlie here would lead us and thought I was the captain.

"Yes, yes. I will lead. Nice walk from here. Nice walk, you will see."

"Mike, stay in line, and have everyone all step in each other's tracks. Briefing said lots of old land mines put in this area from the French. For the first mile inland, maybe more, stay alert, men. Stay the hell alert. Let's go, Colonel C."

We walked for around four hours, footstep into footstep, meticulously walking step by step through brush and grass, around bamboo trees, staying off the beaten path. Easier going the farther inland we went, sure as hell easier, but far from a cakewalk. The team was amazingly quiet. They knew I didn't like this situation, so they were on their toes as much as I was.

When I figured we had made it about halfway to where we would ditch our gear, we took a short break. It was around noon, and the walking was easier for sure. I figured we were still behind the eight ball on this outing, but so far so good. I looked at my team as they watered and dewatered. They looked a mess, their wet clothing sticking to them. To hurry wasn't the answer. We could make up time someplace—where, I hadn't figured out yet. We were making steady time, so no need to change clothes yet. We would do it at the ditch of gear, as we called it. Yes, then we would take food, change, get down to just the necessities of the game—extra ammo always. It was just our nature to have more ammo with us than the book said was allowed, but the guy who wrote that book had never been out here with us—if he had ever been on a mission at all.

We hadn't been walking again for more than a half hour when John signaled to us from his rear position to bunch up. Seems he had heard someone coming up on us, dogging us from ten yards or so to our flank. John was factual but very concerned that we were being followed, maybe about two hundred to three hundred yards back.

"Mike, you guys go with Colonel C. I'll stay back and go poop, if you get my drift, OK? And watch that gook—he wasn't supposed to be out here on his own. In all the briefing I was in, he was supposed to be with the SEAL team. He could be part of an ambush, so keep him close. If he asks about me, tell him I needed to poop. Take off."

"OK, Duke, will do. But we'll go no more than around three to four hundred yards and then stop to wait for you. You got thirty minutes, then we dig in for a fight. We'll be here for whatever happens."

"Nice. Mike, remember the birdcall? I'll use that for signaling when I get close. Got it?"

"Sure, I remember. Been working on them, for sure."

I hunch-walked back to Allen. Looking at John, I nodded to him, saying, "Good job, kid, good job. Now, go to Mike and do whatever he says till I get there. Let's go, Allen. We'll walk back a bit and see if we can set up a nice welcome for whoever is dogging us."

We walked a few yards. I looked over my shoulder, and the group was already gone. We both hunch-walked back a little to where we were concealed in tall grass, downed dead bamboo, and some other kind of trees. We could see down the path for about, oh, say, fifty yards. Kind of a clearing in front of us, not far enough for this sniper to feel good about. My earlier kills had always been at a farther distance for, so this would be a first.

"Now, Allen, don't panic. Just keep low, and don't shoot, even if I do—not till you can see the whites of their eyes, as the old story goes from our forefathers. I don't know if our tracker will be a scout or what, so if there are a lot of them, you'll see me shooting like hell, and then you can join in anytime. But I might elect to just pop one and see, so don't tip your spot away. Got it?"

"Yeah, sure, Duke, sure, but...Oh, I see. You're putting on your silencer. OK, got ya. I'm going behind that log and watch. I'll make sure they don't try and circle us, OK?"

"Yep, that's good. Watch both our backs, and I'll take care of the front."

We watched for what seemed like an hour, and still there was no movement. Damn, John, what did you see, hear? Was it a pig or a rabbit? I knew we were on high alert, adrenaline running wild in our veins, but what did you hear, John?

Then I saw something moving. Couldn't make it out. Very slow and deceptive along our trail to the side, about three to four yards off. I looked at Allen, and he made the "all's clear" sign. I hand-signaled back, "Something coming up the trail three to four yards to our right side. Be ready."

Now it was about one or two yards on my right side of the trail. Keep alert over there, city boy. Stay jacked up on your adrenaline—it's all you got. It was still about one or two yards to the side of the trail, being very sneaky. I could have dropped him anytime, but I was still not sure about him. Looked like a jungle fighter, maybe another gook—not sure yet. He was now about ten yards from me, and I knew he was one of ours. I could smell the difference at this close proximity.

"I say, there, mate, got a smoke?"

He fell so hard I thought he was having a heart attack. I looked at his greased face; that must be what I smelled.

"No, don't smoke, asshole!"

"Well, mate, sure could have used a nice smoke for an old asshole like me! Come on in. Keep low. You alone?"

"Yeah, sure. Fuck, you just took the life right out of me, mate. Dang, I think I might have broken a rib on that dead bamboo stick."

I motioned to Allen to stay low and out of sight, to watch us, not move, and be very cautious until I give the signal for whatever way this was going down.

"Was following you guys since you met up with that gook, Charlie. We had a rough time of it about two nights ago. We were able to hold the river spot but had to dig in deep to the mud, just like toads. Good thing they didn't have the best weapons. Don't know if we could have held them off otherwise. Killed around thirty-five of the dirty little bastards. Anyway, that's when we made the decision for you to move upriver two more spots to disembark.

"Here is all we know: not a lot of info, but every drop helps, and we must maintain radio silence. Think they have our frequency and are listening. If you have a radio, I would say don't use it—not now, anyway. There are a lot of Charlies out and about, around thirty-five to forty in a bunch, looking for what we can only guess. Seems they're intent to get someplace.

"We think they're getting ready for a big push. Not sure yet, but there are a lot of them moving around. That's as much as we can tell you. They are thick as thieves in and around the river. Best guess is they're going to try and hijack our barges so they can get our weapons, but don't know for sure yet. When I left, our interpreter was still talking to some we captured. They're not talking much. They will soon, though; we sent for some Aussies.

"The Aussies will take them back to their camp and will have them singing like long-lost friends soon after. They're a nasty bunch, them Aussies. Been told the reason the Aussies cut the ears off their kill, always the left ear, is that the Australian government gives them a bounty for each one. Dirty bastards. The Aussies hang the ears around their necks. Now, that is plain gross! Just wanted you to know they're out there, so get farther inland as soon as you can. Here, remember this: the new pass code is going to change in one week's time. Don't expect to see you before then, so here it is: *mule, jackass.* Got it? *Mule, jackass.* That's funny, don't you think?"

While he was talking, I motioned for Allen to come on over.

He was surprised to see Allen and said so. "Must be getting old."

Mostly thinking out loud, I assumed, as he wasn't looking at us but at the ground as he shook his head. "I hate this cat-and-mouse sort of shit. Hate it." He then told Allen the new pass code and said it was going to be in a week's time.

My Seiko self-winding watch made a sound as I popped its cover open and checked the time and date.

"So, you're saying that it goes into effect on Monday. How often do you change it around if we get caught out here for more than a few days?"

"Good till you get back."

"OK, got it. Good till we get back. That's nice to know."

"Then we'll change it to something even more humorous, bet ya," he said with a grin.

"Where you from, mate?" I asked.

"Chicago, the Windy City."

"That's nice. I hate the wind, but it's nicer than this place anytime."

"Yup, mate, it is that. Good luck on your mission, whatever it is. Just glad it's you and not me. Oh, by the way, that Charlie is one of the best guys they have. You can trust him for sure. He will die with you if need be. Been shot up some but still a real go-getter. Listen to him, and you might make it. Good luck, mate, and thanks. You better give those smokes up out here, ya asshole." And with that, he was gone into the brush, this time quiet as a church mouse.

I whistled like a songbird, and sure as hell, Mike gave a nice one back. Missed me, didn't ya, Mike? Allen and I caught up with Mike and Colonel C.

"Colonel C, it was one of my mates that Allen and I just had a pow-wow with. He's gone now. Said you were OK, so if he likes you, we like you. First order of business: we need to find that spot to unload this extra gear, dry off, and change our clothes. You, too, Colonel C. You smell like cigarettes. Can smell you a mile away. We need to eat some food, restock our water, and go over the mission that you want us to provide some help with. OK, what you say, Colonel C? You're the boss."

"What 'boss' mean?"

"You're in charge. You tell us what you want us to do to help you complete the mission."

"OK, we go about another three or four hours, and we be at my safe place. No patrols there. It's a burying ground. They don't like. They have lots of superstition of the burying ground. If they spot our digging, they will not look. They think us crazy for not burning our dead like they do. We go now, yes?"

The walk was easier the farther inland we walked. It was also a lot hotter then—and as humid as being back at Fort Benning, training in what the army called Little Vietnam. What a story that was. Finally, we arrived at the spot Colonel C liked. Sure as shit, like he said, an old burying ground for the French. Who would have thought it? His dad was a French soldier buried here in this cemetery.

He wouldn't go look at either of the headstones of his parents buried side by side. Bad sign, bad omen, he believed. If something did happen to him, we could bring him here and release his soul to be with the souls of his mom and dad. They had died together many years ago. Too much pain to reminisce, he said. I asked him what happened to his folks, why they died.

"My dad, he French Foreign Legion, and my mom, she housekeeper at mansion. That where my dad be commander of the French troops to protect estate from locals that threatened to attack the plantation of the French. My mom and he, my dad, they love each other very much, so I was made.

"They married under protest of her father, but with me in her belly, it was not very loud protest. My dad was well liked by the locals after that, and things were pretty calm till I was around twelve years of age. Then some villagers had a dispute about the French—they say didn't pay them for the land, was not paying all their wages, also stealing their portion of the food.

"French say something to do with bad crops, villagers not good workers. So I was told French not able to pay. One night, villagers sneaked into the plantation and killed the guards, the whole house of workers, and my mother's parents as well. The French masters die in their beds. My father and mother wake up with the screaming and gunfire, and my mom took me with her to the old cellar.

"My parents' house was behind the mansion. My mom, she hear them fighting upstairs with my dad. She was crying. Tells me to be quiet and stay down in the hiding, and she runs to my dad. They shot him, both of them, dead. Before they shoot my mom, they have lots of evil fun with her. She not scream like other ladies; she too brave and don't want them to know where she had me hid.

"The good villagers from a place beyond the hills," he said, pointing south to the hills, "took me there, to my mom's brother's family. They raised me, and when I was old enough, I went to the French government in Saigon.

"French government sent me to military school. I get my dad's pension still this day from the French, and now I am his rank as well. That why I hate the North. They ones that killed my mom, my dad.

"But while I was in the cellar, I could hear them having fun with my mom. If I knew their names, I would have wanted to kill them all. But was in military school, so couldn't go shoot them. You can trust me. I good Charlie soldier. I find their names in military records, same ones now we go kill. I wait long time for this. I good man. I get them now, see them die."

I listened to his story and didn't believe a word of it. Colonel C's eyes didn't match his mouth. Mike and Cap as well as John and Allen were sucking it all in. Tex and I, well, we just listened. I thought, We'll see how good a soldier he really is when the fighting starts. And it will. It always does.

We ate, watered up, dewatered, redid our supplies, dug our hole, and buried our stash. And then we moved it out. Colonel C and I had a talk as Mike took point. Seemed we were going to an old farmhouse—not the one where Colonel C was born but a different one. The one where he was born had burned down many years ago. We were going to outbuildings of a long-ago plantation—workers' housing that had been owned by the French.

The house where the two men were selling information to the North was well built, fortified by the North. They had used this house for many years, it seemed, for meetings about trying to get into the arms race. Colonel C knew both men from pictures at the French military school. The same ones we had looked at in our briefings.

The French military had tracked their movements for years but had never had the manpower to act on it. Then, as America took up the fight, the French moved out. It seems these men had been French trained in that same military school.

The rub was not whether they believed the South should or should not be independent but that they shouldn't have taken the knowledge from the French military school and sold it to the North along with arms they got from Russia. That made them traitors and spies in everyone's eyes.

They were being blamed for many deaths, and as French naturalized citizens, it put everyone in a tight jam. Colonel C wanted every last one of them shot and would like to have them more than shot. He wanted their teeth for his pocket as well as the teeth of all the men who were with them. That was why he was so disappointed at the size of our group.

I told Colonel C we could shoot only the men marked and only those others we had to just to protect our own hide. That was all the mission was about. Colonel C asked if he could shoot others there who were also bad. Told him there was nothing in my orders to stop him from shooting anyone he liked.

"I tell you, Colonel Charlie, look at me, and listen well. If you put me or my men in harm's way, I will not hesitate to shoot you at that very moment."

He looked at me and then laughed. "You shoot me but not other bad guys. That make me laugh."

"All the same, Colonel C, I tell you now, don't underestimate me. I will do as I say, and any of my men will do it as well."

The grin left his face, and his face became hard. It was a face I had seen many times after a target was shot. A face that understood that death was closer than it could ever have imagined. A face that knew it was drawing its last breath.

We walked for two more days. Not as tiring as before now that we had dry clothing and lighter packs. We didn't take a path. The best way, Colonel C said, and for me, I really liked that way of doing things. The North patrolled all the roads and trails. Even with limited aircraft, they watched as best they could.

So far, no aircraft had been overhead. Colonel C said he thought that was a good sign, that the targets were feeling safe in their little haven, which meant we could shoot them very easily. He asked if we could sneak in and blow them all up, but he knew that wouldn't happen. Not this time. Not with our limited attack force.

Would be lots of regulars around, but if we shot their commander, Colonel C believed the regulars would go back north until they were regrouped under another leader. Could mean as many as four or five months.

All I asked of Colonel C was that we be at least a half mile away, five hundred to eight hundred meters away, uphill some would be very nice, so that we could get a good look at their entire layout. He questioned me, thought a half mile was too far away. I showed him my big sniper rifle, the one I called Old Betsy, giving her a nice pat on her butt. He really wanted to make sure those guys were left truly dead. If we missed, it might be the last time we ever saw them again. They would disappear forever, he feared.

Mike said to Colonel C, "He doesn't miss—not with that big gun. We could be a kilometer away, and Duke could get them all."

Colonel C was afraid we would fail. We walked on, putting him at point. When we reached the spot, we stopped, and I took a look. Colonel C wanted to sneak closer, but I said no.

We positioned our guys around us. I told Cap to stay back and wait till we were in position. We crawled the next hundred yards to a nice spot that I liked a lot: a sniper's dream spot—lots of cover yet enough openings to see everything. With Colonel C getting nervous about the distance we were from the targets, I told him he could watch through the spotting scope. That made him a bit easier to deal with. When he saw the targets sitting on the porch drinking tea, I could see the beads of sweat come to his face, just like the first time we'd met. Then that death look surfaced again.

I was not sure what he thought he saw. He tried to jump up, but Mike grabbed him in time before he gave our position away, body-slamming him to the ground so hard he didn't move for quite some time. We knew he was all right, as he was blinking and watching us set up our gear.

At this distance, I wanted to have the best control of my shots, so on the end of my silencer I put the muzzle break for more weight. I didn't want Old Betsy to do any jumping. With this cover, we would be almost impossible to spot from the targets' position anyway. I was nervous as hell, looking for signs of a path the patrols were walking. With that in mind, I sent Tex to look around and see if any lookouts were in this area. If there were any lookouts, they would have to be our first order in this nasty business. Then I sent Mike to have the guys do a little recon on their own as well. The targets were too calm down there. Dirty Commie bastards. Didn't they know there was a war going on here?

Finally, Colonel C sat up. "Sorry," he said. "It has been a long time coming to this part of my life. I just want them dead—dead forever, like my parents are dead. Sorry lost my head for a moment. Won't happen again. I have been hunting these guys for so long that it was almost too much for me, seeing them. Do you know what I say or feel? It has been many years that I wanted this chance!"

"Remember what I told you, Colonel C. I shoot you if you put me or any one of us in harm's way. Remember, next time I just shoot, or worse, I put my knife in your throat. I eat your heart raw while it still beats in my hand. So be good, Charlie, or die here all alone."

Mike and Tex both returned.

"All good, Duke. Back door closed. Looks like we're alone—as much as we can be out here."

"Thanks, Tex."

Looking at me, he must have seen my anger building as I nodded at Colonel C. With a nod back, Mike took over taking care of Colonel C. Mike knew how I needed to get in the moment before a long shot. He started explaining the process to Colonel C and letting him help so he could get into it, measuring the air, the humidity, the wind, and the elevation above sea level. All that could make a bullet fly more accurately—or make me miss the target.

"We don't take any chances, Colonel C. We just pop them and then get the hell out of here, so what we need from you is positive ID."

Colonel C got back on the scope and did that. Then he asked a weird question: Could he pull the trigger? I looked at Mike and said, "He must be fuckin' kidding me. Fuck, no, Colonel C! But we will tell everyone that you shot them both." Boy, he was fine with that. I could really see the spark come back into his face. Then we brought the captain up to make sure of the targets. Colonel C was surprised that I was not the captain.

We were ready, and Colonel C told us that the two men at the table were not the big brass. The big brass must have gone back inside. So we waited.

Mike had Colonel C read the numbers from the scope chart that pops up when everything is in focus. "Duke, six hundred and twenty-three meters. Wind, two clicks to the right. Elevation clicks, four up."

Colonel C was enjoying being part of our team. Finally, he said the man who had just come out was the main man. Then another came out, followed by two women. "They are local ladies," he said. "We should shoot them because they're not nice ladies."

We laughed at him, and he became red faced.

"You Americans like to fuck our ladies, don't you?"

"Well, we don't deny that, but for sure we don't do that. We respect you and your people."

The women had walked back inside. They must have been making tea for the brass. As the women went back inside, I looked at Mike and then the captain. The targets were affirmed, and Cap went back to his post.

"Colonel C, which one you want shot first?"

"Big, bad guy."

"Mike?"

"Duke, it's your call. Which one do you want first?"

"You can number them, Colonel C. I will do it in your order."

And I popped them in Colonel C's order. He was amazed at how easy it was to watch from here, and no one even knew. Then the women came back out and started to scream, so I looked at Mike.

"Your call, Duke."

"Colonel C?"

"Shoot them all. It will help us get away."

The women fell on their lovers as they were looking at them. Hope that last time was the best one; they were all in heaven together now.

Mike handed me a Willy Pete. "Let's get this place ablaze. Could really confuse them."

I took the one he handed me, and I lit the place up. There must have been some kind of gas bottle or something inside the building that we couldn't see.

We picked up our gear and made our way out. John and Allen brought up the back door, making sure we weren't followed. To make certain of this, we went about a half day's fast walk, almost a run, before we stopped and regrouped. Tex took off, scouting the back door even farther back, maybe a mile or so.

"Duke."

"Tex."

"No one is following us close enough to count."

"Good deal."

We finished eating our rations, watered, and dewatered, ready to head out again.

TWO

MAKING OUR WAY BACK TO THE SEAL TEAM

"Good job, guys. Colonel C is happy. He made some great shots out there."

They all looked at one another and then grinned as they understood why the credit went where it did.

We knew we had a long haul back to the burying ground, and the closer we came to it, the more we would encounter the patrols. Stragglers mostly, I was thinking, as we lay in the tall elephant grass.

"Tex, what's up with you?"

"I don't like this, Duke. Not one damn bit do I like this. Bad feeling I got. Do you feel it?"

"Yes, I do, Tex. What you got in mind?"

"I say we skedaddle this place and forgo picking up our stash. Hell, if these jungle monkeys pick up our trail, we're done for."

"Got it, Tex. I'm thinking the same as you."

We talked about our options. Cap, Mike, Tex, and I agreed we should make a wide circle. Colonel C wanted to get the stash. We finished watering up and dewatering.

"You guys ever find the guy who made the C rations, let me know. I will cut one of his fingers off. Dang, I hate this shit, and I don't care how much they say it's good for us. Let's move in five more. You guys ready?"

Some guys will tell you they have to piss bad during a firefight. Not me or the guys I served with. You're so high on adrenaline that all your blood goes to your brain. You never think about pissing. Afterward, yes, when you come down. Sometimes I amazed myself by how much I really could piss. Seemed like a gallon.

One guy I knew during training at Fort Benning, Georgia, well, he didn't dewater when the rest of us did. Said he didn't have the urge then. The story was that when we hit the little stream we had to cross, he let it go. Could smell him a mile coming up on you. That's the story, as told to me.

So, we decided we had enough ammo at present, seeing we hadn't shot much—just seven shots from Old Betsy. To avoid the dig—smart move, I was thinking—we moved around it. We were low on water and C rations, but we did have our backup survival food, our last-resort food. Colonel C was hesitant at first, but later he said it was fine with him. He could go back at another time, dig it up, and use it. We didn't care. As far as we were concerned, if the army wanted it back, they could send someone for it.

Colonel C set out in the lead, followed by me, Tex, Mike, and then the captain. John and Allen held back around fifty yards with a twenty-five-yard spacing to close the door. I was starting to like these guys a lot. A bad feeling for me because I knew that if I got attached, then something would change my mind. It had the last time into Nam. Oh, well, we'd all made it then, and on this trip, so far so good.

We were nearing the first drop zone, around eleven hundred meters from the river. We came upon a clearing that looked like a napalm bomb had landed there. The place was starting to grow again, but the shrub and grass were only around a foot tall. We thought it must have happened a month or so ago, as the jungle grows fast here.

It was covered with North Charlies.

We moved back. Colonel C said he thought for sure they were part of a company of North, the same ones the SEAL team had been fighting the day we were to land here. The North must have had some reinforcements come in, as they had been mostly killed off when Colonel C left to sneak off to find us. From where we sat in their back door, it looked like they were getting ready to mount another attack. I wondered if the SEALs could handle yet another. Had they slipped away, not waiting for us?

We had to make our way to the river, and that meant either going through them or taking another route. That thought generated a lot of stress. It meant three to four days to walk around this spot, and no telling what we would run into. The SEAL who had dogged us had said the North Charlies were getting thick as thieves near the river. I talked to Mike, the captain, and Colonel C, and we made a decision. Well, it was mostly my decision, as I had not been in a good mood from the get-go on this fucked-up, easy-peasy mission. Colonel C was grinding into my brain. Had he led the SEAL team into this ambush? Had he led us here to die with his North buddies? My mind was running through so many scenarios of why, how come, and how did they know we were to land here? The navy was good at their drop-zone shit. How did anyone know about us from the start? Or were they still waiting for us to make a push? Did they know we'd hit the targets? Like the mate said, hate this cat-and-mouse bullshit! I wished we had a line to defend like they did in World War II. Not so much sneaking around. Made me an old man before my time. I didn't want to lose anyone or have to carry anyone out of there with a bad wound. It was not in my makeup to lose a team member. Fuck, this was what we needed to do, had to do, got to do. Now or never. It was the only way. Better here, now, or never have a chance to succeed, with not a man to lose, not a one.

"Listen up, guys. We'll make our stand here, like a doubled-headed ax, and if the SEALs are here, then we're sure to make it out with no casualties. So, stay cool, and keep your heads. We'll start the fight when they start theirs. As of now, we have the advantage of surprise. They think all the enemy is on the river. They don't know we're here at all. We need to make a semicircle, be no more than three yards off the shoulder of the guy next to you. Back away enough to make this semicircle but not so far back that your barrel will crack his ear. You can do this by making sure your shoulder is in line with his rib cage. No one will fire until I give the word. Are we all on the same page on this?"

I noted general approbation all around.

"OK, then. The seventy-nine on the outside. John, you take the left; Allen, you take the right. Make sure you have smoke rounds of red, green, and yellow. Red and green will be used for letting everyone know the position of the North. Red if within four hundred yards, green if within two hundred yards, and help with that side if at all possible. SEAL team will know it's us if you put yellow out—it's to say we are losing the battle and need help. Divide up the grenade rounds along with the smoke rounds. Everyone knows their colors, so divide up the hand grenades along with the smoke. I will be beside John, then Mike and Cap. Captain, you sure you can handle John's sixty?"

"Sure, Duke. Was the team marksman at West Point with it?"

"Captain, you and your sixty will be in the middle. We'll make sure you're safe so you can take them out if we are charged. Until then, just use your fourteen, as we are a sniper team. We pick and pop. No misses. We need all of our ammo, as we cannot sustain a firefight.

"Colonel C, you're on Cap's right, then Allen. Give us around thirty minutes to get set up and dug in. I then want you to drop back and take some of the hand grenades and commo wire. Make us some booby traps around four hundred to five hundred yards out, then some more at two hundred and fifty yards out, and yellow smoke at two hundred yards as well. If we see yellow smoke, we know we are to make a circle.

"Allen, Cap, and Mike will make the back of the ax head. We will be a force to survive. John, Colonel C, and I will shuffle to our right when that happens, making two semicircles about fifteen yards or so apart. Now, water up, dig into your main spot and then your next spot. Be very quiet, and don't make any dirt to be seen from the North Charlie side. When you're done, help your buddy make his better. We need to not lose a man, or we are all lost. Everyone will walk his own dog tag out, got it?

"As soon as we are dug in, Mike, let's check this place out. Looks good. Now, spot me the far side. I want to pop some of their snipers, nail them to the trees. They'll be hiding from the front assault, not the rear."

"Seven ninety-three to the far trees, Duke; six thirty-three to where they're at now; three fifty to the large termite hill that's in the middle of the clearing. Think you should pop some white rounds into the far side of the trees and brush, burn them all out?"

"Not till the fighting starts. Then we will. I want the SEALs to start a counterattack first, then we know we're not alone out here. If that never happens, then we'll be silent as mice and hope they move on far enough so we can slip by. Do you agree, Colonel C? And you, Cap? We are way too outnumbered to take the fight to them, but if the SEAL team does start some shooting, then we will pop the snipers first. At that point, Mike, your idea of a burn will be nice. We know that their command is in there someplace—it's their MO. They'll be interested in leaving. It could be a long rest of the day and night if we are on our own.

"OK, guys, looks real good. Let's all get some shut-eye, and I will take the first watch.

"Mike, I like this. We have two seventy-nines, one sixty, four two by fourteens, and our two two by fourteens—not the best sniper equipment past six hundred yards, but we have Old Betsy to even things up some. We could be set for a nice fight if we need to. Get some sleep, buddy."

The day seemed to drag on. I was marking the snipers one by one—five so far—when Mike woke up. I showed him the targets but told him I'd continue to watch, as I wasn't tired. Too much of a rush for me to sleep.

"Wake Colonel C and have him sneak on back and make sure our back door is posted, shut for visitation to all visitors. Tell him no traps to the south—not yet—as we might need to get away in a hurry. Have him set his watch by yours, and tell him one hour only, or I'll come get him, so don't be sneaking away."

"OK, Duke. Colonel C is on the back side of us doing his thing, and we are ready."

"Good. Need my numbers, Mike. Let's start with the right side first, the side I marked, so I will be ready. I checked out the ammo. Old Betsey is ready, I'm ready, my team is ready. What the hell are they waiting for? Those damn SEALs would like it dark so they can use their new night scopes. Bet that's what's going on. Mike, check out Colonel C; he's been gone a little over an hour and ten now.

"How's it going, Tex? Looks like we're in for it this time. We're sure in a hell of a mess. What do you think? Sure not looking good, is it?"

"No, Duke, it's not, but you listen up. As long as we're together, I won't let something happen to you. Got it? Yes, sir. So now we have one sixty, four fourteens, two two by fourteens, and two seventy-nines. Well, hell's bells, bet old Custer would have loved that much firepower when he was surrounded, bet ya. So here we are, Duke—about three p.m. I would guess by the sun. So here's what we do. Let me go do some scouting, check on the SEALs, and give you a report."

"You want to do that?"

"Sure, why not, if you ask me to? I'll do anything you ask, Duke, you know that. I'll find out if the SEALs are still here. Think they would be, or why would so many Commies be getting ready for this kind of action? Then, if the SEAL team is still here, we let these Commie bastards have it full force. Got it, son, you and me. I am, shall we say, like a guardian angel. OK, lie down and rest. You're too drawn up, tighter than dried-out Wang leather in the desert. Be right back. Now, you hear me loud, son. Rest up, like you told the men. They're good guys. They need you strong, at the top of your game."

I don't know, but I been told,
If you're left, you're right
Crown would taste good now; let the beer flow
as your memory is torturing to me,
I want a girl just like a girl like my mommy used to be;
It is a mean old world, I am a mean old man,
and shooting you would be a joy like whisky from...
I don't know but I been told
Eskimo girls' hearts are cold.

OK, boy, listen up, here. Wake up. You awake?
   Yes, sir. "Oh, Tex, what did you find out?"
   "The SEALs are dug in deep for some real fighting. There are fifteen of them, so looks like they're going to wait this out and be ready to strike when you all make it happen. They have some of them there rubber boats hidden in the brush and looks like they're armed to the teeth. So here's what I think we should do: Let's take those snipers out. There are eight of them. See the trees to the far right, almost on top of the SEAL team? There are two in there. See them? They're set back in, on some kind of rope slings like parachute harness, just waiting for their commander to give the word. Seems like some general inside a dug-in foxhole is the one in charge. He's this side of the termite hill. Heavy bamboo for the roof, but I think the seventy-nine will break through and do a job on them, so let's get Mike on board and get ready for the sniper shots of a lifetime. Let's take those Commie bastards out and send them to hell where they belong. You ready, Duke? Let's go! Here come Mike and that sleazy lowlife Charlie Charlie. I don't trust him one bit. When you and Mike start the fireworks, I'll sneak back and look to see what he's done back there for us anyway. You good with that?"

"Yes, go, Tex. Go! Now, Mike and I will take out the snipers as you said, and for me, keep an eye on old Charlie Charlie, as you call him. Yes, he makes the hair stand up on the back of my neck too."

"Mike, glad you're here. We can't wait till dark; we need to act now. If it gets dark on us, no way can we hold this spot. So let's take the snipers out, and then work on the command post if and when all hell breaks loose. See the guy sitting there in front of the termite hill, maybe about twenty-five yards closer to us? He isn't sitting; he's standing in the command post. Take your spotting scope and look. There are also three more snipers hiding in the trees to the right side. OK, see? There they are; they just moved. One just lit up a cigarette. See them there talking, like this is a Sunday go-to-church meeting?"

"Yes, I see them. The scope said eight hundred and seventy-three yards. That would be a great shot if you pull that one off, Duke."

"Yes, for sure. There's a lot of brush to wind my shots through, but I'll study those as you get the guys ready for this mission. Zero those seventy-nines in. I want every shell they have to go into that command center! There is more than likely all kinds of top brass in that foxhole with radios and who knows what else. Their antenna is more than likely a commo wire, so thin we can't see it. Zero them in, making every shot count. When the guys are done with that—and only then—send the smoke, as that's when we'll need to know if the SEALs are with us.

"Before the SEALs start chiming in to the fight, we need to be done with the tree snipers. Signal John and Allen to start sniping the outer edge on their side. Stay low, working to the middle. We don't want to give ourselves away. Here's hoping they think that the SEAL team has climbed a tree, and with our suppressers on, they can't figure out where the shots are coming from.

"We can give them some good old-fashioned hurt before they realize we're here. When we give them the seventy-nine and then smoke, we will wipe those Commie bastards up this day. When the fighting gets heavy, I want you to go back door. By then, I might have some insight as to what's going on. If you need help, come back and get that Colonel C bastard. And be careful; I have a feeling he's one of them. Second thought: Take Allen, and leave Colonel C here. If the booby traps go off, take Allen at that moment and back door us. Just leave Colonel C here with us, OK?"

"Got it, Duke. OK, off to get the guys ready. Are you going to start without me?"

"Got to, my friend, got to, but hurry. After I set up, I'll wait. Need your help, for sure."

"We're all ready now, Duke. Let's get those guys out of the trees."

"Well, Mike, I've been thinking about using some white rounds. If I miss those guys and hit the trees, there's a good chance to fire the place up. That does a lot of good. Even if they're still alive, those guys become a liability. If they're wounded, they'll be yelling if only one speck of the white gets on them. At this range, these are still highly accurate, don't you think?"

"Yes, Duke, that sounds good. But just a leaf at that range could ignite them, you know."

"Yes, I know, but the object will be to make them make a lot of noise. So the diversion will be working if any of this stuff gets on them. It will make them scream in pain, and then we can get the others easier as they swing out to see their buddies burning and screaming. Then I'll switch to black rounds, so if I miss, the SEALs will see the trees split wide open. That will help the SEAL team see and get the ones I can't.

"When you have the seventy-nine, Mike, start dropping in rounds. Here's hoping they'll think the SEALs have dropped in small mortars. If that works, we can just pick them off at will. I know there's a lot resting on you, but we can't forget the back door. Still a lot riding on that Colonel C."

"Got you, Duke. I'm going to tell Allen the plan, so if something happens to me, he will take the back door. Let's get the plan in motion. I see you have all your clips loaded half and half."

"Hell, Mike, that all I've got. That's why I made the decision, but I think it'll work. Here's hoping! It's straight up one o'clock. Let's start the parade now."

I pulled the target up, looking through the scope on three-quarter power, but the power was too great. All I could see were enlarged leaves and brush. My crosshairs were too crowded to put it on a clear spot like I had hoped. I switched to lowest power, and then it was hard to clearly pinpoint my mark on the target with any kind of accuracy. Didn't want the standard head shot—wanted to see them shout in pain—but the foliage was too much. I brought the hairs up a touch, 873 yards, two more clicks up—still not a clear shot. OK, two to the right. I studied the foliage. No wind, nothing moving. Not even the smallest leaf. This would be easier—no side drift. There, I was dead on his heart, more to the right by a click. No, should be a half click. There. Now clear. Better bring it down so more of a belly shot.

On target, I pulled the trigger and rested. I let my air out slowly, slowly. I needed to get into my mind-set—in with a big breath, slowly out, slow, slow; in again, again out slow. My heart was down to lower than normal now, and my shakes were gone. One more time—big breath, hold, more air in...not ready to breathe out, hold for a nano-second...slowly now, all air out. I released the trigger. God damn, that was a good shot. Look at him squirm and holler. Next one. Yes, swing out and look at your buddy.

Pop, pop, she's a wicked old woman
and a mean old bitch.
It makes me happy to shoot like this.
Take that, you bitch.

"My God, Duke, you threaded the needle on those two! Looks like a double whammy—got them in the belly. Both of them, and white is working. It went through them, and now they're on fire and screaming.

Their tree is on fire too. Looks like the SEALs are there, as they are firing from that position."

"Yes, Mike, I can see it in my scope. I see them screaming. Think I will stay with the whites until they're gone."

"At this rate, we'll have them all with those clips. The SEALs know what's going on now, for sure."

"You're right, Mike, and look at those boys hopping all around. The SEALs are peppering the hell out of them, and all they're trying to do is find their release rope to hit the ground."

OK...

Pop! Pop!

Sweet dreams of you,
Oh, how I like to dream of shooting you.

"Duke?"

"Yes, Tex."

"The so-called Colonel Charlie made some booby traps, all right— so open that the bastards could just step over them. Like making a highway to us. So I fixed that all up. Listen, I think he has a radio hidden back there someplace. A direct line to them in the command post. That's what I think. Couldn't find it, but will keep on looking, if you like."

"No, Tex, stay with me. I need you here. I got four down and four to go. Let's shoot some and let Mike go check the back door. He's good at that stuff."

I hand-signaled Mike to come to me.

"What's up, Duke?"

"Mike, I can finish up here. Tell the boys to make some noise now with those seventy-nines of theirs, OK? Then slip off, don't let anyone see you, and check the back door. Be careful. I think Colonel Charlie set the traps for us, not the Viet Cong. If that's so, redo them correctly, and then come shoot that bastard in the belly! Or tell me, and I'll do it. And let's break his hands while we're at it! Anyway, when you're ready for Allen to unload, I'll tap John's shoulder to start his popgun up also. Then sneak off. Colonel C will be distracted and amazed that we're giving the correct place so much fire. Go, Mike, and watch out, be careful. Watch every step very closely. Be careful of that back door. No telling what he's done to us back there."

"Got it. I'm out of here."

I watched Mike crawl off as the boys started the seventy-nines. Mike had them zeroed in perfectly, for sure. The first two hit dead center. I took a fast glance back to old Colonel C. He was watching the snipers now, four of whom were still screaming and thrashing around like they were in a fire pit. Well, hell, guess they were on fire, for sure. The seventy-nines placed the shells so accurately that it was a miracle. Really, they were that good. God, we were a hell of a team. Cap caught my eye and shrugged at me. I motioned him to be alert but to stay calm. We were sure to need that sixty at any time.

Then I got back to the business at hand. They were wide open, now more than ever. They must have been thinking they were hidden behind the trees from the SEAL team, not realizing they were more open to me. They were watching their buddies, not the front line. I moved over to the far left of John, lying on some soft grass, barrel propped up on a small mound. I started doing my thing again from there, breathing in deeply, out slowly, pulling the trigger.

Pop!

Oh, baby, baby, come dance with me,
You're so ugly horseflies could never take your place.

Pop!

> *Sweet dreams, baby. Oh, how you dream.*
> *Hold your pillow and squeeze it tight*
> *As papa put it all right in your gut,*
> *Sweet dreams, baby.*

"John, you out of the grenades now? OK, let out some smoke. I think we have it going our way. Make sure it's to your far left so it will draw fire away from us. That's it, Allen, smoke. Both you guys are doing great. Another one far out. It's working. Now sniper those Commie bastards. We have them really confused. I think you guys got their command center. Great job lobbing those damn things at that range. Make your shots count, guys, and I'll make some more fires with old whities here, then I'll switch to a two by fourteen and help you out. OK, Cap, spray a small burst now and again at random. They don't know where to hide now. Just like Custer's last stand—got them surrounded, and the SEAL team is doing a good job. Be careful now, they're likely to…Mike, what's that? OK, take Cap. He's full of ammo in the sixty. Never even fired but one short burst. How many are there? A lot? Oh, God, let's close that back door. Take Allen too, and leave Colonel C with me. Go, Mike."

I crawled over to Colonel C and pulled out my forty-five auto from my shoulder harness. As he looked at me, he noticed that Allen and Mike, along with Cap, were leaving. With their disappearance, I stuck the forty-five in his ass.

"You set us up, you son of a bitch." And I pulled one off. Didn't make much noise. He looked at me, wild eyed, as he felt the flesh part until the bullet come out at his neck. He was choking now. He was in lots of pain as he stood, grabbed his neck with one hand, dropping his rifle, and started running toward the Commies' command post. He wasn't able to speak.

I knew this wasn't going to go well for him. Had the wrong uniform on.

When he was about 200 yards from me and 150 from the North Charlies, they noticed this guy running full blast toward them. He waved as he slowed down his pace. He was humped over, and he turned to look at me, blood covering most of his shirt now. Going slower than before, he turned back toward them, started walking toward some of them, waving but unable to speak. They turned their rifles on full auto, and man, they made Swiss cheese of him. As he lay on the ground kicking, one guy jumped up and ran over to him, shooting him in the eye with a pistol that from where I was looked like a German Luger.

I pulled Old Betsy up with a white round in her chamber, my last one, and let that guy have it. He made a hell of a racket screaming. That did a lot of good for me, and it drew a lot of his buddies out of their holes. *Pop! Pop!* My fourteen was so hot by the end of the hour that I thought for sure the barrel would start drooping from the heat. I knew for a fact that I had shot the barrel out. It would never shoot another accurate round again—not for what was needed by a sniper anyway. John slid into Cap's place.

"What the hell did that Colonel C do that for? We have them pinned down good. He didn't need to charge them! He was crazy—crazy, Duke. Why did he do that?"

"I have no clue, John, what the hell he was thinking, but by the sound of things, the big fight is behind us now. I'm going to slip off to the right side and hold down the spot from there. Take half of Colonel C's rounds, and go help Cap, Mike, and Allen. I'll be OK here. Tell Cap to return as soon as he can."

"Got it, Duke. Anything else you want me to tell them?"

"Yes. If I lose this spot or you guys lose yours, throw your yellow smoke, and get back here. If I throw mine, that means I am coming to you. Now move it.

"Tex, what do you think? We can hide here and still pick off anyone coming from any direction. I'd better use Colonel C's fourteen for a little while. Mine is so damn hot I think the barrel is shot out. Man, I don't smoke, but I could really use one now. A good shot of bourbon and a cigar would be a dream come true—the best thing for a guy at this moment."

If I had a dollar, you know what I could do?
I would take you to the movies and spend it all on you.
I got a hot-rod Ford and a million-dollar smile.
If you want to have fun, come along and do it with me;
We will have a bucket of fun.

Well, I was down to forty rounds, and it sounded like the back door was quiet. It looked to be almost six o'clock—lots of shadows. It was hard to believe that we had been at it hot and heavy for five hours. Seemed like a few days. I wondered where the hell that Mike was.

"Tex, can you go find Mike and tell him it's time we moved out?"

"Sure can. I'll find him and be back in a jiff."

I'm Duke the eighth, I am. Duke the eighth, I am, I am.
I am a mean old man in a mean old world,
Oh, baby, I got to have some good lovin'
Need your good, good lovin'
It will make me feel right after popping gooks all day long.

"Mike, what the hell? You guys all OK? Are there any more Commies out there?"

"No, Duke, we got them all, we think. Was about fifty of them. Could have been a few more. Didn't take the time to count the bodies. They were walking slowly. We waited for them to trip the first wire. Surprised them, along with the grenades that took out a few for us. Thought Colonel C said it would be all clear, but it wasn't. We held our fire until they crawled up to the last wire. They were looking at it when Cap opened up on them with the sixty and sprayed them. Then they were down to around twenty-five. By then, we had the high ground, so we just picked them off. Cap is a hell of a shot with that big old thing.

Had it on semiauto, not full auto, so we chose our targets, and he let out bursts of three at a time. He was awesome, man, just awesome! Where's Colonel C?"

"John can tell you."

"John, where's Colonel C?"

"Mike, it was the damnedest thing you ever saw. He jumped up from his spot—a good spot, Mike, looked safe as hell. He just tore out after the Commie bastards like he had a fire in his ass. But after he'd run for about a hundred and fifty yards, he was so tired he was barely moving, and the dang smokes got to him, is what I'm thinking. He almost made the command post, but there wasn't much left of it after Allen and I had seventy-nined it. A Commie bastard saw him and unloaded a complete clip into him. Then, when that was done, one of them was still not happy, so he runs over and shoots him in the eye with his pistol. Then Duke shot that guy with a white and let him scream. That's when I left to go where you were, like I was told to do, and Duke just picked the guys off one by one as I was crawling to your spot."

Mike looked at me. "Hell of a story. How did you get him to do that, Duke? Tell me, how did you get him to run out there when he knew he would be shot, and he was safe here like a baby in its mother's arms?"

"Not now. Later maybe, but not now."

"Duke, the SEALs are coming. They're flanking us. See them?"

"Thanks, Tex. Yes, have them in my sights. Look, Mike, there's movement. More than likely the SEAL team. Let's get ready to get the hell out of here."

"Mule."

"Jackass."

"Hey, army, how you been? Need some water or C rations? We got plenty, though it looks like you guys got lost. Thought we were going to have to go find you and show you the way back home. We've been waiting for you for a week past your time. What took you so long?"

They turned and looked at each other, looked at each other's dirty faces and muddy, wet clothing, and then they both turned to me with a grin.

"Hell of some shooting from you guys. Hell of an idea to pop some Willy Petes into the trees where their snipers were. They sure do jump when that shit gets on them. We never saw a one of them until you pointed them out to us by lighting the trees and them on fire. We knew the tracer rounds could do that—you know, start some fires—but hell of an idea using the whites. They don't leave a trail when you use them like tracer rounds. Hell of some shooting! You guys are the best sniper team we've been around—next to us, that is. SEAL Team C. And how did you know they were in the trees and where their command post was? It couldn't be seen from our angle. How did you know?"

"Yes, Duke, tell us how you knew that stuff? How did you know?"

"Mike, you were here with me. We spotted it together, the guys coming and going. You saw it with your spotting scope. You spotted it, not me, Mike."

Looking at me, he said, "Yes, we did." He turned his look to the SEAL team. "That's why we are the best sniper team the Special Forces has ever had—next to you SEALs, for sure."

"When we were walking out to our mission, I had a long talk with Colonel Charlie, and he told me you guys had run into some trouble. That was how we knew their MO, how they like to set things up and position their troops. Hell, he went through military school with most of them."

"Well, let's go. We'll be debriefed aboard the Cleveland. You can throw your C rations overboard when you get there and enjoy some real navy chow. You guys one man short? We were told there were six of you to bring back. Where's your other guy?"

Mike looked at me and then said, "Yes, we were to be six, but Colonel Charlie took off after them. He's over in that pile someplace. You see, those Commie bastards shot the shit out of him and then shot him in the eye. What a bunch of bastards those Commies are. Bastards every last one of them."

"I tell you, Duke, I'm for sure the shit ready for us to get the hell out of here. How about the rest of you guys?"

"You got it, John."

We walked single file behind the SEAL team to the boats and then rode to their ship, the whole time Tex and I singing our heads off. Of course, no one could hear us, but we were damn happy. And for the first time, I realized how much I depended on Tex. He always was able to do the impossible task at hand.

Oh, Betsy, oh, Betsy, I love you, oh, Betsy girl,
If you're left, you're right, left, left, right, left…
Ain't no sense in looking back, Jodie has your Cadillac.
Ain't no sense in lookin' down, ain't no discharge on the ground.
I don't know but I been told
Eskimo girls are mighty cold!
Oh, Betsy, you know you want to be true,
If you started back doing the things you used to do
I would have to break you in two.
I am a mean old man, righting the wrong in a mean old world.

What was that noise?

Bolting out of bed, I realized I was safe—safe in a bed, on a ship, in a room—my room by myself, not in the bush but on a ship. Quickly processing why, what, where, I knew why I was there. I went to the wall locker and started to get dressed.

As I put my pants on, I saw that my rifle and forty-five were not in my wall locker. Routine, my ass! They wanted me to pay for old Colonel Charlie. Commie bastard Colonel Charlie just about got the SEAL team killed and us along with them. Commie bastard!

All the damn briefings before this mission and now debriefing afterward. They're the fuckups. They should have known he was a bad apple! Maybe they did, and we were the expendables—another number on a clipboard someplace in DC or the Pentagon. Hell, I wonder if Johnson got his briefing on us, or were we too far down the list for anyone to really give a shit about? One or two teams not making it is of no consequence if the end goal was achieved. End goal. What was the end goal? Must have been to flush out old Colonel Charlie and not really having anything to do with the targets. That's it—Colonel Charlie was a flush job, and we couldn't know that they were sure he was a bad apple. To tell us would have been a distraction. That must have been why Cap went along: to make sure we didn't pop someone who was not checked out. Hell, maybe we even had a snitch in there with them. But figuring all that shit out was way over my pay grade. Well, maybe we were a worthwhile asset to the top boys back there in their armchairs figuring who lives and who dies. I would stay there, fighting in the bush. It was a lot safer than being there and doing all those assessments of all the angles. Hell yes—a lot easier on one's heart in the bush, for sure.

My mind was still retracing the steps there in the wet bush of Nam, waiting for him or some other Commie bastard to shut my door, but the thing that was hard for me to think about was that if I missed the step, my buddies could have paid the price. I did what I had to do for them.

When I was on a mission, I had to focus. I knew we had the captain to rely on, but the team and I trained together, ate and slept our mission together. When I looked into their eyes, I could see their confusion clear into their souls: "Duke, don't leave me here!" and "Don't let me die!" And I didn't! I told them that you walked your dog tag in, and you walked it out.

Yes, I was wound up tight with the pure pressure of it all so that they could sleep in my trust. And I looked to try to find the correct answer for them and tried to keep them all from going to hell.

I was on the ship—here, on this ship—we were on the ship, all of us on this floating tub, and we were all safe, resting for another round. Where that would be only the brass knew.

God, I loved my room. And those SEALs, knowing they were so close every day to going to hell. Yet when the mission was over, they were back in their rooms, eating good chow, taking hot showers until the water ran clean, the mud out of their hair…Clean, hot showers. Lucky bastards.

What a mission! One moment trying to figure if I would have enough ammo, if the back door was safe, and then the night came, and I was sleeping in soft, clean sheets, safe because of this navy ship. The SEALs, who didn't say no, stood their ground and waited for us. God damn, they were brave guys to risk it all for me, for us, for my team!

God, I could have fallen back on that bed and hoped it had all been a dream. But I knew it wasn't. And old Colonel Charlie: the truth I would never know about him was the real story of his childhood. Damn, who the fuck cared? He was gone, and my team and I were here—hot chow, hot showers, resting for the next big bang of whom we would lose next. I know I should never have gotten this close to the guys. It was a hard one to swallow when they were gone—my fault, their fault, no one's mistake, just the luck of the draw.

Reality was a strong thing to wake to, the realization that my heart was beating now like…like I was hiding in the bush, worried I could do nothing if they did find us. I looked in the mirror as I buttoned my shirt, making sure all the lines were as straight as they could be. Just hours ago, I was deep in shit, and now I was on a ship, as safe as I could ever want it to be—could ever be—and still be in the army.

Opening the door, the MP who was guarding my room was spit and polish. Bet you his rifle had too much oil to even fire a shot.

"How goes it, buddy? Ready for some chow?"

"Yes, sir. We have one hour before the debriefing starts. Are you ready to go back to your unit when this is over?"

Is it ever over, ever over…ever?

Looking at his name tag, I asked him, "Tell me, what's the correct pronunciation of your name?"

"Just call me Scat, sir. Most all do. I'm Polish and from New York, so not many ever say it correctly anyway."

"OK, Scat, let's scat down to the mess hall. I am very hungry this morning."

While I was eating, Scat stood at attention an arm's length from me. Made me hurt looking at him.

"Hey, Scat, relax yourself with me. No one would ever say anything while you're with me. Go get some coffee and sit here. Where do you think I could be off to on this tub?"

"Really? You think it's OK, sir?"

"Yes. Sit. You make me nervous, and when I'm nervous, someone has to be shot. So relax, and let me relax."

"Thanks, sir."

"You don't have to call me sir. Duke is my name. I work in this army, the same as you, and yes, I am ready to be off this tub. I feel like a sitting duck, don't you?"

"Coffee is good on these ships, not to mention the chow. I think I could live on this ship forever. So is today your last day here?"

"That's to be seen. Have to be debriefed, as you know, before I can go anyplace."

"The word is, Duke, sir, that you're some kind of badass hero or something."

"No, not I. Looks like the brass are moving. Guess we better scat to the room there, Scat. If I get kicked out of the service, we could be a standup comedy act. What you think about that, Scat? No, I'm no badass, Scat—just a soldier doing his job. Maybe a little better than the average but just following orders. Did you know I started out like you, up from the ranks?"

"Here we are, Duke. I'll be outside. Good luck, sir, Duke."

"Good morning, Lieutenant. I am Captain Paul Ford. You're here for your debriefing, and I will be handling it. Are you OK with me doing so?"

"Yes, of course. You did three or more on me already. Yes, no problem, sir."

"Then, let's begin. We've talked to the rest of the team, and now you are the last. Did you know that?"

"Do now, sir."

"You know the general, General Pat Wright?"

"Yes, sir. He's been in charge of all my missions from the first to date."

"Good. Let's get going."

Debriefing with General Pat Wright
Friday
0900, 4/19/1968
Aboard the USS *Cleveland*
Doctor: Paul Ford, MD, PhD, PsyD
Second Lieutenant: D. (Duke) Moore, platoon leader
This is his story of the mission from the beginning until he and his team were back aboard the USS *Cleveland*.
Captain Tony Marks was the officer in charge of observation and verification of the targets.

"Give me your name and service number."

"Second Lieutenant D. Moore, RA one eight nine zero two three six nine."

"You go by Duke, is that correct? And you were team leader? Can you, for the record, write down for us your best detail of the mission?"

"Yes, sir. It's the paper I just handed you."

"Do you have a copy?"

"No, sir. Just what has stayed in my head."

"So the mission was composed of the team members listed here." He showed me the page of the report showing the personnel list. I looked it over.

Captain (Cap) Tony Marks, RA-13307288
LT D. (Duke) Moore, RA-18902369

SP-7 Jerry (Mike) Mikes, RA-92628315
SP-3 John (John) Phillips, RA-11281424
SP-3 Samuel (Allen) Allen, RA-11854924

"Lieutenant Moore, is this correct?"

"Yes, sir. I was team leader on this one. General Wright said to give Mike all the room I could to see if he could make a leader if I should get hurt or something. That's what we did most of the time anyway. And after we were into the mission, Mike and I always teamed up. Like the old saying, two heads are better than one. You see, sir, we have been in the army together since sniper school. I tend to take charge, as the captain will tell you, and as you will read in my report. But at no time do I feel that Mike is left in the cold. I tend to keep him up to date with my thoughts, direction, and decisions, and he keeps me informed of the men's progress. So, you see, sir, without Mike there, I don't think we could function as a team. I do believe it takes two, if you're really asking that as a question, sir. Team leader, sure. Cap, I mean, Captain Marks, was ranking officer, so we kept him up to speed as well. But his answer to me was that he knew what he was doing so just to tell him what I wanted him to do and he would, like any other guy on the team. So you see, sir, you can call me team leader, and I guess I am, but I don't believe there is just one guy in charge. It's all of us as a team that makes us all come back. No one can be a part of this team and feel he is superior in any way. We all are a team; no one more important than another—that's when we are able to function as a team. You get that, don't you, sir? The team follows me, sure, and when I bark, they jump. A leader, for sure, but not better or worse than any man out there. I just have a different job than they do. And they know that I take it all very seriously, for sure. I don't want anyone on my watch to have their dog tags not walk out the same way they walked in."

"So, Duke, do you need help from us in any way, whether psychological or medical? Anything we need to know about?"

"No, sir, not that I can think of. Why do you ask?"

"We're just making sure you're OK with the shooting of a lot of people. More than shooting but with Willy Petes. Your team says you look happy when you shoot the enemy."

"Yes, sir. Them or me—yes, sir, not a problem. And I am happy that I have the skill set to be able to do a good job and to keep our team safe, both mentally and physically."

"OK, Duke. I'm finished here."

"General Wright, sir..."

"Yes, doctor, I've got this. You're dismissed. Duke, at 0400, you and your team will fly to Japan and there pick up your new orders."

He stood, saluted me, as I did him, and then with a handshake, he said, "Godspeed!"

"Thanks."

I turned to salute the other officers in the room and left.

"Let's go, Scat. Let's find my team."

"They're in the mess hall, sir, with the SEAL team."

"Scat, what did I say about that 'sir' bullshit? You need some airborne training, Scat?"

"Airborne, sir, Duke?"

"Yes, airborne. Like, over the side of the ship, if you get my drift."

"No, Duke, I think...well, no, I don't need any airborne training. I'm sure of it."

"Then, Scat, it's Duke from here on out so I don't have to holler 'Man overboard.'"

I entered the mess hall as Scat opened the door. They all stood, saluted me, and then clapped. I turned for a moment so they couldn't see the tears in my eyes.

"What you guys doing? The SEAL team is the hero here. If it weren't for them, we wouldn't be here."

"Sure, Duke, whatever you say. But we'll go to hell and back with you any day."

◆　◆　◆

After all of us were finished eating, most of the guys left. Mike and I talked about a lot of stuff. Nothing important, just chitchat—his girl back home, our cars, stuff like that.

"Let's find the rec room, Mike, and shoot some pool. What do you say? Ready for me to kick your ass at pool?"

So we wandered down and listened to music and shot pool until around 17:00 hours, and then Mike and I headed to the showers just before chow. A mite early, 0400, and we figured we'd better not miss the chopper.

"Mike, this here shower is sure nice. How you doing over there, Mike? Mike, what's wrong with you? Why are you crying? We're safe now!"

"Duke, you know. Doesn't it bother you, shooting those guys and watching them suffer? Well, it does me. I hate it, and I don't know why it makes you so happy to do it. I see the smile on your face. How do you live with yourself?"

"Hold on, Mike, let's clear this shower room. OK, you guys, clear this room, and I mean *now*! You, yes, you. Last man in, you stand guard with Scat. Scat, don't let anyone through the door, not a soul, or the two of you will be mine. Got that, jarheads? Say it!"

"*Yes, sir!*"

"Now, Mike, let's talk. We're alone. I smile, that's for sure, Mike, but the reason I do is that I know I just did a horrendous shot, and it makes me smile to think that, whoa, I am pretty good at this shit. If it weren't me, it would be someone else, and maybe they would be better at it, but I don't know that as a fact. So, Mike, we just follow orders. We didn't make the war or the rules, but it's my job to bring you all back safe.

"Mike, you're the best on the team, and we work well together, so just put that shit out of your head. And remember, they want the best for the tough jobs, or they would let the SEALs do it or some other team. We work well. You're the best spotter in the army, and with that, you make me the best sniper. Hell, Mike, I couldn't do it without you. I would never get the yardage right, would always be off—but not with you. You give me the edge. You are so exacting with everything. So, Mike, please don't break up the team. Say, 'We are a team forever'!"

"We are a team forever, Duke, and I won't be the one to break us up. But, Duke, you have to be honest with me, OK?"

"OK, Mike. What is it?"

"My first question is, how did you know that the back door was in jeopardy? Second, how did you know about the SEAL team being in place? And third, how did you know that the command post was where it was? Don't give me the same cock-and-bull story again that you gave the commanders. It was *you* who pointed it out to *me*! And finally, I could barely see those guys in the trees with the scope on full power. So tell me, how do you come up with all this shit? I know you have better eyes than most, but you cannot see five hundred to eight hundred yards to your rear in tall jungle grass, so cut the shit. You're always telling me this or that, amazing me with the things you know. So tell me, Duke, without the bull. OK?"

"Mike, the SEAL team guys were our buddies. They knew we depended on them for our lifeline back to this old tub. They would have stayed there till the end of time for us, and that's how I knew they were there. Besides, if they hadn't been there, why were there so many gooks there looking like they were getting ready for a big fight? We would have done the same.

"Mike, what the hell? Stand up. What's going on? What? Don't cry. I know it was a rough one and that we lost Colonel Charlie, but Mike, don't do this. Mike, Mike!

"Good, Mike. Here, let me help you stand up. Lean on me, man. Yes, that's it, put your hands on the sink here. It's hot. Let me splash some cold water on your face. That's it, good. Stand up, Mike. You're my bro. Don't ever scare me like that. I thought you were going to go into shock. We can't talk here where there are ears. As soon as we get back, they'll let us have some leave time. We'll go to Frankfurt, have us a good time. Hell, as much as I hate it, I'll even buy you a shitload of girls, if that will help. Just hang on, Mike.

"Mike? No, don't fold! Stand up, Mike. Mike, you listening to me? Just stand tall. We are the best that America has. We can't let these jarheads see us this way, Mike. You're with me, bro. Mike, look into my eyes. Listen, bro, I did what I had to do to make sure *we* got back safe. No bullshit. Mike, look at me. You've known me now for two years or more. You know that we are brothers more than anything. Don't do this, Mike. Let's go out of here heads high."

"Duke, yes, I'm OK now. It's just that…all the killing! Seeing a person up close, not like it was before—you know, snipering them, I mean, and all. The sound, the look as they gasp for that last second of life. It was a horrible thing, Duke. Just…well, anyway, I like being a spotter with you. And I don't really—not deep down, really—care about all this. It's just that as my bro, I think it hurts too much to think that you really like to hurt people. To take their last breath and breathe it for yourself. I guess that's what I don't stomach. Just can't walk past that, bro. Just can't do it, not if you're happy with the pain and hurt. And yes, bro, I know we didn't make the orders. There's something to that, but still, bro, you don't have to sing and like it. Don't do it, Duke. Don't become their killing machine. It will eat us up. It just will."

"Yes, I know, Mike. I really don't like it, but what I do like is to think, 'Damn, that was a hell of a shot.' Not trying to set any records. We took a stand, swore an oath, but it wasn't to brag about it. Let the guy out front get the glory. While we, my brother, are here to help save lives. If we didn't do it, who would? It would get done, sure it would, but at what cost? For now, it's just another red-blood-stained rage in our minds, that's all. We will survive this, as we do all missions."

Mike was quiet, seemed more settled.

"Mike, you OK now? Ready for some beer? Let's go. What do you say? Ready?"

He nodded, and we gathered our stuff.

"OK, jarheads, good job. Thanks. My bro here was just feeling a mite sick—too long in the jungle. But with some good beer in his gut, he'll be just fine. Thank you, guys."

◆   ◆   ◆

At 0400, we took off for Japan. From there, they sent us to the Philippines to train in their jungle (of all places) with the Filipino elite marines. It wasn't a bad job. We went to the jungle, killed a wild water buffalo, and sat around eating barbecued buffalo. We talked about what we should and shouldn't do to make ourselves better fighting machines. Those boys knew the jungle and taught us how to get around in it more easily by reading natural signs. We taught them the art of long-range shooting, how to breathe and squeeze the trigger and not jerk. They taught us how to keep the bugs from making us into dinner. The damn mosquitoes were big, I mean really big. They were large enough to pack a full-grown man back to their nest.

THREE

1987
NO MORE

"*Tex, I think I should go find that doc.*"

"*What doc, Duke?*"

"*You know, the one who's done most all our debriefings. What do you say, Mike? I feel worn out from all this. Should we all go see him? Damn, what's his name?*"

"*Doc Paul Ford, like the car.*"

"*Yes, that's it. Doc Ford. Thanks, Mike. What do you say, guys? Should we go find this guy Ford?*"

"*Yes, let's go find that guy, Duke. Last I heard, he was in private practice in Spokane, Washington, near where your dad lives.*"

"*Thanks, Mike.*"

"*We're with you, boy. Yes, we're here for you. We don't want to split the team up now after all this time.*"

"*Thanks, Tex.*"

"*You know, Duke, that if you go to him, he could have you locked up again, like they did in the days just before the war ended.*"

"*I know, Tex, but he isn't army now. So we could have a chance of being safe from that padded cell. Not like before.*"

"I'm just saying, Duke, that if we go, we could find it a lot harder to climb our way out of it this time."

So, we found this guy, Doc Ford, and checked ourselves into his safe house for vets. After a while, they moved us to a secure jail for PTSD vets in the Walla Walla VA hospital. With other vets like us, for our own good, they said. The more we were around this so-called doc, the more the three of us disliked him. The mistake was on my part: I let him in, and I should never have let him see the inside of me.

I knew in short order that he was not working for me. He was part of the system that had taken my youth and my mind and turned me into something I couldn't change, something *they* couldn't change. It had always been my decision to be what I wanted to be—or so I was led to think. In reality, it was the system that used my good nature. I just wanted to get along and get the job done, God and country, as we were raised to. I was an idiot not to listen to my fellow soldier buddies—those who went home, got on the GI bill, and then marched against the war. I knew it was a rich man's war. Their minds were full of money, and they wanted all it could buy. The average Joe like me, well, we thought it was God and country and all that bullshit stuff. And we thought that it was for the truth, for the American way, that we were giving our blood. Tell me for what, really? Tell me that, and I will be happy.

So, here I was down the road—alive but not really. My insides hurt with fear. My mind was nothing but a fighting machine. Every move, every sound made me jump and think I was going to die this time. I wanted to do what was right for the good of the country, but I didn't know what that meant anymore. Should I just have gone and blown up Washington, DC? One Commie bastard falls, and there are two to pick up his weapon, to march toward us. What the hell was I doing there now? It was a mistake. Mike and Tex gave their lives for me, but in reality, I had never been as true to them as I should have been.

How was I going to become just an average Joe? Who was there to help me walk the path that had eluded me for so long? There was no one who could give me back my youth, my childlike ways of thinking. Hell, they couldn't even undo what they had done to me physically, let alone mentally. We fought like hell when we were in the army, and then we fought like hell when we got out to help them realize their promises to us that they would take care of us. It fell on deaf ears. I guess I couldn't be one of the "walk the line" kind of guys. No, it was never meant to be. My dad had been right: I was not only worthless to their world but to myself as well. That was what he'd meant when he hit me for the first time when I was four. He knew then that this was what I would become: a number on someone's page that let the stats look good someplace—but not this place. No, not here. I would not bend again.

◆　　◆　　◆

"Do you know why you're here?"
"Yes, Doctor...Ford."
"Well, then, tell me why."
"Because you had me transferred here for safety—my safety, I was told. What a crock that was. You make me puke, Doc. You've known me for more than twenty years. You know what they had me do for them, and now you say 'for my safety.' Eff you, Doc, and the horse you rode in on!"

Oh, when the saints, oh, when the saints;
If I had my rifle, I would ring her in the morning;
Oh, when the saints go...
Oh, when the saints go...

I could make it ring in the evening,
I could make it ring in the morning,
I would ring it so my buddies could hear it all through the night.
Because I got to get the ringing in this place if it's the last ring-
ing thing I ever do.

I'm so overwhelmed with joy I could cry,
The people on the river, they couldn't get me; big boats keep
on running the river
As that big diesel motor is playing my song...thank God and
the navy for them boats.

Oh, where, oh, where can them boats be now...
The boat was stalled, the engine was dead, that's all I can
remember
of that firefight that started one morning till late that night,
Runs into the rain, rain coming down, beating me on my head;
The crying boys, the bustin' caps.

Early morning ra-ain; yes, early morning ra-ain, fogging up my
lenses,
Those big iron boats going down the river;
Your sweet lovin' boy ain't a-coming back;
Body bags full of your sweet lovin' boys,
Never to kiss your face again. I could just cry.

"Because I was caught. Give me a break, Doc. Give me a break. No, I was tired, needed to clear my head—still need to clear my head. But no, never mind—I surrendered. Guess I just gave up. A damn quitter. Doesn't that just beat all? Me, a no-good quitter. A good-for-nothing quitter. What does the captain think of that? Me, just a no-good son of a bitch. Effing quitter. Is that why you're here, Doc? 'Cause like me, you couldn't take it anymore?"

"Well, more than that, Mr. Moore. You turned yourself in to me, and then the court put me in charge of your case."

"The court? How come you didn't tell me they were looking for me? You're supposed to be on my side, aren't you? You told them, didn't you? You're a big tattletale, Doc. Isn't that a breach of your oath? Oh, yes, I forgot—you don't have an oath, do you? You're just one of those…you—you worthless piece of shit! Yes, in charge of my case, but if I hadn't turned myself in, you know they would never have found me!"

"I am the doctor in charge of your case, to see if you really understand the reason you're in here. The way the court looks at you before the sentencing. Do you understand that?"

"Not really, Doc. What should I call you?"

"Just call me Dr. Paul Ford. And you go by Dwight?"

"No, D. Moore. Hate to be called Dwight. My effing dad called me that. No, don't do it. If you need a name, call me D. Moore or Duke, OK? Just plain old Moore. Not sir or Mr. Moore—just D. Moore. And is it all right to just call you Doc?"

"Yes, I guess so. D. Moore, tell me why you did what you did to those people."

"Well, Doc, I must tell you that in reality, I was a perfect soldier. You know that—you were in on a lot of my debriefings. As for the way I was raised, I have no conscience. Couldn't really give a damn what other people feel. Pain or death—doesn't matter. I liked my job, and I enjoyed it too much, I guess. You could say that I really enjoyed it. You know, hurting people. Most anyone—didn't really matter. Mike told me it would get to me one day. Guess he was right about that. Well, Doc, I did what I did. Just following orders."

"What, D. Moore? Whose orders? From where did you get these orders?"

"Top brass, Doc. Who you think?"

"You're not in the army now."

"You think not? Tell that to the brass. You know, once in, always in, Doc. You know that. God, Doc, you really aren't that naive now, are you?"

"So, D. Moore, no more of your bull now. Tell me who gave you the orders? And why? From the top, from the first—the whole story. Let's get it all out in the open, if I am going to have a smidgen of a chance to help you."

"Well, I guess I *should* start from the first so that you can under-stand, seeing how you didn't know. Guess you got top clearance to hear all this shit, or you wouldn't be here now, would you? General Pat, I guess. He's in charge of the CIA, you know. Not sure, really, where the orders came from. I just always got them and then burned them. Shred them—that was what we were told to do. The first, Doc? Where is the first? What first? My first? Tell you, Doc, can't remember where the first is without telling you my whole life story. The first of my career...no, not then. Guess I'll start with telling you about my old man. Can't say that I want to visit the old home place again. How much time do we have? But you know, Doc, I told you and them when you all marched me over here that I'd done it, so why don't they just hang me and save us all a lot of time?"

"Well, the court wants to know why so that maybe it can help other vets and you. All the time you need. Pat, General Pat, is dead, if you mean the General Pat who died in 1979."

"That's a laugh, Doc. Hell, they made us, and now that they don't like what we became, they think they can turn back the clock. Don't make me puke, Doc. They just make me vomit with their untouchable ways. Is this a laugh or what? I have to admit you're one funny SOB, for sure. Did you see him in the coffin? Did you, Doc? Was all for show! He's still out there someplace. Give me two months, and I could find him. Bet ya I could."

"So, D. Moore, let's just get to it. Let me know the story, your story. Not the other bullshit you think you know, but just yours. The facts."

"Well, how much time did you say we have? You know, we take an oath not to tell or else be hung, face a firing squad, all that good shit, but I guess it's OK. How much time?"

"All you need. All the time in the world."

"So, Doc, the longer my story, the longer before I hang. Is that it? They can purge their souls and have no guilt. It was just me on a rogue mission. No sanctions. If caught, we were just deserters. No name tags, just out there on our own. Got it, Doc?"

"Yes, got it."

"So I guess I can tell you all, seeing how a long time has passed. So no security breach now. Should I really tell you all? How strong a stomach do you have? Do you really want to hear the truth about your government? Really? The whole truth and nothing but the truth?"

"Yes, of course. I am here to help. So is it OK by you if I record the conversation we are having?"

"Sure, why the hell not, Doc? Sure, go ahead, get it all on tape. If I tell you too much, what are they going to do to me? Hang me? I think it's time for me to just puke. Save their bacon, and this is what I get. No offence, but really, I should have a medal. So I'll tell you, Doc. Maybe you can decide that what I say is the truth, but for now, who really gives a shit?"

FOUR

YOUNG WARRIOR

"I have a lot of memories growing up in the fifties—some are very good, and some are hidden in the dark side of my soul. It's easiest to say it this way: my dad was a pistol, so I am a son of a gun. Better yet, my dad's dad was a pistol, so I guess that really makes me a son of a son of a gun.

"You don't find that funny, Doc? I like to laugh, and I'll keep this on the humorous side of my life. That's really what life is for me: a big laugh. As a child of German, English, Irish, Scottish, Italian, and Russian stock, I guess my grandma had it correct when she said we're American with Heinz 57 blood in us.

"Anyway, as a child of the fifties, I think that time was the best of the best of what America was: the boys were home from the war to end all wars, the country was united, and I had to fight only two days a week at school. The best of the best. I was never one to care if I was liked much, and for sure I did my share of fighting. As a little kid, my dad had broken my eardrums, so I thought—no, Doc, I knew—the other kids were making fun of me all the time. If I saw someone laughing and then look at me, I would just walk up to them and punch them in the mouth. 'Now laugh about that, will you?' That's all I would say. Most of the time, the kids were a lot bigger than I was, so when I would hit them, I never had to fight. They were stunned that a skinny younger kid would dare do that to an upperclassman. Yes, Doc, I see the look on your face. I did get kicked out of school a lot, but that was fine with my old man. He always had a ton of work for me to go around wherever we were living.

"My memories go back as early as eight years old, but my stronger memories are at the old age of eleven and being raised by a boomer. That's a construction worker who went from job to job, chasing the big bucks. My dad, he thought I should always be the toughest kid on the block. Size or age didn't matter—I was to be the toughest kid. Hell, at eight, he broke my nose, hitting me while he was teaching me to box. Jack Dempsey boxing gloves. Of course, *I* had the gloves on, not him. At eleven, my dad tried to kill me one night. I can't remember what set him off. I got away by crawling downstairs to the basement and passing out on my bed. My grandpa started protecting me from that day on, but hell, he couldn't be around me all the time. And when he wasn't around me, the old man would fly off the handle and hit me. One time when he hit me, it was almost a week before I came to my senses. When I did, I ran away from home for the hundredth time. It was a very simple life for a young boy—never having to settle down, never having close friends, and never playing ball on a team. No need, hardly, to unpack. No stress on a kid of that age, right? And you know what, Doc? All you bastards knew my buttons and how to punch them. That's why I was so dang good at being your shooter. You all played with my mind, and now that you think I am out of control, now you want to try and help? Hell's bells, Doc, do you guys see your way to admitting to a mistake, ever?

"So walk back in time with me. Far, far back. Back to yesterday. At my age, yesterday is as far back as I care to walk. Ha! So let our minds drift back to the days when men were men, and horses still would kick the shit out of you if they had the chance, not to mention biting. The sayings were different then too: a joint was a place to get a beer, but all sorts of things change. I need to go lie down now for a spell, Doc. Can we pick it up tomorrow?"

"Sure, D. Moore. No reason not to."

FIVE

NEXT DAY

"D. Moore, where were you? Did you hear the question? Your eyes seemed to roll over and became glazed. Do you understand the charges against you here?"

"Yes, sir, I believe so. Your name is?"

"Dr. Paul Ford. My name is Paul. Can you tell me why you would do such a thing that you did?"

"What did I do?"

"You don't remember talking to me yesterday?"

"Did I talk to you? Yesterday? What day is it? Yes, of course, yesterday before chow. Of course. Just rattling your chain some, for sure, Doc. Tell me what I did, Doc, so I can see if you're legit."

Yes, Tex and Mike, I know this guy for sure is a lamebrain, good-for-nothing government puppet.

"Well, you shot up a family and killed a fireman and a policeman besides all the property damage you caused."

"If I did all these things, why are you here?"

"Because you asked for me, and we talked about the things you did. And you...we...decided that you should give yourself up. I am here to help you get a better idea of why you would do such a thing.

And to tell the court what I think is going on in your head, why you are the way you are about this thing."

That's a laugh, isn't it, guys? They want to know what's going on in my head. If he really knew, he would just puke. Bet my bottom dollar on that one.

"Did I do it for sure, Doc? You must know that I did. Thought about it a lot. Premeditated, I think you call it. Yes, I did it, so why talk? Let's just get it over with. Let's put the rope around my neck and do it. Get it over with."

As the saints go marching in, we will meet in glory
As the saints go marching in.
I will lay down my rifle and take up the Bible,
As the saints and I go marching into glory.

"Well, we don't use rope anymore."

"What a shame. Could scare some into going straight. Use the firing squad, then. Must be a thousand guys who would enlist just to be on that squad if they knew it was me they would get to shoot."

"Would it have you?"

"Would it have me what?"

"Would it have scared you straight?"

"Hell no. They wanted me to carry out their orders. Ask Jim—he gave them...or at least sanctioned them."

"OK, I know you think you had orders and all, but setting that aside, tell me your story, and remember yesterday you said I could record you."

"Yes, record it all, Doc. Just for you, correct?"

"Yes, just for me. I will transcribe it for the court, in my own words as a doctor. Not your words, just your story. Let's start now. Ready?"

"Yes, sure. I don't think I'll be going anywhere. But just for you. Like doctor-patient records. No telling, yes?"

"That's correct, D. Moore. Tell me why you did what you did. Take all the time you need. I have the recorder on, so tell me your side of it."

"Yes, so my story. Yes, my story. First off, I didn't do anything that I wasn't told to do. Or was told it was OK to do. Just want that clear, Dr. Paul Ford. Just want it made very clear. In case I forget to tell you, I am telling you now. Got that, Doc? You really got that?

"My story is just about a good soldier doing his job. You know, God and country and all. They took a good, naive farm boy and turned him into a killing machine—their own assassin, per se. Made us into nasty people. They knew how, and when it was over, they wanted us to go back to being kind, gentle people. Love thy brother as thyself.

"They think we did it for God and country. The truth is, we did it for the guy next to us, not for the guys giving the orders. To save one of our brothers so he wouldn't have to come over and go through what we were going through. That's it, plain and simple. For each other, and the hell with the rest."

SIX

D. MOORE (DUKE)
JUNE 27, 1947

really liked being outside and being very much alone, as I was for some reason always in trouble.

I would comb the beach when we lived in California and pick up driftwood. One day, I found a perfect spot to build a fort. My fort—my own place, a place to be safe, to leave the world behind. What did I know of the world back then at around eight years old?

It never occurred to me until then that I could do this. And do it in such a way that no one would ever know I was there.

So I did it. At age eight, I was becoming a loner, a person of self-reliance. I built it on my own, and I would lie inside, out of the sun, and stare for hours at the ocean, at the blue waves crashing into the land. I could daydream for hours—about what, I don't know.

As a young boy, I would dream, imagining that if I could live here for the rest of my life, letting the world turn past me, I'd never have to see my folks again. I knew then that I really hated my dad, right to the depths of my soul.

One day, I saw a young couple walk out to the old tree stump that was near the water's edge, around sixty yards from me. They started making out. It was fun to watch, as they would look around and look right at my eyes and never really see me. That was fun, and they really were getting quite carried away.

At an early age, I had figured out that people could look at you and never really see you—if you were quiet, didn't move, and just wore stuff that blended in. At that age, I was the color of sand. I knew this as a good fact: that people could look and not see you. It was movement they were accustomed to seeing.

The fort was invaded by sand crabs. I went home with bites all over me. Mom was as mad as I could ever remember seeing her. She sent me to the washroom to take a long, hot shower, as hot as I could stand it, and then climb into what seemed like boiling water to kill them all off. The next day, I went and burned that place to the ground. Good riddance, nasty crabs!

Hated school. Never in the same place twice. Never had a good friend. I didn't mind beating up on the other kids. I never really got to know their names. From the fourth grade on, I never started school at the first of the year, never finished school at the end of the year, and went to five different schools in between. I had an older half brother two and a half years my senior. Never liked him much, as he liked to make fun of me. He was a mouthy guy who got his comeuppance. We fought a lot, every place we went, and when we did fight, we fought like a pack of wild dogs. When there was no one around to beat on, we beat on each other. My dad would chime in every chance he got. He would beat us up at will, for the fun of it, I guess.

When I was eight, my grandfather gave me my first rifle, a twenty-two long J. C. Higgins. We would go shooting almost every day in the summer.

"How old are you, son?"

"I'm eight, Grandpa. Why do you ask? You know that I had my birthday last week. You were there when Grandma gave me a cake, and I blew out all the candles."

"Yes, you're correct. I just wanted to hear you say it. Now that you're old enough to handle a rifle on your own, here is a present just for you. And I don't ever want to see you misusing it, or it will be mine from that day forth."

"Thank you very much, Grandpa. But how will I buy the shells for the new rifle?"

"When we go shoot the ground squirrels, I supply all the shells. The reason we shoot the squirrels is they ruin the ground for pasture and the hay. When you shoot on your own, and I encourage you to do so, here is the deal: for every blackbird you bring me, just the old crows, and for every gopher you bring me, I will give you one shell. For every bird you bring me that we can eat, I will give you two shells. Now, those birds only count if you shoot them with the rifle, not a shotgun."

I not only learned to shoot better but to be very shrewd about it as well. The blackbirds would sit on the tules that were on the edge of our man-made lake. They would sit there and talk, and I would line them up and shoot them at the base of their heads so they wouldn't fall off. I could get two very easily, but the game for me was to see how many I could get. Five was the maximum I ever shot with one shell. My old hunting dog would hold down the birds until I was ready and then let them fly off. At first, I could never hit them, but when I figured out how to do it, I very seldom missed.

My grandpa was good to me. When we went shooting, he would always quit just after we reloaded. My gun would hold around twenty shells, and if he had an open box, he would give it to me, saying the box would just turn over in his old car and make a hell of a mess. After a while, he told me to just bring back the left wing of the old crows or magpies rather than the whole bird. He also told my dad that he should chip in as well, and he did, so I got double the shells. I could just sneak up on the sage hens, so that made them easy to shoot— just plink their heads off. The ducks were OK, but my grandpa said I couldn't shoot them out on the water, so I never did that except a few times. The geese were not so hard to shoot either, as they would focus on my dog. He was well trained and would never go after them until I was in place. My grandfather told me to be careful on the water, as a goose could drown a dog with ease. So I wouldn't let him chase the birds if they were in the water, because I loved that old dog way too much to take the risk.

While I was at school, my grandpa would sit in his chair out by the barn and shoot his pellet gun at a post some thirty yards off. He could put the pellets on top of each other, and that, my friend, was some dang good shooting. I think my dad got very jealous of his dad and of how much time my grandpa and I spent together. As time passed, my dad would get mad at me over nothing and hit me for it. My grandpa and my dad would have lots of words over that, sometimes getting into fistfights about it.

Because of that, my grandfather took me in when I was eleven, so my dad wouldn't beat me so much. My dad tried to kill me when I was eleven. He had broken my eardrums when I was four by slapping me around. My grandfather died when I was sixteen, and then my dad had no one to hold him back. The funniest thing about my life in those days was that my dad was considered "a pillar of the community"!

At seventeen, I left home, and my dad followed me. I first went to a friend's house, and my folks found me there after a week. Then I went over to my uncle's—my dad's half brother's—place. My dad was mad when he found me there. I awoke one morning to find him standing over me, glaring. I thought he was going to kill me for sure this time. Every time I moved, he would follow me around, place to place, just scaring me, mostly. So two weeks before my eighteenth birthday, I joined the army.

I loved the army from the first day I got there. When I was growing up, my mom's cooking was so good that I thought the army chow was great.

SEVEN

"I know that you guys have been through a lot in the last year and a half, from boot to advanced infantry training. But my goal, my job, was and is to make you into the best damn team this army has ever seen. Yesterday, a lot of your buddies didn't make it through the endurance test, and yesterday, you were just soldiers. Today, you are Special Forces. You thought that boot was hard. Well, now you know it was a cakewalk when you compare it to me making you into the hardened Special Forces you are now. You'll no longer be looked at like ordinary men. You're special. You will honor the legend from this day forth. You will go on to learn to do many things no ordinary person could do. But you will get the job done—and done with pride.

"My job is finished, and you're all on your way to the next phase of your training. I want you to remember me when you're out there in the world and things get tough. You can rely on your instincts from this training camp. Some of you will go on to a different school, and some will stay here and go through sniper school. It is all based on your test scores from the many different tests you were given.

"You in the back of the class with your hand up, I will no longer be your instructor. Good luck to you all, and keep your ass down—it hurts when you're shot there. Your bars are soon to be on, and you're soon to outrank me. But listen up: as long as you're in my house, this place, you will always give me due respect. Otherwise, you could wake up some cold dark night to find a shadow looking down on you just before *your* lights go out.

"All the orders have been cut, and where you're going is posted on the board outside. Sniper class groups are posted on the board as well, and teams are picked. So now, have at it!

"Remember to grab a root and growl!

"Di-i-ismissed!"

Fellow called Mike was on the list as my buddy. We were to bunk together and do this class together as a team. I had a hard time putting my arms around all that, as I was a loner. Sure, we'd done team stuff before now, but each one of us was graded on how we did as an individual. Now, a team, to hold someone close. I was wondering about this shit in my mind, pondering whether this was the end for me. Could I do this stuff?

This guy named Mike was to be my spotter, and I was to be the shooter on the team. He had just graduated from "shake and bake," as it was called. It was a school like this one, but instead of turning out second lieutenants, they turned out NCOs.

"Hi, there. My name is Mike. And you're Moore?"

"Yes, that's correct, but everyone calls me Duke. You can call me that, if you like, and if you don't like, you can call me Sir Duke."

He laughed as he stared at me, lying on my bunk with my feet up on the foot rail. We had our own room, a nice cozy corner one. I had to tell some guy I would bust his head if I couldn't have that room, so he said, "Go for it." I started toward him, and he said, "Stop! I mean go for it; it's just a room."

"Mike, that bunk is yours. Stow your stuff, and let's go for a run."

I began to really like this guy, and I learned a lot about him and his family. Unlike me, he came from a good home—an only child. His folks had died when the car his dad was driving hit a horse, and so Mike enlisted.

We went to school as buddies and learned to work as a team, firing old M1s, with Mike doing the spotting. I learned a lot from Mike. He was a smart guy when it came to knowing and understanding bullet trajectory. He struggled some when he pulled the trigger. We worked together just fine. He was a city boy and not good at hiding, but spotting was easy for him. It took many hours to teach him how to be quiet like an Indian and not to move even if your hand was stepped on. We were at the top of our class: eighty-eight points out of a hundred. A few teams were better in other things, but when it came to the test of hide-and-seek and shoot, we finally mastered that one as well. We were in first place in the field of spotting and shooting at all times.

We were a good team, and the time went by quickly, until one day the captain said, "This is the last day of field training. Tomorrow you receive your new sniper rifles, and with them, you will need to pass or go back to regular forces to be reassigned to a team you don't know."

The next morning, we were out the door early so we could be on line before sunup. All of us who had graduated from field training were to get our new sniper rifles. Let me tell you, those guys I was with were a tough bunch of SOBs.

So we were out on the line, me and Mike, my spotter. He was good too. He could take that handheld device and check everything we needed to know. We were handed our new fifty-caliber sniper rifle. I called ours Old Betsy, after my grandpa's old car. That's what he called the car, because she would never let him down. We filed through the armament building and signed our names to a million forms for every single thing.

We were given instructions on the weapon and were told that if we needed anything changed on Old Betsy, we could go to the warrant officer, the guy standing in the rear. He could fix or adjust anything we wanted to have done.

"Mike, go pick a bench and start taking Old Betsy apart. Clean it up, as this old girl is your life now, and she's the only thing between you and the devil."

So, this was my new rifle. "It's for shooting, and my gun is for fun," goes old army saying.

As Mike and I were taking it apart, cleaning every inch of her sleek body, we both marveled at how heavy she was.

"Hey, Duke."

"Yes, Mike."

"Maybe we should call her Two-Ton Tilly."

"No, Mike, it's not nice to call your mom that."

"Not my mom, you bastard—Old Betsy."

"Yes, for sure, but she'll love you better than anyone else in this world. And I'll teach you to shoot her proficiently, just like my grandpa taught me. I can, you know. There's a knack to everything, and I will show you. So clean her good and oil her up, and we will love her as she does us. I'll be right back."

"Where you going, Duke?"

"I need to see the warrant officer."

So it took him almost three hours to do what I wanted him to do.

"Where you been, Duke? If I clean this thing any more, I'll rub it in two."

"Went to that warrant officer to get the trigger fixed for me—a pull release and set for eighteen ounces' squeeze to set her."

"Whatever you say, Duke. That's above my pay grade."

"So let's put her back together now and go out and boresight her in at a thousand yards. What you say, Mike? And then let her plunk some targets. So give me the lowdown, Mike: How far is the last target out there?"

"Range finder says three thousand yards."

"You sure, Mike? Think about this before you use that gizmo. The one thing the army does is never give us an even number to work with. It never happens out in the field and for sure not here in training. If that's a mile to the crossroad and another to where you turn and go behind the targets, behind all the bunkers, it must be halfway back, so let's just say a mile and a half. At this distance, we can't be guessing, so let's practice on our range some, OK?"

"Yes, for sure, Duke. Getting better readings now."

"Well, then, Mike, it's just like I thought—never an exact number. It wouldn't be as much fun for the target masters, now, would it?"

"My scope said with a few clicks that it should be around seven thousand nine hundred and forty feet. You got that, Duke?"

"Yes, got it. Now, let's dial this baby in and make her talk to those guys down there. With my power set to max, looks like the mark is the size of a quarter, but you're the bullet master. What do you have?"

"I read now, with the dust out of this thing, is it...or...I've never looked that far before, Duke."

"The best thing for your eyes, Mike, is to look far, focus in, and then come toward yourself. Things will adjust faster and more accurately. Has to be that way for this distance shooting. Far target is two thousand six hundred and sixty yards, so now midway, what do you have? I say just under a mile: one thousand six hundred and ninety yards."

"Yes, right on, Duke."

"Now the close one, Mike. What do you have—one thousand yards?"

"More like one thousand two hundred and sixty-eight."

"OK, Mike, I have that. So now we have that all done. Let's adjust Old Betsy up again. Start with the far one."

"OK, got it, Duke. Six full turns up, that's twelve clicks to the turn if you want to count. Wind: four turns to the right, max forty-eight total right, seventy-two up. We're going to be the best team out here. Where did you learn this stuff, Duke?"

"My granddad loved to shoot and took me with him every day. When we would go, we shot at least two hundred rounds every day, each of us, at ground squirrels. So now give me the clip with the highest velocity, Mike. OK, now plug it in, and let's start over. If we have the right info on this ammo, what's the wind and droppage going to do to us?"

"Same, Duke. Six full turns up and four clicks right side for wind."

"Can't do it, my friend. Look, the wind here is blowing left, and wind there is blowing somewhat to the right. Read again?"

"OK, six up...and now two for right wind. Agreed?"

"Yes, agreed. OK. So let's fire one for getting our bearings in. Ready?"

"Yes, I am, Duke. Earmuffs are on. Are you ready? Have your ear-plugs in?"

"Mike, what did you say? Yes, ready. Wave at the instructor to let him know."

Seeing our signal, the instructor approached us.

"OK, you boys think you got it figured out?"

"Yes, sir."

"OK. Ever fire a scoped rife before?"

"No, sir. The M14 was open-peep sights. Liked it that way. Why?"

"I just think you have your eye a little close to the lens. Might want to readjust it, is all I'm saying."

"You think so, sir? If we do, we'll have to use the laser-bore thing again and resight it if we move it. Is that the correct way?"

"Yes, just think one rule: three fingers from the edge of the scope is the rule of thumb. OK, hand me your folder, spotter, and let's go bang a hole in some metal."

"Sir, metal?"

"Yes, Sarge, metal. These targets are metal so you can see them better. How you doing?"

"Yes, sir, locked and loaded."

"Well, looks like you two are in the lead to be on the top of the list."

"Yes, sir, we try."

"Shooter, it's your game. Let me know, and we'll clear the field and make ready for you. You're sure you're ready? No one else is."

We nodded.

"Well, OK. Let me know when you're going to pull one off."

"Yes, sir. We're ready."

"Shooter?"

"Ready."

"Spotter?"

"Ready."

"Mike?"

"Yes, Duke?"

"Check to make sure everything is the same. Sir?"

"Yes, shooter?"

"We are going for the far one first, then move into those closest to us, then back to the far one, then to the first, and then the middle. Five rounds. OK?"

"Whatever you want. You're the shooter, not me, but you know this one is just for fun, right? No scoring today, shooter. Just want to see how you're going to handle the fifty, is all."

With that, he cleared his throat and shouted, "Ready on the firing line!"

'Yes, sir, ready as we will ever be. Mike, keep your eye in the scope, and let me know where she lands. Want to know if adjustments are needed as we go."

I pulled the trigger, and to the officer's surprise, nothing happened.

"Did you put one in the chamber?" he asked.

"Yes, sir, I did. Mind not talking? Need to let me concentrate here for my first one."

"OK, shooter, but—"

Blam!

I released it. Next thing I knew, I was dazed, and my eye was bleeding. Hurt like hell. Wouldn't tell him, though. Looked at him, and he just held up three fingers. Mike looked at me and also held up three fingers.

"Guess my eye was a little too close, huh?"

"Well, you think so?" they said in unison as a black haze tried to take me away.

"Spotter, fix your man, and let's see where he hit it. Wait. Move it, spotter. Who told you, shooter, that you could have a release trigger?"

"No one, sir."

Just then, a black blanket was pulled over my face. The next thing I knew, Mike was picking up our stuff.

"Mike, where we going?"

"Hell, glad to see you're over your nap. We need to go—have to get that eye looked at and resight the Two-Ton—I mean, resight in Old Betsy. Need three fingers, wouldn't you say?"

"Yes, we do. My head hurts like you've been beating on me for a while. How did we do?"

"Hit her dead in the center of the heart, Duke. They say never saw it done before at that range."

Yes! We did it! I thought to myself.

Mike and I were a good team. He carried a lot of extra ammo for us throughout the war. He had memorized all the ballistics of every round. We really liked our Old Betsy. Wish I could have kept her, but they kept upgrading us to better, faster, lighter, with tripods. All this fancy-dancy stuff. But not one of them could outshoot my first old love, Betsy. One thing I did like was the silencer. Well, not really a silencer—a noise suppresser and blast redirector as well. It was heavy, giving us a nice counterbalance for muzzle jump.

We didn't make first in class at sniper school. It was very disappointing to me, as I wasn't used to being second. I did finish best shot, but because we had to do another bore setting with the scope (seeing it was not three fingers from my eye), it put us behind in paperwork, and that cost us points as a team. Mike made first as best spotter, and that was great. They kept us together as a team!

EIGHT

This was our first jack-off mission! The high brass had it all wrong. From the get-go the mission was all screwed up. This was my first mission out of the box—and the first time I came to the realization that the words *calculated risk loss* applied to me as much as to any man in this one-man's army.

"Well, here we are, guys. Look at your maps. The blue dots are the ammo dumps that have been hit. You can see they're kind of in a horseshoe effect. We need to make contact with these guys. We don't know who they are, so think about this: If you were to hit these dumps, where would you go to get back into your homeland? In red, I marked the route I think they all would take going back home. Yes, you guessed it correctly. We are going into Czech to find these guys who have been raiding our ammo dumps. They're tough men, really tough. They've been killing the guard dogs, along with our guys, without a sound. Be sharp, and don't wear anything that tells who, what, or where.

"Men, at 0800, we meet at spot alpha on the map. If we get caught, we are just some guys that the USA doesn't know anything about.

Now, look again at the maps, all of us together, and see if you think there's another route they might want to take that I have overlooked."

"Got ya, Duke."

So we looked and planned our route. My fear was that we would come across the Commies on this side of the border and get into a real firefight. We weren't going to be armed that heavily, so I asked the commander if we could have a tail to the border, maybe even thirty minutes at most behind us. If we did get spotted, we would need help for sure. And if we could catch the Commies on this side—well, then they were spies. And we could deal with them the way we knew we would be dealt with if we got caught on the Commies' side: dark holes, water up to your knees, loud music, and a few beatings, until one of us cracked. I would have liked to think that none of us would crack, but then I only knew the ways I had been trained to get *others* to crack. I was sure the Commies were less civilized than that.

So we stole a car that had been arranged for us to take. The keys were under the fender skirt. It was a normal-looking car, but it was from the past. It had belonged to a German diplomat and had some added weight. There was armor around the back so he couldn't be shot from the rear, the gas tank was oversized for longer range as well as protected, and there was some added driver protection. We had to have the car back by 0600 the next day, or the new owner would report it stolen. Normally, if we were going to be inside the border, we would have had an old commando car that had hideaway compartments to keep our unmarked rifles, cameras, and the like. Those cars were also bulletproof to a degree. Anyway, my Old Betsy along with some armor-piercing shells would make it inside the diplomat car.

We were crossing into an iron curtain country. Nothing we had, or seemed to have, could or should be found on us or the car. Our government needed to be able to say it knew nothing about us or about any mission we might have thought we were on.

We drove for hours to make the rendezvous with these tough guys. We thought the CIA must have had it wrong, because they never showed. We had a beer at a guest house across from the meeting place in the market square. We spread out individually rather than sticking together so that we wouldn't be conspicuous. When they didn't show by two hours past the meeting time, I got spooked. We then beat feet. We didn't know if the CIA was setting us up, and we weren't going to wait around to find out. Being caught behind the iron curtain wasn't what I or any of my guys had signed up for.

We had been told the guys we were to meet were the Commies behind the ones coming across the border and stealing arms from our depots. We were told they had killed a lot of our guys. The brass, the CIA, really wanted us to get this done. They had told us to make any deal we could to put a stop to the stealing and killing, offering to supply them with arms directly if that was what it took.

We made it back to where the car was to be dropped off with an hour to spare. On the way back, we had wiped it down, and we had our gloves on. We hoped it would not be checked. We put the envelope that had been left for us in our get-home vehicle into the glove box of the diplomat car, and that was it.

With the mission failure, I talked to the brass about letting us reinforce the depots and change the guards to some Special Forces teams. With all in agreement, we formed a plan to set those Czech guys up so we could catch them. We each took a team of Special Forces newly assigned to us and built our plan for every depot that had already been raided as well as for the ones close by that looked like good targets. We kept it as secret as we were able. We fortified the ammo depots, putting in a lot of listening devices, armor plating the lookout towers, burying the telephone and electric wires so they couldn't be seen and cut, and putting in backup automatic generation so the power would never turn off. The last touch was putting new, better-trained guard dogs—and I mean *really* mean dogs—into every site inside the compound. These dogs couldn't be touched, even by their handler. I had never seen such hatred in an animal, then or since.

We then broke up and staked out the depots at random. I was the only one who knew where we would be at any given time. I trusted my guys, but that was the extent of my trust. We had radios, but in those days, they were as much use to us as tits on a boar hog. To say the least, they were unreliable. We moved around a lot, trying to outguess where they were going to hit next. They never did come back on my watch with any success.

We never caught them, but we came close one night at the place where Mike and I were staked out. Close, as they say, but no cigar. They were able to shoot and wound our lookout-tower man. All I saw was the flash. I slapped Mike and pointed. I took out after them, in the lead and running like a crazy rabid dog, with Mike close behind me. There were four of them. I have great night vision, and I had my forty-five ready, silencer on, but I could never get close enough to take a shot. In the woods, where they went, I knew the only thing I would do if I pulled one off was blind myself, even with one eye closed.

We chased them for most of the night until early the next day. I could get close enough to smell them and hear them talking, and I wanted to shoot one just for good measure. They split up on Mike and me, and we had to stop to dig in, waiting for the light. That's when we heard the car: doors opened, closed, and diesel motor started and sped away. We still stayed low, not wanting to give a sniper a shot. I figured that was what I would have done in their place—stay behind and get the SOB who had scared ten years out of me. We finally left, found the tire marks, and discussed and cussed it. It had to be a diesel Mercedes.

Cat and mouse ended soon, and the guards were OK left by them-selves. Our time in Germany was well spent. No more body count for either side, and from what I was told later, the Russians had mopped up and left the Czechs to themselves. Their goal was to disarm the Czechs, and they had done it well.

NINE

VIETNAM
JANUARY 3, 1970

We went to the Japanese base on a nonstop flight from Germany. We were briefed there.

As Mike and I were told about the mission for us and for our team, I looked around the room at all the brass. Hell, even General Pat was in on the briefing. That they had Mike in on this briefing was very puzzling to me. Thought for sure I was about to lose my bars for the way the last mission had gone down. Everyone was cool. They said they just wanted Mike to get his feet wet on this easy one. Easy, my ass. They say all of them are easy peasy. Well, it ain't them out there, for sure.

We were to be choppered in to within about eight miles of our targets. Mike could change that later, if he wanted to, when he briefed the pilots. We were told that we would go to an old French estate and pop three guys who were selling arms to the North. There were arms from China as well. Not just small arms but antiaircraft guns, like the one Jane Fonda had had her picture taken on. That photo confirmed that the North had at least one antiaircraft gun, and the State Department could see the make and model. They traced where it had come from, and that had led us to this mission. What a bum rap she got for doing our reconnaissance for us. Name of the game, I suppose. She may not have known for sure what she was doing, but it was a big help all the same.

From the base in Japan, we went by plane to an aircraft carrier and then were choppered out to the drop zone. I was glad of that. I didn't like the idea of going into the river first thing off the bat. We had walked for four of the five days. It was slower than we had thought it would be. The jungle just flat wore us out. It was so thick in spots that it seemed we were walking backward, but there was still no hurry to my mind. That's when, for no reason, the heavens opened up and swallowed my heart.

"Don't move, Mike! You're on it. Don't let it up!"

"I know, Duke. I'm a talking dead man."

"Don't say that. We'll figure it out. The rest of you guys, step back slowly in your own tracks until you pass mine, and then walk to me. OK. Now, you guys know that Mike is on a land mine, so be prepared. There is a stream bed up there about two hundred yards. Go get in it, and don't make a lot of tracks. If this thing blows, they will come running. So then, drop down, and give us fire cover. Got it? If it doesn't blow, then we'll get the hell out of here. So move it!"

"Duke, we're all screwed. If it goes off, we'll be heard for five miles, for sure. And Mike is team leader on this mission. I think we should be going back the way we came in and rethinking this mission. Besides, who died and made you back in charge of the mission?"

"You, if you don't get the fuck on the move, *now*."

"You heard him, guys. He's in charge. I release my team leadership to Duke. Move it now, as he says."

"Thanks, Mike. You're going to be OK. You know, that's the first time the guys have ever questioned me for one second. Shows how much they rely on you to keep them sane. We both know that, and you've always been our team leader from the start of them all."

I watched as the guys moved slowly to the riverbed. They knew I was always in charge and that Mike was always my right-hand guy.

Second, for sure, but he took care of the guys, and I took care of the mission. Out here, it didn't make a hill of beans what the brass said or didn't say. "Fuck the brass," I said under my breath. It was I who had brought their dog tags home on their own feet walking, and this mission was not going to change one dang thing—not as long as I drew breath. Not if I had anything to say about it. With my heart in my mouth, I hoped to hell all the training we'd done would pay off for us now, as we didn't have any room for a mistake.

"Mike, I will come to you. Sit down on your foot so that you are relaxed and calm. Now, that's it. Take all your stuff off and hand it to me."

"Stay back, Duke. This thing could just go if there is a timer besides the release button."

"Mike, if there was a timer, it would have gone off already. It's been more than a minute, and that's maximum. So now hand me all your stuff. We can do this, Mike, and if we don't, I want you to know that I love you, bro, so don't do anything stupid like try to run, OK?"

"Love you too, bro. We've been through a lot tougher, and no, I am not stupid. Would do the same for you if the shoe was on the other foot."

"Mike, OK, got it. Take your stiletto, and slide it between your foot and the sole of the boot. Don't worry about cutting your foot. You need to keep the pressure the same. You got it. Now, here, take mine and cut the boot laces. Now the tongue. When you can get your foot free of the boot, slide it out on my command. Got it?"

"Yes, Duke, got it. Ready to slide my foot out on your command."

"Mike, now put your hands on each side of the knife, and slide your foot out. Do a handstand, kind of, and then lie flat on the knife."

"Got it, Duke. Dwight, *don't leave me!*"

"I am here for you, bro."

Mike was a big kid. At six feet and 220 pounds, he could pick up a VW and carry it a mile. After sliding the one knife under his foot, he slit the laces and then did a handstand. His foot free, he lay down on the knife.

"Good, you got it. Can you hear a timer?"

"Yes, I think so."

"OK, Mike, I'll go to the stream, and when it goes off, we'll be ready for whatever."

"Duke, don't let me die this way. Just shoot me in the top of my head or something. I will lie here till they come and get me, and then maybe it will explode. Then, only then. Please, Duke, do it. I would for you."

"What are you saying? Shoot my best buddy?"

"Yes, shoot me, Duke. Please do it. This old land mine—the chances are it will not kill me, and I'll just lie here and die a slow one. Do it, Duke. Just do it. Think of the mission. One way or another, this will go off, and then the rest of you guys will not make it out of this hell."

"OK, I will—from the bank of the stream. OK, lie still now, very quiet. If it doesn't go off in an hour or so, maybe you could run for it. What do you think?"

"Not a chance, Duke, not a chance. If and when I move, this thing will give our position away."

I moved away to join the rest of the men in the stream bed.

"OK, you guys find any more mines? Look good just over the bank, under the leaves, dead grass..."

"Nothing, Duke. We didn't find a thing."

"OK, walk upstream in the water. Don't make any footprints; step on the rocks only. Be careful, don't slip. I don't want to see any mud. Go now, and for God's sake be quiet. Go now, at least three hundred yards. Here, divide up Mike's pack. We will need all of it."

I watched them until they were out of sight upstream. I looked for any movement, upstream, downstream, in front, behind, over to where Mike was—and nothing. Whistling at Mike our signal indicating that all was OK, I put the noise suppresser on my two by fourteen. He whistled back that all was OK. I had to shoot him but not move him an inch off that mine.

"Tex, what do you think? We safe here for a time?"

"No, boy, we need to move. I have scouted around. Nothing in a quarter mile, but they have tunnels all over this damn country, little tunnel rats that they are. Listen, Duke, don't leave Mike this way. Let me go talk to him. Then, when and if he whistles, then do what you must. But not if he doesn't whistle. OK, boy? OK?"

Mike whistled, and a sharp pang ran through my body, tearing into my heart and welling into my eyes. I hesitated for the first time in my life, knowing I should pull the trigger.

"God damn you, Mike!" Tears clouded my vision. "Why? You done did it this time, damn you!"

◆　◆　◆

The next two days were rough. No one said a word to me, or I to them. We walked nonstop to our place of contact. I had a bad feeling, very bad. Tex, John, Allen, Tom—all of them just looked at me. We used hand signs to talk until the time was right for the attack to start. We whispered how it would go down: John and Allen were to the right; Tom and I were in the back preparing our gear for the shot; Sam, the gook, was covering our rear door; and Tex was out scouting the area. Sam was between Tom and me and the other part of the team. I started walking forward to the left, half crouched, far enough to the left now so that it was hard to see Allen and John in the tall elephant grass. Both groups were now walking in a V from our point of departure. I stopped and lay down behind some young bamboo. Mike was beside me.

I turned and said, "Mike, you ready?"

"Tom, Duke. I'm Tom."

"You ready, lad?"

"Yes, Duke. Ready as I'll ever be."

Before the words were clear of his mouth, all hell broke loose. Small-arms fire was coming from all around us. We were surrounded. Tom lay flat beside me, looking at me.

"I say there, old chap, we've been set up. Let's get the boys and get the hell out of here."

I crawled backward, popping a shot now and again and hitting one with every shot. Tom was scared. Turning around, he started crawling quickly. I watched to our right side and then to our back, which had been our front two seconds ago. I could hear John and Allen doing the same. "Must be like Custer's last stand" was the only thing going through my mind, and then it happened—a thought past dying. If ever I find those SOBs who sent us to our graves, they were dead. Tom stopped crawling. Lying beside me, he rested his head on my rump, and I rested mine on his.

"Duke, I think they got Allen and John. I don't hear them moving or shooting anymore."

I slowly turned my head. I couldn't tell from my position, lying flatter than a pancake in a skillet.

"Tom, I can't tell, but let's hope not. Let's leave this spot. We need to keep buddy-crawling. When we hit the ravine, we will find that gook and shoot him if he's still there."

"What about Mike? Is he there also, Duke?"

"No, Tom, he isn't. He went home to secure the drop zone."

We buddy-crawled, with me still set on silent, hitting everything that was near us. It looked like they were intent on getting to the ravine before we did. In the ravine, now walking half crouched to stay hidden and Tom still holding back his firepower, I continued to pop them. They were well aware of someone killing them but weren't sure yet where it was coming from.

"Oh, God, Duke, look! Sam the Gook! Look! Putting out a lot of lead to help us."

"OK, let's move. Stay down, and don't shoot yet. Let me do it. I am on silent, and they don't know that we're here yet. They just keep seeing their guys fall, is all. This could give us the time we need to get out of here."

"What about our mission, Duke?"

"Well, it's over, but if you like, you can go it alone."

"Not me. I am out of here with you. I'm not letting you leave my sight again, ever. If I am to make it, it will be with you."

We had crawled for an hour buddy style, our feet hooked together, he pulling me along as I shot very carefully. Slowly and methodically. Didn't want to give our place away. The tall elephant grass, the young bamboo, and my silencer were our godsend. We were finally to Sam the Gook, and sure as hell, he had shot most of the guys who had stood up to try to see me. Looked like we had them now, but a firefight in the jungle could be heard for miles. And, hell, who knew? They might have a tunnel with another brigade of a million of these little Commie bastards. Sam, Tom, and I finished the last ones off, and then I turned to Sam.

"Sam the Gook, how did they know we were coming?"

"Me don't know. Just a patrol, is all, maybe. Me don't know, sir."

"Tom, let's drink up, fill our canteens, take our pills, and move out of here."

"Tex?"

"Back door still clean, Duke."

"You go get the dog tags for me, will you?"

"They're in your backpack already."

"All of them?"

"Yes, all three."

"Duke?"

"Yes, Tom?"

"We're going back to where Mike is waiting for us?"

"No, Tom, he's gone. Sent him back to the drop zone. We'll go to the northwest, not where anyone would expect us to go, especially the gook army. I think I shoot you, Sam, in the guts now. Gook, you die very slowly. You a part of this, Mr. Sam Gook?"

"No, no, not a part, no! I not know this patrol was here. Don't shoot me, please, sir."

"Then lead Tom and me to a safe spot, and I will let you live. But if I think you are leading us into a new trap, I shoot you. You be first shot out of my gun. You hear me, Sammyboy Gook?"

"Yes, me hear you very loud, very clear. Where we go?"

"The place they'll never look: northwest."

"Duke, our supplies—we need them."

"No, not now, Tom. We live off the land, like him, but you do what you like. Me, I'm going north three or four days, then southeast. Map is here in my head. I know where I want to go. Now, follow or not, but if you don't follow now, don't change your mind. From this moment on, I will shoot whoever and whatever gets in my way to being safe."

"No way am I even thinking of going it on my own. No way."

So we ran three days and nights. How, you ask? Because we were so scared. We were crazy scared, in our finest hours of youth. We'd left for war as boys; we came back from war as old men. Yes, twenty and able to climb the tallest hill, crazy scared. You don't shit; you don't pee. Not while you think there is the slightest chance they will find you. We were taught how to change our breathing, change our heartbeat. But me, I was so crazy scared that I knew for a fact that if anyone came within a hundred yards of me, they would smell my fear and hear my heartbeat. My heart wouldn't slow down, and I couldn't relax to let it. My mind was on high alert. I could see around things, see into tunnels that weren't there. God, I was so scared that I was shaking. As the old saying goes, like a dog shitting peach seeds.

"We are safe for now, for the moment. But we need water and rest, Sam the Gook. We need to find a hiding spot to rest, and then we will part company. You have done a good job, Sam the Gook. But look at me. You're not out of the woods yet. Not till I am. Got that, Sam the Gook?"

He was bent over, hands on his knees, almost in a sitting position, taking big gulps of air into himself, letting it out slowly, some blood dripping from his chin. I knew he was done for. The blood on his chin was from his lungs, which were bleeding from trying to produce air for his body if I said we needed to run some more.

"We hide in tunnel, Duke. I will find one for us all to hide. There are plenty in this area. We find one they store stuff in to hide when the bombs come. They will have food in some, and we get water. You like rice ball, yes?"

So we hid, still too scared to move, so tired, but sleep didn't come. We covered ourselves in mud and dirt so the dogs, if they had them, would have a harder time smelling us. I hadn't seen many in this country, but that's how my mind was working, being so damn scared. I was trying to calm myself down, breathing correctly from my diaphragm, not regular breathing from my stomach. I could hear thunder and then feel the lightning strike. I was sure we would all drown from the rain, as the vault door to this grave was just a piece of grass sod. Then it struck me: it wasn't rain and thunder I was hearing; it was our own bombs. The lightning was the earthquake that was shaking the ground. A hell of a way to die: in a man-made grave from our own bombs.

I had to pee on the second day in the tunnel, but if I did, it could give us away. So I peed into my canteen cup, just enough to make the pain go away, and then I drank it. Don't ask what it tasted like—I was too scared to know. After a few days, three or maybe four, we left. Sam the Gook went farther north. We took all but one clip of his ammo, leaving him twenty rounds and all he had for his forty-five auto. In this jungle, a pistol was more useful than a rifle. We headed southeast. I knew we would run across our guys, and hopefully that would be before another firefight happened.

We finally found an outpost. They had had some really tough firefights, so they were very wary of letting us in. Finally, after a long jaw with their commander and his spending time on the radio, we were let into their hell hole. What I remember most about the marines was that they were well dug in but didn't have enough clearing between them and the rest of the top of their little hill. We stayed and worked the night shift with them. God, the rats were so bad you had to wrap yourself in a blanket to keep them from coming up on you and trying to eat your flesh while you weren't able to do a thing but try to shoo them away. The next day, a medic chopper came in, and we rode out with five body bags. They were replaced with ten guys who looked so young I didn't think they were even shaving yet.

One looked at me and said, "You the Duke guy everyone tells us about? Duke the Legend?"

"Hell no, marine. Just a guy who likes to keep his head and ass down, and I'm telling you that you should do the same."

I was very dirty when we got back on the navy ship. Same one, the USS *Cleveland*—who would have thought? Chopper dumped us off and then headed back to a carrier or someplace for the body-bag drop. That's when I showered. The water ran brown forever, it seemed. Soaped up three or four times to get clean.

"God, this shower feels good. What do you think, Mike, Tex? Is this the best dang life ever in this here military? Next life we join the navy. What do you guys say?"

"Yes, for sure, Duke. Mike and I are really enjoying this hot water. Feels very soft as well. Did you know that regular sailors shower in seawater, not the stuff from the boiler? Rank has its privilege."

Then we were debriefed and sent back to our base in Germany. In total, the longest five weeks of my entire life. Hardest day was turning in those dog tags. Didn't say much. Was too dang mad. I felt then that we had been set up. Today, this day, I know *for sure* we were set up.

TEN

LOVE OF LIFE

"Hello, there. Can I help you?"

"Well, hello, there, skinny! Yes, you may. My car needs some oil and gas. Can I pay you inside here for the entire amount? Seems I don't have a credit card. You do take cash, don't you?"

"Yes, we do. Where're you going? My name is Connie. What's yours? And what's with this 'skinny' thing anyway?"

"Sorry, didn't mean to upset you. My name? Well, most call me Duke. Headed up to the dance over on Third and Post. Left my wallet in my room. Why? Is that a problem, with me going to that dance?"

"No, not really—not with me anyway. Just with the owner. Seems like two years ago some asshole bought the place, and now all goes by the book. Some old army vet is who bought it, so I am told. Hires nothing but vets to run the place. They think us kids are too rowdy sometimes and card us all the time, even though they know we've been there before. You know, I'm off work in five, so if you like, you could follow me there. I'll be ready by the time you get your gas pumped and the oil added. What do you say? Not a date—just thought you might like to follow, is all."

"Sure, why not? If I don't have to call it a date or anything like that."

"Why? You married or something?"

"No, I was just joking with you. Using your own words, is all. Which car is yours?"

"The faded-pink bug over there. It's not much, but it's fun to drive. It's a stick, very gutless but very cheap on gas. Don't make much of a wage working here."

"Will follow you there. I don't dance, so don't ask. OK?"

"Man, Tex, this gal is some looker. Don't you think so? And man, what a set of hooters. I could dig this for a long time...When the saints come marching in; oh, when the saints come marching in..."

"Thanks, Connie. I don't think I could have found this place very easily without you. I need to do an errand before I go in. Maybe I'll see you inside later?"

"Hope so. See ya...Duke."

"See ya, Connie. Say, you got a steady guy?"

"Nah. Guys, they seem kind of like prudes to me anyway. Why? You looking?"

"Hell, I'm probably one of those prudes. But was asking anyway. Maybe yes, maybe no."

"Hell yes, we're looking. What you think about going to our place after the dance? God, that Connie is a looker. Five foot two, I would think. Man, what a build. Blond hair...but who knows but Miss Clairol? Guess she doesn't like vets. Better not let her know I'm the asshole who bought the place two years ago when I was down here for some training. I really like San Diego, but it's just not a place to hang my hat. Place seems quiet enough tonight. Look, there's Connie over at the far table. She has a lot of guys around her. She doesn't have a steady, and I am not a guy with a bulge in his pants, my ass I'm not. Look at her. The flirt...Everyone gets up to dance but her. Well, maybe she is single, after all. Looks like she's headed to the restroom. Better not be caught staring."

"So, hey, there, Duke. I've been looking all over the bar for you. Thought you might buy me a drink, and then I will buy you one. What do you say about that? Why're you in the corner here?"

I waved to the waitress. "Will you please get this lady a couple of drinks for me? She's my friend."

"Sure thing, Mr. Moore."

"She knows you, Duke. How does she know you?"

"I work here. First day on the job. I'm the new bouncer."

"So that's why you don't dance...'and don't ask me.'"

"Yes, that could be one of the reasons. But really, besides the work, I don't dance."

"Here is your drink, miss."

"Thanks. Just put it on my tab, will you, please?"

"Sure thing. Anything else?"

"No, it's too close to closing. Better have the barkeeper call for last round."

"So this is a nice song by Patsy Cline, Duke. We could dance one slow one. Can't you at least dance one slow one with me?"

"Yes, one slow one. Just this one. Then I need to help close and see everyone makes it out. You know, safe and sound and all by the book. God, Connie, you really feel good in my arms. Been a long time for me. Well, maybe not a long time, maybe forever."

"Nice dance, Duke, and you're not half bad at it either. Maybe if you come by the station tomorrow, we could talk some on my breaks and all. What do you think? OK?"

"Nice meeting you, Connie. But I don't know. We'll see. Good night for now."

"You too. Good night. Oh, and by the way, you're a good dancer for a guy who doesn't know how."

I started hanging out at the beach, early in the day mostly, as that's when it was vacant for the most part. Walking, thinking of my past, where my future would lead me. Walking one morning on the beach, thinking about what to do with my life, I made my mind up to join the ranks of the Black Ops. They were sure offering me a shitload of money to do the same job I had been doing in the army, and almost all of them were retired Special Forces or Green Berets. A soldier but yet not one. But still taking orders from the army; the same old guys still in charge. The base pay was very good, and the bonus plan for each mission was great. The way I figured it, in a short three or four years, I would have a few million stashed away and be able to live anyplace I wanted in the world.

My three-month leave was just getting started, and with two weeks gone, I was feeling the pressure of it being over before it had really got started. It was going by far too fast. The job on Friday and Saturday nights helped, and then it didn't help. For sure, it wasn't my cup of tea as a job, but it was a good investment as long as my old friend Frank was alive and taking care of it. I was backing out of the job, telling my old buddy that I was going to be gone again but longer this time. He was good with that. I told him I wanted to hook up with Connie and see where it might go, but for her safety, I didn't want to let anyone know. If she asked about me, I asked him to tell her the beach on Baja was my favorite place.

I knew that this line of work—being a bouncer—was not for me. Too much temptation to just pull out my forty-five and shoot some of those loudmouths. Stupid, drunk jarheads, mostly. Sure would help clean up the gene pool a bit. Was offered a job from a large insurance company that entailed recovering bail jumpers. No, thank you. That would be like stepping into a ring with five guys twice your size guns when all you had was a knife. Walking down the beach, trying to clear my head, running all the old missions through my mind, knowing the Cold War was getting worse not better, and now, at twenty-six, feeling quite old for that job. I was feeling somewhat good about my next path in life. Songs, nice old songs playing in my head. Mike talking to me, telling me the only thing for us was the army. "Guess you're right, old man," was all I could tell him. But the songs were playing louder.

"Tex, what do you say? Tell me what you think I should do."

"Look there, Duke. There's Connie. Play cool, boy. Don't spook her."

"Hello, there, D. Moore. Hey, wait up! Hello."

"Oh, hello, there. Connie, right?"

I knew she had gotten hints from Frank. He had called me, and he was the only one who knew where I was. I told him, "Hell yes, tell her where I am, but don't let her know that I set this up, please." So here she was, my sexy little angel. God, she was so dang good looking. I was hoping she wouldn't mind when she found out I was a vet.

"Yes, you're correct, Duke. And what are you doing out here anyway? It's far from the bar. Don't you work tonight?"

"No, just Friday and Saturday nights, when it's busy. Why? Besides, I told that Frank guy to take that job and...Well, I told him I quit. He said that was fine with him, as I was a lousy bouncer anyway."

"Well, I was running after you, calling to you, and you just kept on walking. What was so on your mind that you didn't hear me call you?"

"Just my life, wondering what to do with it. That's all."

"With what?"

"My life. See, I am still army and on leave. Took this job to see if I could fit back in. Doesn't look like it..."

"Tex? Yes, Mike. Boy, oh, boy, just look at those jugs. Sure would like to get my hands on those. What you say, Duke? Let's take her for a drive and make out with those."

"It really doesn't seem to be working out for me."

"Well, I can see you need some company. Want to go to dinner?"

Hell yes, we do.

"No, don't think so. But thanks anyway."

Damn you, Duke. What's up? You need...we all need...a good lay.

"Well, then, how about we just go for a drive and maybe a movie? No obligation from you or me. Is that OK?"

"I don't know, Connie, maybe a drive. No movie for sure, not today anyway."

Yes, yes, yes. Tex, speak to Duke and wake him up. Can't he see this gal really likes him?

"Well, OK, Duke, just a drive. Maybe we should take my car, as my mom says to watch out for you army guys. You all have Russian fingers and Roman hands."

"I don't have those kinds of fingers on any sort of a hand."

That made her very sober, very fast.

"Well, dang, I was sure hoping. Then guess there's no need to go for a drive in my car. If you're not going to make out with me, we can stay and walk here on the beach some. Want to tell me what is on your mind?"

"You don't need to know any of my stuff. Besides, if I told you, it would probably scare you off. You'd probably go home crying."

"What is it that might scare me off? I don't cry, and nothing about you or what you say would scare me off. I already know you're Special Forces, a sniper. You kill people for the army."

"How do you know all that? We never talked before, not about *that* stuff."

"Well, see, my dad was an officer in the army. Died in Korea— friendly fire, they say. Can you believe it? Who's a friend that shoots you? Besides, my mom is well connected to some general. I went to the bar to see you. Then Frank told me that you were down here and that you were in the army. You told me your name, and I knew you were about six years older than me, so I asked Mom if she could pull some strings. I knew she could, seeing as how she has been banging that general since Dad went missing...or died. He never showed back up, and we just buried an empty box."

"So you did all that just to find out who I am? What for?"

"Are you stupid? Can't you see I really like you? I did the first day at the gas station when you were so polite to me. Well, here we are at the parking spot. Which car is yours?"

"You tell me. Seems you know a lot more about me than I do about you."

"The maroon Corvette is yours. Has your plate DMB 69 V on it, and that is how I know. Besides, you drove it to the store and followed me. Did you forget?"

"Did I? Just checking on you. Would you like the top down or up?"

"Down, please."

"Thought we were going to take your car so I would be able to use my Roman hands on you. Where you want to go?"

"You pick. Just as long as I can feel the warm breeze in my hair, I'm good to go."

We dated for two weeks, going almost everywhere together. Spent almost every night on her mom's porch. She knew that the way to a man's heart was through his stomach, and she could cook, let me tell you. She would hold me tightly and say, "Don't go. You can stay. Mom likes you." I never did. I wanted to very much. I just never could.

One day after picking her up from work, I asked her, "Where to tonight, sweetheart?"

She slipped in as close as she could with that damn old center console in the way and said, "Let's go south. My mom has a home in Mexico. We could be there in a few hours, if you like. Could stay a few weeks. How long are you going to put me off anyway?"

"What about your job?"

"Off for a week—inventory. I don't have to help with that. And it doesn't matter. I would rather be with you."

"OK. Well, I don't have anything better to do. What about your car?"

"That old thing—I should put a sign in the window telling people to just help themselves to it. The radiator leaks, the transmission slips, the tires are bald. Have to steal it as is. No warranty implied."

"Now *that* is funny, very funny, as it has an air-cooled motor. But what if they do steal it?"

"Poor suckers will bring it back inside of ten miles. Anyway, no worries. My mom will be by later. Told her you were going to pick me up and that we were going to her place, so don't come down."

"Who knows about us besides your mom and General So-and-So?"

"No one who knows me, and Mom won't tell a soul. Why? You on the lam?"

"Hardly. Just trying to decide what to do, and you're not making life easy on me. You know that, don't you?"

"Why not? How, Duke, am I not making life easy for you?"

"Well, I am tired of the shooting, killing, all that stuff. Hard to talk about it. Besides, I am getting older, you know, and for sure can't talk to you about it. It's just the army and its ways of doing things. They want us to be as mean as any soldier in the world on any given day, and then *bang*—the next day we're to be normal and just blend in with regular folks. And if anything goes wrong, it's never their fault—it's always ours. Doesn't matter if the info was bad or not. Still our fault. I'm thinking for sure we are...I am going to join the Black Ops team. Most are ex–Special Forces, and the pay is like nobody's business."

"How old are you, Duke?"

"Just turned twenty-six two weeks ago. I called in yesterday and told my captain that I needed another month to decide this stuff. He said I had the time coming, so sure, take it. You had this week thing planned for how long?"

"So, the radio works. Can I?"

"Help yourself, but don't act like you didn't hear the question."

"Country and western? You listen to this shit?"

"I'll have you know, my grand—Anyway, yes, but play what you like."

"You listen to KOOL 1420? It's hopping. That's *cool* spelled with a *K*."

"Oh, God, let me out at the corner."

"And while you're at it, me too."

"Listen to this one. It's good. Elvis."

"We gotta get out of this car."

"Yes, let us out at the next corner. It's the only hope we have."

"What are you laughing about?"

"Oh, someday I might tell you, if I'm still around."

"Man, does he have a *voice*! It is so musical! Don't you think so?"

"What? Who?"

"Elvis. Just listen to him."

In the early morning rain in Vietnam,
With a rifle in my hand,
Humming along, laaaaa laaa

Out in hangar number twenty-nine,
Big old bird being loaded with boys in bags set to go...
Humming and singing along where the morning rain don't shine.

"I just love to listen to his songs. Do you like Elvis? Of course you do. Who doesn't? What about Gordon Lightfoot, CCR? Who's your favorite singer?"

"Johnny Cash."

"Yes, I know him. 'Folsom Prison Blues.'"

"She ain't half bad on this song stuff. Guess you don't need to stop for me any longer there, Duke."

"When we get to your mom's place, what do you have in mind?"

"Oh, just thought we could talk a spell, and I could see what she has in the fridge. See what I can cook up for you. You like Mexican, don't you, now?"

"I like anything that's not from a brown sack that's got a big C or K on it. How's that? Besides, what have we been eating the last two weeks at your mom's house?"

"Yes, I know, but there is a difference between being polite and eating and actually liking it. Here's some tequila. Want to drink some with me? I love this stuff. Don't do the salt thing. Come on, just a little to loosen you up."

"Connie, if I didn't know better, I would think you're trying to get me drunk so you can have your way with me."

"What's wrong with me? Don't you like the way I look, or what? Come on, tell me the truth. I'm a big girl. I can take it."

"Well, I do like your wit, and you're pretty good looking, at that. But see, I'm not a free man. Don't you get it?"

"I get you're army, but that's all. What do you mean 'not free'?"

"Well, I have lots of demons, and, well…Let's change the subject. Yes, I like you, but if I do this with you, will you still like me in the morning?"

"Hey, that's the lady's line. Here, have another drink, eat some more of these tacos, and then let me jump your bones. And we'll worry about tomorrow tomorrow."

"I like the way you make love to me, Connie. Are you sure it's OK?"

"Yes, more than OK. You're my first, you know, and it's all the dreams I had come true. You're the best, Duke."

"You can call me MD or Doc. Just for us, OK? Only when no one else can hear you, OK? It's a special name from my granddad, you see. My initials backward."

"OK, I see. I will call you Doc. Just the name for my man."

"Connie?"

"Yes?"

"Why didn't you tell me you've been saving it for your wedding night?"

"No, not my wedding night. Saving it for when *I* wanted to. Not because *he* wanted to, whoever he would be. Besides, I like you, and you're so cute."

"Cute, my ass. I'm a lean, mean, fighting machine."

"In the army maybe, but not here. Here, you're my sweet guy. Come put your head on me. Let me kiss your ear, your face. Let's do it again."

"What? Three times is not enough? You're from the other side, aren't you, and going to kill me with sex. That's it—you're working for the Commies. They sent you to kill me."

"No, I just like to feel you inside of me. You're good, you know. But what do I know? You're my first and my last, if I can keep you. Can I keep you, Doc, MD? Can I?"

"Sure, but we have to keep it a secret. If it gets out, you could, your mom could be in danger."

"Hold my hand again, just like you did the first time you let it go inside me. Made me want to cry with joy. This all is so special when you did that to me. You know I love you, Duke, Doc, MD, D. Moore…my Doc, big tender pussycat. So this should be our safe house. No one's ever going to know about it."

"No, Connie. Your mom knows, and we cannot take the chance with your life or hers or mine."

"I know the perfect place for it, Doc. Down the road about fifty miles, just off the beach. I think it has beach access and its own dock as well. I know it's for sale. We could buy it. No one would know. But now, let me on top. I want to kiss you more, play with you until you're ready for me again."

So we went to look at it the next day. I was so sore I could hardly walk.

"I like this place, Connie. We could make it look really nice inside but leave it alone outside. Seems like it's an old drug lord's place—well built. Could stand off an army from inside. Bet it has a tunnel out of here. What do you think?"

"Yes, I like it very much. My, I mean, *our* first home."

"OK, I'll buy it for us as soon as we are married."

"But how can we do that? Can you do that?"

"We just get us a priest in a local church someplace we'll never go back to and have him marry us. We'll say we have to, otherwise your good name will be disgraced."

"Sounds good to me. Are you sure about this? Are you really sure? But what I meant was, can we get married with the army and all? Do we have to get someone to sign off for us, or what?"

"Yes, Connie, I've never been more sure. And I never felt so good in all my days. And no, we don't have to involve the army in any way. The less they know, the less trouble we will have."

So we went back to the States, got us a license, and found a little chapel. We were married that day, and it was the best thing in my life. Then we went to the bank to draw money from my account, and that is when she saw that I was the "asshole" who owned the bar. The Fender Benders was a good investment with Frank at the helm. I set up Connie's own account and paid cash for the house we had decided to buy in Mexico.

"So now you're my wife, and I am your man, but life will never be the same for us until I can see what the future is for me, I mean us, dear. Always, just us."

"You can do the army, Doc, or whatever until we die. I don't care what they have you do as long as you leave it at the door when you come home."

"I will try, my love. Will try with all my heart and soul, as I love you more than life. And that, my dear, you can take to the bank."

The drive back was way too short, leaving the house we just bought and stayed in for six days. The lovemaking in those few days was something else. When we left, there wasn't a place in the house we hadn't christened. We talked about everything: lives, kids, family, her mom, what I would do for the next five or so years. We made up our minds that it was better to be Black Ops and make a ton more money in a shorter time. So I made the calls to put it in place.

"Wake up, my angel, my wife. We're at your car. Looks like you're still the proud owner. Where do you want to go? Over to be with your mom?"

"No, let's go to my place. It's our place now."

"Hold on, I can't take my car home. I'll put it in the storage shed near my rental and meet you at the back of the bar. Then we'll go home."

"What did you just say?"

"Go home. Yes."

"Yes, those are the words I dreamed about: go home with the man of my dreams."

◆　◆　◆

"Wake up, Duke! Wake up!"

"What's wrong?"

"You were talking, crying, in your sleep again. Oh, my poor dear, we need to get you some help. Want to talk about it?"

"Just one of those crazy dreams I get. Seems like the same one over and over. My dad is standing over me with a gun in the darkness, laughing, ready to pull the trigger. Then a dirty-toothed gook pointing his pistol at me and saying, 'This is going to make you hurt like I did.' Then Mike has a rifle, and he's talking crazy stuff like, 'Payback is going to be fun.' Then one of the other guys, I can't make out who, has a flamethrower and says *I* will burn in hell, not him. Then I woke up, you lying on top of me and kissing my face. I tell you, Connie, it was a bad idea, us getting married. What if I don't wake up and I hurt you, kill you even, thinking you are my dad or some enemy I don't know? All this goes on, and I am still asleep."

"First thing in the morning, we should take you to the nearest VA hospital, Duke. There is one close, I am sure of it. We'll check you in and let them help you."

"Been down that road. The only help the VA or the army has for you is a pill and a padded cell until they're sure you won't hurt one of them or yourself. No, thanks. I will work it out. It's just in my head, you know. Just in my head."

"My love, I know, but don't you think you should go see a professional?"

"No, they don't know how to fix us. Just fuck with us is all they ever know how to do. If it can't be cured by a pill, they're lost. And for sure they don't understand why we are the way we are. Hell, they're perfect, so we should be too. They know how to overcome whatever's going on by meditation and a relaxer, so they tell us to do the same and not to drink. Well, my love, you know I don't drink much, and when I do, it isn't the trouble that they say it is. It's just in my head, that's all. I will deal with it, and that's that. So for now, we need to find you a safe place to live, and I think I know where it could be."

ELEVEN

Civilian Life

I called my first-line guy and told him I was sure I wanted to join their team. He said they had a job for me, a team job. He said I could be a contractor and would not have to reup in the army, but the time would all count toward my army retirement. They took care of all that stuff with the army and got my pension in place like a transfer. I think anyway, but not sure. One thing I am sure of: that pay was out of this world.

◆　◆　◆

"Now, my love, we'll go find you a safe place, a place to blend in. Lots of Latinos there, so no big deal. You know I love you more than life, and someday we'll be too old for this shit, so we'll need a big nest egg. We will go and live forever in the house we just bought. But, my love, remember you're married to a spook, and we do get even, so no messing around when I'm not at home."

"Oh, Doc, you're crazy! I wouldn't even think of it. So where are we headed? It doesn't matter to me as long as I have you. You know, we talked about it, but you never said. Do you want kids or not?"

"I've been thinking about that. I'm not sure. Guess it's OK. I'm just scared that I'm too much like my old man—get mad and take it out on our child. But then I think about how my dad hurt me, and I know I would never hurt you or one of ours. So for now, yes, but just one, OK? No more until we talk more and we see how I am with him or her. Winnemucca—you been there?"

"No. Where is it?"

"Nevada. A small-to-midsized mining town. We will blend in. Can buy us a place there pretty cheap, and you can get a job waiting tables. I know you won't like that, but for now, it will help keep us under the radar. OK?"

"Yes, OK. For sure. You're the boss. Yes, I'm good with that for now. But later, I can do something that will be more meaningful, like go get my college degree, right?"

"Yes, I agree. For now, though, I think we should put your car at our place in Mexico and buy us a pickup to help blend in."

◆　◆　◆

That's what we did. Took her car to our home in Mexico and bought us a pickup in San Diego. The next few weeks were hectic, as they wanted me down there in Texas, so the new job was making me feel pressure before I even got started.

"Yes, for sure, my love. I got all your stuff in the pickup. We're ready to go start our life together where we aren't known from our past."

We bought a garage across the alley from the bar and asked Frank to keep an eye on it. In it, we stored things we weren't taking, along with the Corvette. We knew the Vette would make a good ride later when we came back. We would take it down to our Mexico place. With the kind of money I'd be making, we figured we could retire in about three to four years. Retire from this job anyway. We made a pact never to have too many monthly bills or debts. So we were on the road with a week to spare before I had to report to Texas.

"What about Mom? She'll need to know where I am, where we are. Don't you think that's only fair? Tell me, Doc. I can't just leave her with no word at all."

"No, no one you know now can know anything. Or else when you have our baby, they could find you and could hold you and our child against me if something ever went wrong. Hell, I went to Iran and shot a top personal aide because he was talking too much. I know these guys. We have to hide you. Never let them know that you're my wife. Your mom can call you anytime. We'll get a new mobile phone for her and give her the number she can call. Tell her the less she knows, the safer she is. And tell her not to tell the guy she's banging. Nothing. No one. Tell her to tell them you went abroad to study. That's it—went to Munich, Germany, to get a degree, and she can call only on Sundays, like three or four o'clock in the morning, so the shift change will not be so apt to pick it up. Hide the mobile phone. Only use it for her to call you."

"OK, Doc, my love. But what if—"

"What if what? I told you I wasn't a free man before you said I do, and you agreed. It's my way, my love, or we need to turn this truck around and just drop you off at your mom's. Stop crying. It's for the good of both of you."

Oh, when the saints come,
Yes when the saints come in,
Oh, when the saints come in,
And the dog barks at the moon, is when I will lay down my soul
and exchange it some day for a sword.

"Oh, funny. You guys are very funny. It's not the song at all. You're so far off it's hilarious. God, you guys are going to drive me to drinking."

"Well, here we are in the dusty old town of Winnemucca. Let's find you a place to stay. I'll leave you the pickup.

"There now, all unloaded. You can drive around and look for a place to buy after I'm gone. Make sure the place is a good deal. And remember: sign my name to take cash out of the bank account I set up. Then put the cash in the account you set up. Leave it for a few weeks, then cash some out, and open an account here. Deal only with cash. If it looks like the bills are marked, not old used bills, take them back in a week or two and redeposit it back. Be very alert. You must keep a low profile. No showing off, no new anything. Live very poor but clean and nice. If you find a place to buy and get the cash for it, deposit it so no one will be the wiser. Get a loan and then divide it by eight months. Get the loan paid off in that little bit of time. This place has the rent paid up for a year, so don't be in a hurry. Never use the mobile phone unless it's an emergency, and then leave me the voice message that we practiced."

"Yes, Doc, I got it. Leave the message, in this order: 'Just called to say happy birthday, as I forgot to when I saw you last week' means I'm scared and going to our safe house. 'Called and just wondering about dinner—are you going to make it?' means we need to talk. And if I call and say, 'Dad has died,' you'll know that I'm going to withdraw everything from the bank and go to the place in the hills in Nicaragua, so it's bad, and I destroy the phone at that point, and the next call will be on the first Monday of the month. Then I'll give you the number by saying it backward and adding two, four, three, five, seven, two, four, three, five, seven—last number first, the middle one the first, all in reverse order. You will call me on the following Saturday and will let it ring twice, then you'll hang up, call again, let it ring four times, and then hang up. When you call again, I'll answer by saying…um…just a minute, I got it. Then I will say an old kids' joke, 'Mel's Meat Market—you stab them, we slab them.' How's that? Good?"

"You should have it all up here in your head."

"Should I write it down?"

"If you do write it down to study, you must find a way to keep it, like, in a plastic bag, and double it up to hide it at night out on a road close by. If someone does find it, they won't know the code if you just write enough to jog your memory. OK?"

"Yes, I got it. I'll do that so that if I get busy, I won't forget it."

"OK, you're set. I have three days to get back to Texas. Just take me to the town down the freeway called Reno. That's where the big bank is for money withdrawals. Drop me at the airport. I will make it in plenty of time."

"Oh, Doc, kiss me one more time. I so love you. Hurry back to me, OK, my love? Yes, just like that. Here, put your hands up my dress. See, I didn't wear any panties so you could feel me and know that I'm all yours, only yours, from day one until forever. Love you, my sweet man. Hurry back to me. I need more of your sweet lovemaking. Promise me you won't do anything dumb. Come back to me. Oh, please, promise me."

"Why we jogging so fast? Where we going that we can't walk there?"

"You really are in love with this girl, aren't you, Duke?"

"Tex, he's head over heels."

"Yes, I remember my first. You're out of shape. Need some leg stretching, don't you? Too much good home cooking. Feel I'm getting soft right along with you."

"Remember, guys, this is now my wife you're talking about."

>   *Singing my song, moving along, bye, bye, blackbird.*
>   *High up on the mountain, looking down on the city,*
>   *Used to be the mountain of love.*

"What am I doing trying to remember new old songs? We need to switch it up a bit, mates. I'm tired of the old Hank songs."

"OK, OK, we got it, don't we, Tex?"

◆   ◆   ◆

Humming to myself, I rode the bus from the airport. It had been a nice plane ride, very relaxing. The Black Ops had had a plane ticket for me at the counter. Was a VIP, for sure. Anyway, as VIP as Southwest Airlines could give you. The Black Ops office was outside Houston, Texas. A big place with a nice training ground and lots of other training facilities as well, like demo practice, indoor shooting test, and hand-to-hand combat instructions. I'm not sure, but I think some CIA personnel were training there as well. Anyway, they signed a contract with me. It was great—no more Asia. I was going to be in South America. I was asked to learn the language. I told them I had begun and had a very good and reliable teacher. They never got that, and I never let on. I was going to be assigned to a team, but I told them I would build my own. And as far as they were concerned, I was the only one on the team. They didn't like it, but they said they understood. They gave me a credit card for missions only that had a ten-digit access code. I could give it to you to this day, but I won't.

The first assignment they gave me was guard duty over some celebrities. No big deal, but I didn't like that job—until they assigned me to the former president while his regular team was on a training mission. I liked that, as he was also the ex-chairman of the CIA and had given a lot of the orders to the general for me to carry out. Then I was back to watching over smartass young rich kids who thought the world revolved around them.

One day my boss, Jim, asked me if I had taken the kid to a sex shop for some fun.

"Yes, I did. Why?"

"Seems some girl, maybe the same girl, is trying to blackmail him."

"Well, Jim, I didn't know I was in charge of his zipper as well."

"That's not funny, Duke. You better start being in charge of his zipper, and did you check out the girl's place? Apparently not, as he was sent a video of him with her. Can't see her face, just him and his Johnson. Now, take Greg, go find this girl, and bring her to our safe house out on the outskirts of town. If you don't know where it is, Greg knows it as well as the pass code for the locks. We need to mop up this damage control as soon as possible—all of it. No more traceable evidence left out there. ASAP! You got that?"

"Yes, sir, loud and clear. And if she doesn't want to come?"

"Use any force you need to. But I need some answers, so don't rough her up too much."

◆ ◆ ◆

"Look, Greg. There she is on the corner, the dark-haired beauty. Let me out here, and go park around the corner of that building where you can't be seen."

◆ ◆ ◆

"Hi, there. You remember me?"

With a frightened look on her face, she said, "Yes, I remember. Want some more fun?"

"Hell no. We need to go for a ride, and you're going to tell me everything you know."

She looked up and down the deserted street. "What I know about what?"

"There doesn't seem to be much happening out here for a Tuesday night around three o'clock in the morning. I don't think you're going to miss out on any tricks. And that was not a request. You're coming with me."

"I don't think so. I don't think I'm going anywhere with you."

I turned. This great big guy, who must have been three hundred pounds, looked me square in the eyes. Same height as me—six foot two. Looked like an ex-linebacker for some football team. I knew I was going to get roughed up a bit. Dang, this was not what I thought this day was going to be this morning. I knew I had in my shoulder harness my auto forty-five, 1911, in place, but never a shell in the chamber. And it would make a hell of a sound in a narrow, deserted street like this one, especially at this time of the morning. Better to use the old Fairbairn maneuver, a move taught to Special Forces by a Brit, no less, in World War II. He'd developed it for the silent kill. "Can't breathe, can't scream" had been his motto.

"You don't bother one of my girls without paying. Got it, buster? And now I think I'm going to teach you a lesson."

I let him punch me first in the stomach. As I was bent over, I pulled my pant leg up and grabbed my eight-inch stiletto knife from the sleeve strapped to my leg. He raised me up, saying, "You're not going to let this one little punch take you out, now, are you?"

I blocked the next hit with my forearm and inserted the blade deep into the belly just under his rib cage, pointing up toward his heart. It was like popping a balloon. I felt the knife push the skin inward a bit, and then inside it went. The blood immediately poured out of the fat fuck, all over my hand and the cuff of my shirt. He was still pulling on me to raise me, and that gave me more force. So in essence, he inserted the knife into his own belly, quivering and beginning to shake, as I was fully upright now. Legs under me, feeling every jerk his body made, I made a slight right-to-left-angle movement of my wrist to make sure I got his lungs.

With this movement, the guy's eyes widened and locked on mine. No, sir, not one little punch to slow me down, not from you. Jerking in pain, his mouth was wide open, showing he was out of breath. Knowing I had hit the spot needed to keep him from screaming in pain, I grabbed the back of his neck. The girl covered her mouth and just watched as the tip of the blade sliced through most of his lungs. He couldn't get his breath as his air escaped into his chest cavity. As his knees buckled under him, I pulled him close with a little pressure to his neck that enabled me to insert the blade deep enough to cut his heart. As his weight was full on my right hand, the slit was large enough now to let my hand slide inside him. I felt his air rushing past my hand as I turned the blade and tried to cut his heart loose from his body. As I found my mark, he jerked up, and his knees locked. Again, his eyes opened wide, and I saw the pain in them. His eyes clouded over as he jerked harder, trembling all over, nearly taking both of us to the curb. I pulled him close and put my lips on his, as if I were to kiss him. Instead, I blew into his mouth. I didn't want to hear any last words. He was too far gone, and blood appeared in his mouth, and I pulled away in the nick of time. None of his blood was on my lips or in my mouth.

"Looks like you fucked with the wrong group of people this time, my friend."

I felt his knees buckling again, and I looked down to see his bloody shirt. Blood mixed with his air, running down his fancy pants into his cowboy boots, so much so that one of his boots was full, running over. I knew he was dead as his eyes rolled back and turned milky gray-white. I let go, pulling my stiletto out of him. Like a jellyfish jerking out of control, he slumped down into the street by the curb in an unusual position, his head under him, belly sticking out, and the blood running out of his boot. As he lay there, still trembling and jerking, I turned to the girl.

"I would suspect that you'll come with me at this moment without any trouble. Yes?"

As I walked toward her, I grabbed the newspaper from the top of the stand that had been left there three days ago, judging by its date. I wiped my stiletto clean and put it back into my boot sleeve. She pointed to her pimp. I dropped immediately, crouching lower, going to one knee and grabbing my 1911 forty-five auto from my shoulder holster, expecting to see one of his buddies appearing. But not so—just a dog out of nowhere that had begun licking up the blood. The poor bastard dog looked like it hadn't eaten in a very long time. I stood, holstered my weapon, wiped my hands as best I could, and discarded the paper into the gutter. Another dog appeared from the alley across the street, and there was a lot of growling as they fought for what looked like their first meal in weeks. One dog grabbed the belly wound and pulled some flesh loose. The dogs looked at each other in an unspoken language, and the growling stopped. It was fair game for those two, but there was plenty to go around.

The girl bent and vomited into the gutter, and I grabbed her raven hair and pulled it back. Her hair felt silky smooth. She looked at me as I talked to her in a low voice. "No one will hurt you. We just need to talk about the other night." I helped her straighten up. We walked to the end of the block. I wasn't in a full state of mind at this point, as a million memories had flooded my mind. Would she ever talk? I thought about the first time I had used the Fairbairn manuver. It had been taught to me by a crusty old veteran of World War II, a mean old Aussie. No—a Brit. I was not sure of his origin, but he was a mean old bastard all the same.

I saw Greg standing next to the wall, shaking his head. "You're one sick SOB, Duke. One sick SOB, for sure. Why did you kiss the guy as you let him fall? One sick son of a bitch." He turned, walked to the car, and got in.

I opened the back door for the girl to get in. I saw her short skirt slide up her tanned thighs and noticed she had no panties on and was clean shaven. I sat next to her. Greg pulled away from the curb and did a U-turn so that the car wouldn't be seen on the street where the pimp lay.

I looked at the raven-haired beauty and saw her staring back at me. Our eyes locked. Her black hair matched her eyes. What a perfect figure, and what a pretty face, with those high cheekbones and lips any guy would love to have all over his. Then I knew why the kid had had me take him to this slum part of town to be with this beauty.

◆　◆　◆

"What took you so long? Any trouble finding her?"
"Not much trouble, Jim, just a slight delay. Her pimp didn't want to give her up."

I set her in the overstuffed leather chair, flinging my suit coat over the back. I continued walking to the kitchen to wash the blood from my shirt cuff and hands.

Greg appeared from parking the car and told Jim I had killed the pimp with my knife. "I tell you, Jim, he is one bad SOB. Yes, one sick, bad, SOB. He left the poor bastard there in the gutter with two dogs feeding on him."

"The fat fuck asked for it. Hit me first." And I gave Greg my "you're next" stare.

"A sight to watch, Jim. Duke gutted him, and the guy never said a word or screamed. Then this sick SOB kissed him and let him fall to the pavement," Greg said as he stared back at me, trying not to look like he was intimidated.

I finished washing up as Jim talked to the girl. I knew she was thinking she wouldn't live long enough to eat lunch. Jim lifted his hand to hit her, but I caught it in midair.

"I told her she was safe with me and that she wouldn't get hurt. My word, Jim. She will talk, and she will not get hurt."

She did talk, never taking her eyes off me. When we were done, I told Jim to give her the money the pimp had asked for in the blackmail, all of it, and then Greg could take her to the airport so she could go back to wherever she said she was from, or wherever she liked, just not stateside.

"She will never tell anyone about this night, because she knows what I will do to her if she ever even thinks of it." I nodded to her, and she blinked many times. "I tell you, sister, this world is not big enough for the two of us if you ever open your mouth. Got it?" She nodded. Jim gave her the twenty grand, and she left with Greg.

As Greg was about to open the door, I said, "Greg, I will show you firsthand the move I did to the pimp if she is not safe on the plane and punching a hole in the sky when you get back."

He looked at Jim and then back to me. "Sure thing, Duke. Sure thing," he said as he walked out and closed the door behind him.

"Duke?"

"Yes, Jim?"

"I think you'd better go home and lie low for a while, like a year or so. Whatever time it takes for this thing to blow over. You will still get your autopay, and we'll be in touch. See you, Duke. Been a nice year, hasn't it?"

"Yes, Jim. I guess so. Never thought it would end up like this anyway, me a bodyguard and a rich-kid babysitter."

I went to my room and changed into my old faded blue jeans and denim shirt. I put all my suits into my duffel bag, wiped my room clean, and headed for the airport. I was hoping I would run into that raven beauty again and find out her hometown. Sure as shit, I did see her, and she almost fainted when she looked up and saw me in front of her. I bought her some food and some wine and told her I was finished working for those guys and that I was going home as well. We talked for about an hour, and I learned a lot about her. I told her to get married and forget about her past, and maybe one day the wife and I would come visit her. When she boarded her plane, she had a smile on her face, and I was sure I had a friend for life now living in "Costa Rica, almost into Nicaragua." And with all that American money, if she were frugal, she could have a nice life.

On my plane headed for Reno, I thought about how I missed my lady and how I couldn't wait to have her pretty lips all over me.

"Hello, there, Connie. Where are you?"

"Am in the bath. Will be out in a little while."

"Well, maybe I should join you."

"No, not this time. Please have a beer and relax. Wasn't expecting you back so soon. When we talked on the phone, you didn't sound like you were coming home anytime soon."

We had a nice year and a half off. We went hunting and really got to know each other. I did lie low. I got a job working at the tire shop in Winnemucca. It was OK, not too steady, and that was fine with me. Jim came by many times. He brought his wife now and again. We became pretty chummy. He found us some Bureau of Land Management ground, and I along with some help from him built a nice compound. He bought some ground in Kingman, Arizona, and we built him a place up on the hill at the east end of a subdivision, just before town. It was very safe for him and his wife and their two kids. He never asked about that night, and I sure as hell didn't want to bring it up. I never mentioned that I'd seen her off at the airport. Also, I didn't think he needed to know about any of my contacts or my friends.

The compound was very nice, hidden in a mountain, and had good water and a nice place to sleep and eat. We built a bunker of a hangar. I bought an old plane, a Super Cub, and rebuilt it, putting a larger motor in it. Had it purring like a kitten. I put together a nice machine shop there—lots of tools and a below-ground gas tank. The only way into it was from inside the concrete hangar that had every tool in it you could think of, all army surplus. But my sleeping quarters looked like an old trailer. My home away from home was two paces from the bunker's side door. Both doors were very heavy, almost bulletproof.

When Jim and the contractors were not around, I finished setting up another escape tunnel with the contractor's track hoe to make a getaway—a safe, reinforced hatch under my bed that led to an under-ground tunnel to the hangar. The hangar had an escape route already, and at the end of it, I made a small bunker with ammo for Old Betsy and a place for her, so she was watertight and fireproof. With the dirt and sagebrush piled around it, it was nearly impossible to see. Not only was it watertight and fireproof, but it was also a nice place for me to lie prone and be able to shoot anyplace from one end of the area to the other, including the grass runway. I spent a lot of time there, building things and keeping my shooting skills at maximum proficiency as well as just looking over the area. That's when I found the old mine shaft, which I made into a real escape tunnel. No one knew about this tunnel but Mike, Tex, and Connie.

"Connie, why don't you tell your boss that you need a month or so off, and let's go work on the home in Mexico? The compound is complete except for a few things that can wait. I think I'll take the old pickup and buy that camper for it that the guy has for sale at the tire shop."

"Sounds good to me, Doc. We haven't been home now for almost two years, and your old pickup is costing us more than a new. But, yes, I do understand the logic behind it: big motor for fast travel; extra gas tank for long, long trips; some armor in the doors and back panel; and it blends in. But still, we have a fortune in that old thing. Yes, dear, I'll call the shift manager at the Model T and tell him my cousin is sick, so I need to go nurse her for a while. And that I don't know when I'll be back. What do you think?"

"Sounds good. Let's do it. It's going to be a long drive, so let's get started early in the morning."

◆　◆　◆

"Man, I love this place. We should just retire now and live here forever. Wish there was a place for us to land the plane and hide it at the house. It sure would beat the long drive. But oh well. It's a never mind. Shall we swim in the ocean one more time before we go in for our siesta?"

"OK, but no more hanky-panky in the water. Promise me?"

"Well, my love, when I've been dead for a week, I'll still want to play with your luscious body. You don't know how much I missed you. I wanted you every night beside me."

"Well, maybe so, but not in the water. What if someone sees us?"

"They won't, but I promise. I think we should go to the cantina this evening. It's Saturday night, and it will be fun dancing with you. Besides, you need the practice."

"Oh, you. I'll show you what practice means with my skillet while you sleep if you're not good, that's for sure."

Our time at our home was so much fun, and we had it looking great. The escape tunnel was redone, and we now had our fortress fixed the way we wanted it. We had lots of things stashed here and there, mostly in the tunnel for security reasons. I called in every week like a good soldier, but the longer I was away, the more I hated the thought of going back. Connie and I stayed in shape, anticipating that day—running the beach, doing our exercises together. I set up a shooting range in the tunnel for pistols, and she got dang good at it, I will say.

"Connie, I just talked to Jim. Seems our party is over. I have a lot to tell you, as we're now back in the Black Ops contracting business. Pay is for a full team, and that is just us. I told them I had my own team. Hurry up and pack. We have a job here in Mexico, and then we head to Venezuela."

The Mexico job was just a training exercise. Connie did very well. She taught me Latin American Spanish as well as Castillan Spanish, and I taught her Italian. They're a lot alike, so while we were on stakeout, we read our study books and soon became very bilingual. We had it down pretty well and picked up some German as well. When we talked in front of strangers, we started off with Spanish, shifted to Italian, and then threw in some German as well, never any English. We were a great team.

Venezuela kept me hopping. The job was to mark all the drug lords we could and send the info back to Texas along with the pictures we were able to take. As our stakeout grew longer and longer, I could see Connie was wearing thin.

"Duke, I sure do like the way you make love to me, but now sit up and look at me before you go to sleep. I must tell you that I'm frightened a lot now. I don't know how to tell you this except just straight out. I'm pregnant, and I'm worried that my body will change and that you won't love me anymore. I will be fat and look terrible, and I won't be your team member out here anymore. And I will die if you never come back when I should have been with you. Look at me. Have I scared you off? You know I couldn't do anything to hurt our baby. Please don't ever ask me to do that."

"Oh, my love, Connie, I am not scared, and as a matter of fact, I love you more. And we will always be a team. I can do this hide-and-seek stuff on my own, no worries. Are you OK? You look very tired."

"Yes, I'm feeling the effects of the poor food, but I will be OK. This job will be over soon, and I—we—can make it."

"No way are you staying to the end. You heard the boss on the phone—this could take another year. So tomorrow we will send you home to Mexico City first and then on to our home on the beach at San Quintin. I want our baby to be safe, and I want you safe most of all. When you're near time for delivery, go back to Winnemucca and have our baby there, or at the Reno hospital—your choice, my dear. I would even let your mom come visit you there, if you want. Just keep a very low profile, very low, and don't tell your mom anything that she doesn't need to know. But I don't need to tell you this stuff—you have it all down solid in your memory now. You take your satellite mobile phone, and when you're healthy and ready to go back home to Mexico, call me and give me a full update. If I'm not there when you get home, take the battery out of the satellite phone and leave it in our safe in the tunnel. Call me when you're there using the phone in the tunnel, and just keep me posted, please."

"OK, if you're sure about all this, I will. But I don't like to leave you here alone."

"Yes, for sure, I know you don't, but I am never alone. Never have been, not since you've been in my life. I have had you deep in my heart forever and a day. Now, we need to plan how to have you leave without much commotion."

So we packed her up, left the little place we had rented, and moved to a new location. It was time anyway. We always moved around so that no one ever started thinking of us as a fixture in their corner of the world. When I was moved in, I took her to the airport a day's drive from there in each direction.

I missed her more than I had ever missed anyone ever in my life. I could hardly function without her by my side, and it was pure hell for me. Jim was correct: it did take another year for me to send them all the info the Texas office wanted. Hiding and watching, I learned a lot about people and how much we are creatures of habit, no matter how hard we try not to be.

The biggest lesson I learned was that I missed being with Connie every night of my life. I never thought of myself as one to be lonely, but homesick boy was I. I got word that she and our new son were fine and were home in Mexico, passing the time until I returned. I was good with that. The heat had cooled down now from my little thing in Dallas. Just another pimp the police never had to deal with.

TWELVE

TAKING CARE OF DAD'S BUSINESS

My dad and I were never close. I thought he hated me from the day I was born. That said, I always tried my darnedest to be the guy he expected me to be. When I was home, he would always get mad over something from the past, mostly from when I was a young kid.

He was never very well, and I guess I should have tried harder to understand him better. But in my eyes, he was the guy who wanted his family to be like *Father Knows Best*, too much a fairy tale if ever there was one. While I wasn't my mother's first son, I was my father's only son. My leaving home at seventeen took its toll on him. I don't think he ever really got over it. I do believe now that he loved me in his own way but just could never show it, let alone say it. I ran the ranch for him. He never had to worry about that end of the deal: cows, hay, whatever—it didn't matter. I just was always there and did it all. My being gone left him to himself with no help.

When I did go home, just seeing me made him mad as hell. He would curse me and say that if I didn't leave now, he was going to get his gun and shoot me. So I did just that—I left, and the visits were further and further apart by my choice. He never met Connie or his grandson. The funny thing was that he would talk to me on the telephone as if we were long-lost friends, in his mind forever bound by a male duty of some mysterious making. So as he progressed into his dementia, we would talk only from afar. As his only son, his heir, I felt a real duty to him for some unknown reason. I made sure all his affairs were always in order.

He became so bad that he couldn't remember how to drive correctly and would wreck his car almost every time he got into it. After the last wreck he had, he got pretty belligerent with the policemen, and they took him home and took his driver's license away. Now that he was homebound out on the farm, miles from anywhere, we decided to hire a caregiver, a guardian, to see that he was OK. Not a live-in but a couple who stayed in the trailer house on the farm. He fought us on this until he fell and the mailman found him. Then the fight was over, and the court ordered a guardian. I also asked the court to appoint a conservator for his business affairs, and that was ordered as well.

This leads me to the reason behind what I did. It was a sanctioned hit. I was—I am—sure of that. The couple appointed guardians to watch over my dad and the conservator appointed to take care of his business affairs conspired to take him for every dime he had, including his home. And they did just that. They hired a lawyer, a young guy who was as dishonest as the day was long, to change Dad's will to leave everything to them. Their plan was to let him fall again, and it worked. He broke a rib and lay on the ground for some time. "It was just a fall," they said. But he died. The court should have locked them up and thrown away the key, but that didn't happen. So I did what any good son would have done.

It didn't matter that he and I hadn't had the best father-son relationship. The man and his wife, my dad's guardians, needed to be punished. I went to Jim, but he wasn't much help. I called the general and some other guys. They pulled the right strings and got me the go-ahead along with all the needed listening devices, ammo, and equipment I needed to get the job done. They also got me a disguise for my plane, a full map of the area, and satellite maps with exact yardages. Anything I wanted, they gave me, or, I should say, they made it available. None of them actually saw the maps and other materials, but they had to have known of it, because I uploaded from the satellite imagery. I knew beyond any doubt that the higher-ups had pulled strings so that I could make my mark on this family as they had made their mark on mine. I was sure it was a sanctioned hit.

This is how I got that job done. To put my mind at ease, I set it up slowly and deliberately, a little at a time, with long hours of eavesdropping. I became so familiar with their routine that I knew them better than they knew themselves. I knew when she left for work and when he would go out to do work in the shop or just be a lazy bum. Hell, he didn't need to work—he had milked the old man for a million with the place and cash together.

The time was right: the weather was perfect, and the plan unfolded like a well-thought-out and engineered machine.

"Mike, let's take her motor out when she turns the pickup toward me. Check the dew point. No wind? OK, silencer on and armor-piercing shells ready? Old Betsy is ready. Next clip will be white phosphorus, old Willy Pete and us. We're going to have some fun here. Mike, what did you say? 'No, not fun'? Yes, Mike, they need to feel the pain, to hurt. They milked that old man, my old man, and those bastards let him die."

For my eleventh birthday, they had a surprise party for me. They sent me out to check the water in the back pasture, and while I was gone, the entire family came over. Dad called me into the house, and there everyone was—a nice surprise. Then, in the middle of the room, he said, "Bend over and grab your ankles." I did, saying, "What is this for?"

"It's to show you that even though you're a big kid, I am still the boss." And with his belt, he gave me the customary swats with his belt doubled over: eleven for my age, one to grow on, one to be good on, one for the one he didn't know about, and so on until there were eleven more. I looked at my grandpa, but he couldn't look at me. I stood up and with no tears whatsoever said, "Sir, is that it?"

"Yes."

Then I left, went to the barn, and cried—the first time and last time ever for more years than I could count. I stayed out all night.

The next morning, Dad found me and asked if I had any questions for him now.

"Yes, sir, just one: Why?"

"Well, boy, you're a by-product of your mom's infidelity, and my word to her was that if she would stay true, then I would raise you kids until you all are through school."

I never understood it until now, after he was gone and had given everything to those bastards, that it had never hurt him. We were never his. We were just an albatross around his neck.

So my dad and I made a pact at my grandpa's grave, the day of his funeral, to be better that day to each other until I was gone. I was raised mostly by my grandfather. He taught me to shoot, to cowboy, to fix things, and to survive on my own.

"So, Tex, you ready now for this? Tex, what do you think?"

"Yes, let's do this."

Bang!

"Looks just a mite low, but a good shot. Up two clicks. She's starting out of the pickup. Let's close the door on that one through the hood and fire wall into her pelvis."

Boom!

"Yes, perfect. She's swallowed in pain. Let's see...what the hell? She's laying on the horn. He's running to her. White round. Now he's at the back of the truck. Let him have it in the hand. When that Willy Pete hits the truck, he'll get it all over his body. Wow, he is screaming like a smashed cat. And look at the fire in the tank blow him across the lane into the field. Who's that? Oh, yes, their boy. Think I should shoot him in the leg? Reload red shell again, and check the cams, Mike. Make sure all is OK. Mike? Mike? Oh, hell. He went back home. No stomach for this, I guess. OK, boy, here you are. One in the gut. Hope I hit your

spine so you'll never walk again. Damn, missed. Hit him in the leg, maybe both legs. Look at the bitch. She's climbing out the other side of the window. Scared she is going to burn up, bet ya. Mike, want to bet? Think so, do you?"

"No, let's get out of here."

"No, let's play some more. The scanner is humming now. Let's see what the firemen are going to do when they get here. Yes, here they come. Wonder how many of them are old veterans and know what's going on. OK, a nice red round into the front of the driver's side tire, and off it goes. See if I planted that correctly. Yes but a little high. Must be going faster than I figured. Skidding to a stop. They're all bailing out and looking at the tire. Now we'll wake them up for sure, Mike. What?"

"Let's just leave here. We did enough to them. You got your revenge. No need to shoot the firemen."

"No, I don't plan on shooting them, just their windshield. Give me a white round so it can burn whatever is in there. God damn it, Mike! I said I wouldn't. Now, let go of my arm. See? Hit the windshield dead on, and now they're all running for cover, calling for help. Someone is shooting at them! Listen to the squawking babies. Glad we didn't have one of them in our unit."

◆　◆　◆

At sixteen, my dad and I had a lot of words. I wanted more freedom, and he wanted more control, so one day he caught me ready to leave and said, "Where you going?"

"Someplace. No place. Just away from here."

"Think so? Well, I don't think so. You need to finish school."

"I don't need school as much as I need to leave. You're still mean to me in spite of the pact we made."

"Well, let me tell you, I think I will beat you a good one right now!"

"No, I don't think you can do that anymore, old man, and I won't let you. Besides, now that Grandpa is gone, I think I should be gone too."

"No, I don't think so. You might be a big kid, but I know I can take you here and now!"

"Might be, sir, but you're going to know that you've been in a hell of a fight. I will use every trick you and Grandpa taught me. So good-bye."

"Wait just a minute now. You're going to say good-bye to your mom."

"No, sir. I'm just going."

"What? You have only one more year of school, and you're done."

"Yes, sir."

"Then stay. Let's make a truce, and you get your diploma. It's the right thing for you. You will thank me later."

So, I did, and it was better—mostly. The night I got my diploma, I left. Never went home. He followed me everywhere I went, taunting me relentlessly, sneaking into wherever I was sleeping to tell me how much he hated me and how I had hurt my mom. That's why I joined the army—to get away from him. Special Forces was easy. My grandpa had already taught me to shoot, to survive, and to be alone in the woods. To me, the jungle was just the same.

"Look, the air force chopper to the rescue. What a laugh! I am so far away they don't even know where I am. Watch this, Tex. Bet I can hit their rotor gun that's hung underneath the ship. Hit it dead center. Took it clean off the underneath side of that bird. Just like the old days, Tex, shooting ground squirrels."

BOOM!

"Damn! You guys see that? It just exploded. Look, she's going down right on top of that effing fire truck and the fireman. OK, Mike. We still have more fun laid out for these no-good bastards. A few white rounds into the house. It will burn...and then the shop, the outbuildings, and all the equipment. Mike, where're you going? What? You had

enough? Well, hell, then, shut it all down, and let's finish this job and get the hell out of here."

As Mike shut it all down, I popped every Willy Pete I had into the house, shop, and equipment. I made it all burn—burn as I hoped they would be doing in hell that night.

It was just a short haul to the plane on the old four-wheeler I had bought just for this job. An old farmer was outside with his kid and wife, looking at the smoke.

"Hi, there. Ben."

"Who?"

"Ben Franklin."

"Oh. Hi, there."

"What do you think is going on? Heard a lot of clanging coming from where that smoke is coming from. Sounded like a hell of a wreck."

"Well, could have been a hell of a wreck for sure by all the smoke."

Standing by the door of the pickup, his kid stared at me.

"What're you looking at, kid?"

"You. You sure are dirty. And why are you always packing a pistol under your arm?"

"Well, kid, my dad died, you see, and he carried it through the world war, so I'm just carrying it to show it off. Want to shoot it?"

"No, thank you," he said as he climbed into his dad's pickup. They turned left onto the pavement, heading toward the smoke.

"OK, Mike, you happy now? Tex, let's push her out of here and go. Damn, look. The fuel is near gone. Little bastard had a key. Good thing he's gone. Would have given him some pain now as well."

We threw our stuff into the back of the plane. The Super Cub looked small, but with the way I had rebuilt her, she was a mighty mite. We climbed in, and away we went. We took off, heading north to the old field that was twenty air miles from this farm. We landed, taxied up to the hangar, and jumped out.

"OK, if you guys want to stay here, it's OK by me. But just leave me alone from now on. Got that, Mike?"

"Can't believe you're leaving me, Grandpa. Are you sure? Been together near on my entire life. Why now? OK. Well, then, just leave me. I can do it all myself anyway."

I got the doors open on the hangar, rolled the fuel barrels out, and filled her tanks as full as they could be—not another drop could have fit under her gas cap—all the time listening to the scanners, one on local and one on military. Sounded like they were sending some choppers out to help their downed buddies. I couldn't outrun them, but I sure as hell knew we could hedgehop and stay below their radar. Even doing that, I would still have more than enough fuel to reach the compound. It was a good thing I had thought of that old hangar, good as it was for storage and all.

I bet that kid was worried then, thinking I knew who pinched my gas, the little bastard. I knew I needed to fly south at an altitude of about two hundred feet, trim the tabs, and then take it to full lean. I was doing just fine. Then I went over the hill and flew the Boise River before heading on to the Snake River. Then I took her up to the five-hundred-foot level to still keep me out of the radar. The fishermen thought I was the Department of Fish and Game, checking on them. Things looked good, and I trimmed her out. I was starved, ready for some rations. I had plenty now that I was alone. Warm coffee. Only thing worse is cold coffee. I had a stale sandwich and warm coffee. I was going to be glad to get to my truck and trailer in Denio, Nevada. No one would find me there. I picked up some tailwind, and that was good. I needed more trim tab pushing me down. I saw the town of Murphy, and it was time to leave the river and head over the hill. I gave it some more fuel and a slight climb. I'd done that a million times, but the old girl wanted a little more fuel and more angle. She just liked her own way. I knew it was still a little hot out, and that wasn't good for climbing. I put the fuel on full rich, and the old lush liked that better. I turned the fuel value to both tanks and kept her level on weight. Through my mirror, I looked at the cargo in the back, still all nice and tidy. I finished my coffee, as I wasn't going to have time for anything but patting this old girl's back-side. When I was over the first set of hills, I could see I was just north of Sucker Creek State Park. I could feel the chuck holes in the road. I knew to be patient, and we would be over the worst.

She's a rough old ride,
But the old girl is mine
And I like it that a way.

Hate that song. Need a better tune. There it is, old girl. Thought we were lost. You should be able to go it alone as many times as we've done it before. OK, now run south.

South of the border, down Denio way.
She said, "I like the bad boy guys; you're my kind of guy,"
La-la-la, hum, la-la, hum...

Forgot the words. Can't believe it.
We went west and just a mite south but not too much. We looked for the pass. We needed to come out just south of Lake Owyhee.

Oh, baby, come a little closer,
You're my kind of girl
So big, so luscious, la-laa-laa.

"Yes, Lake Owyhee, about another forty minutes, maybe less if the wind keeps blowing up your pipe. What you say, old girl? A little more up tab? OK, OK. God, you're sure full of it today. Yes, a bit more south, then north. Will you ever be happy?"

Oh, sweet Mary, why can't you just be true to me?
You don't like me doing those kinds of things we used to do.

"You moaned like a little schoolgirl when I put the long-range tanks in you and changed power plants. Now what do you need? Just like a lady: never enough of anything. Bitch, bitch, bitch."

> *She was a wild thing.*
> *Always wanted me by her side,*
> *So I pulled her close,*
> *And they said, "Look, her dad is coming!"*
> *So out the back door I ran*
> *And as I did, I heard her say, "Daddy, he is OK…"*
> *If you're left, you're right, left, left.*
> *It's a mean old world that I love to be mean in.*

By then, the air felt cool—nice and smooth. It was a great day to be punching a hole in the sky. We just followed the water until it turned north. Then we went west by southwest. I was doing it tab down, and then dropped down under the radar and leaned her out again.

"Yes, got your fill, did you, now that you interrupted my coffee. *Think there might be some left if you can manage on your own now. Girl, you keep this up, and that old Basque guy will end up with you in a heartbeat. Yes, it's called divorce, so be kind to me. Had a trying day so far. You know Tex? Well, he left me now. And so did my best friend, Mike, after all I did for him. See it there? It's going north. That was nice timing. Some wind but mostly still now. We're ready to go south. You remember the next landmark, or you getting too old to remember your way home?*

You got it—a little tab and shouldn't need any more fuel. OK, well, maybe a little. Your vacuum looks good. What the hell you moaning about now? Yes, I remember: Climb until we see Glove Reservoir, then level out, throttle back, from there to Groundhog Lake, on to Cow Lake, and then what? You remember? Well, come on. What's the answer?"

This lady of mine is so sweet,
She so fine
Got to make her purr for me,
Oh my, oh my.

"Hate that song. Think of another."

"You got it. We turn west again, not to pass over ninety-five. Then we'll hit seventy-eight, turn south, following the edge of the mountain range until we see Alvord Lake."

Somewhere over the rainbow, she will be mine.
Oh, somewhere over the rainbow, only time will tell.
She will be mine, laaa-laaa-laaa
Somewhere over the rainbow, they will get theirs too
Laa-la, hummm, la-la.

From there, we just took the 205 home.

"What do you think, old girl? Going to make it before dark? That would be nice, as there are no runway lights, and we sure don't need to bang you up on some antelope or a stray of some sort."

Giddap, old girl, giddap, old girl, old girl, old girl,
Saved my sawbucks, saved my...
Giddap, giddap, old girl, old girl,
Not the fastest plane in the world, she is my old girl,
Giddap, old girl, giddap...laaa, hum, hum, old girl.

THIRTEEN

LOVE OF FAMILY

The bed in the trailer felt good. I was tired of the long last month. I was very depressed over losing my best friends, but I was sure they would show up one day, out of the blue.

Sweet memories of you,
Oh, how my heart breaks, losing such a good old friend.
Sweet memories, sweet memories of you.
As I am so sad, but I can't cry.
Ever hear a grown man weep,
Weeping because he lost his best friend?
Sweet dreams, sweet memories of you.

The next day started early, at noon according to the clock, but I could have slept until hell wouldn't have it. My things in the trailer looked in good shape. No one had bothered it during the month I'd been gone. I started taking the false-numbered disguise decals off the plane. I was feeling good.

"Boys, the general will be proud of us when I send him my report. Guess the stress is leaving me. Good mission, good job."

I was feeling good, or was it that Mike had been correct? Was I just a sadistic son of a bitch, enjoying killing, liking to see people hurt? As Mike had said, I enjoyed taking and breathing their last breath as my own. Or was it that I was still trying to prove myself to my dead father, make him realize that I was a good son, one who could be depended on. No, none of those—they're all wrong. It was a good job, mission, one to be proud of, just doing the correct thing in life, "manning up," as they say, and giving the sentence that justice must have. That was it. Not my call. I'd just followed orders, doing what must be done. If not by me, then someone else would have done it.

Around four o'clock, I fixed some lunch and then sat and relaxed, falling asleep. I was feeling better than I had in years. In the morning, I would be off to see my lady and my son, the two loves of my life. How could anyone ever say they loved someone or something and then hurt them the way my dad had hurt me? Well, just shoot me if I ever become my dad.

"You lazy kid, get out of that bed now, or I will roll you out on the floor! Didn't you hear me call you, stomping on the floor upstairs? You're late to do the chores. Get your ass out there now!"

"Yes, Dad. Didn't hear you. Getting my clothes on now. Don't hit me. I'll have them done soon and won't be late for school."

"I have a surprise for you this weekend, so get your act together, boy."

"Yes, sir, will do. A surprise? What for? It's not my birthday."

So, the weekend came, and my surprise was boxing gloves.

"So, Dad, you want me to hit you? Is that it?"

"Yes, at eight, you're a tough kid, but I want you to learn how to handle yourself a lot better."

"Yes, sir."

"Keep your guard up. Lead with one hand, your writing hand. You're leading with your left."

"Yes, but that's what everyone does."

"They lead with their left and then keep their right ready for the knockout punch. But you're going to learn the opposite, make you a southpaw, so that will really confuse them. If they dance to the right, you just do the opposite. It will confuse them and leave them wide open."

"This isn't fun, Dad. You're hitting me very hard, and you don't have gloves on. Stop it. You're hurting me."

"Big sissy. Keep your guard up."

"You're hurting me. Stop, Dad, please. No, I can't hit you. You're my dad."

"OK. Well, then, keep your guard up. Look, I can hit you at will. That's why you never win any fights."

"But I do. I win all my fights. Ow, Dad! You hit me in the face. Look, my nose is bleeding."

"Put this tissue there. It will stop soon."

"It hurts, Dad. I think I'm going to…"

"Grandpa, how did I get over to your house?"

"Quiet, boy. You broke your nose, and I had to fix it. Lie still now. I'm going to have some words with your dad."

And they did have words. Outside, they hit each other some and screamed, but I couldn't make out what was going on. Before it was over, I went to sleep in my grandpa's bed with grandma sitting beside me with an upset look on her face, crying softly. I hugged her and told her it would be OK. I went to sleep.

I didn't go to school for a week, and best of all, I got to stay with Grandpa. My grandma was a good cook, not like my mom. My mom opened cans, but grandma made real food such as biscuits and gravy and cookies. I went back to school and never said a word about my fight with my dad. I did a lot of shadow boxing, like the pictures in the instructions showed me, but never again with my dad.

◆ ◆ ◆

When I woke up, I was feeling as tired as when I'd gone to sleep. But I was off to home to see the two people in this world whom I loved more than life. It took two days of driving but no big deal. The back of my pickup was a small camper, and it had an ice chest full of some good grub—no C or K on any of their wrappers. I felt at home in the back of my camper. God, I spent way too much time there.

◆ ◆ ◆

"Hi, there, love of my life."

"Oh, Doc, you're here! You're back! I was so worried about you."

"Where's the boy? Not at school—it's Sunday."

"At his friend's house."

"OK, then. What do you have to eat?"

"Not much. Didn't know when you would be back, and Jim called a few times when you were gone. He said they have another big job for you. I told him you were on a big one, but Jim said he didn't know of any jobs. What was going on?"

"Well, Connie, this was just a job, not a big one. No big deal. Mostly just stakeout. You know I don't like you to know about any of this stuff. Let's just drop it. OK?"

"Yes. Well, I do have some corned beef and some mashed potatoes, if you would like that kind of food."

"You know I do. I've been eating out of my most unfavorite things with big C or K for weeks and think I got diaper rash from staying in one spot too long."

"Diaper rash? What? How?"

"You know, can't leave one's post, so we always wear diapers so we can stay active and alert. Anyway, the ones that I was given must have been old, as the wipes were all dried out. I'm headed off to take a shower. Is Bud staying the night? I sure could use some adult fun tonight."

"Yes, I will call and make sure of it. School is out now since last week, so maybe we can go home to Mexico and swim in the ocean. You told Bud we would when you got home."

"OK, that's a deal. But before I can tell Bud, we'd better call Jim. Man, does this shower feel good. Boy, oh boy, does this feel like a dream come true. OK, no more soap there. My ass is too sore for that. I'm just getting too old for this shit."

"Hello, Jim. Duke here. What's up? Yeah, heard something about it on the scanner. Yes? You think we should meet in the morning? Where? At my airport? Why there? It will mean an all-night drive for me, but OK, I'll be there. But the day after, OK? I just walked in the door."

Bastard was the worst liar ever. I could tell by his voice that he was up to no good, but hell, he was the boss, after all. I thought he had his panties in a wad about the chopper. The Ops were going to have to shell out a million for that old piece of shit and were mad about it. For sure, I get that shit rolls downhill.

"Well, I guess Jim has a job for me, hon, so we'll need to drive tonight and be there tomorrow. Then we can go do some hunting. What do you say, dear? OK, pack us some stuff, and we will be gone. Whose house is Bud at? Yes, I know Mrs. Lopez. Always puts the makeup on so thick. And yes, I will be nice. OK, I'll be right back with Bud."

"Hello, there, Mrs. Lopez. I've come to pick up the boy. Hi, Bud! We need to go home, so grab your junk, kiddo."

"You know, Bud, I work for the government. That's all you need to know for now. Yes, we are going to the airport to talk to your old uncle Jim. From there, thought we could go to the White Hills and see if we can bag you a deer. You ready for that?"

I drove all night, not stopping once. Pushed the old girl a little faster than normal. I don't like to drive over the speed limit as it can draw too much attention. Connie and Bud were asleep, and I was deep in thought about what Jim had said on the phone about a hell of a ruckus up in Idaho. I think, because I report to Jim, they want him to take the million out of his budget, and he wanted me to tell him how I was going to pay that back. I didn't know the words to tell him it was never going to happen. Too close to retirement.

As the sun peeked over the hills to my back, my mind wandered up the old goat trail I had left just a few hours ago. As I turned the corner with five hundred yards to go, I noticed that my security light was on. Had to have been set off by a vehicle, as it's set to turn it on with one thousand pounds of weight. Couldn't have been a deer. I pulled the truck off to the side.

"Look, you two, something is up just ahead, and I need to walk in from here. How can I tell? Bud, look at those tracks. Not mine; my pickup tires are thinner. Those are wide like a SUV. Son, hand me my deer rifle out from the back window, and you two stay here."

I put on my Carhartt jacket and shoved a hand into the bottom-up pocket. Three extra clips and a lot of loose cartridges. As I looked at my gal, I noticed the worry and fright in her eyes.

"It will be OK, you know that. Just stay here. Maybe I'm wrong. Just stay here."

"Maybe it's Uncle Jim, Dad," said Bud, standing on top of the hood to see.

"No, Bud, it's not him. Probably the old Basque guy come to get some hooch from me. Uncle Jim is flying in, so no, it couldn't be Uncle Jim. Just stay here, and be quiet. Connie, please?"

As I walked the path up to the right side of my compound, my mind said it was the old Basque guy come to get some hooch I always left hidden for him. His wife didn't like him to drink anymore, but it was his life. Now, my instinct was getting hard to ignore at this point. I could smell the rotten bastards, and it wasn't any smell I had smelled in a long time. "Smells like a teenage locker room," my nose was telling me.

"Can I help you boys?" I said as I watched them trying to pick the lock on the side door of my hangar.

The one closest to me jumped, as he had been intent on watching the fat one work on the lock.

"No, can't say you can help us, unless you got the key to this here place."

"Right nice place it is," the other said. "Never seen a lock like this since I left the army back in seventy-three."

"Well, boys, I do have the key, but this here is government property, so you best get your asses back in that there SUV of yours and head on down the hill."

"And if we don't?"

"Well, like I said, this here is government property, and I am just a caretaker, but the real boss is going to be here anytime, and then you will be in some trouble. So I would just leave if I were you."

"Well, mister—didn't catch your name—but the truth of it is, we are here on government business ourselves, so just come over here and open this door, and we won't have to hurt you, you old sheepherder."

"Well, I'm going to need some papers from you all to do that so I won't get into trouble," I said as I moved to their right, my left, so that the sun would shine directly in their eyes.

The one in front laughed some and held up his pistol.

"Here is all the proof of identity we need to show you. This here is my cousin, old Smith, and my friend here is first cousin to old Wesson."

The fat one held up his thirty-eight short nose.

Good. It will be hard for them to hit anything with those peashooters at this range.

"Listen, friend," old fatty said, "we don't want any trouble. We just need to check into this here place and see if you've been poaching any of our government meat."

He moved to his left to get the sun out of his eyes, and the other one moved to my left.

"OK," I said as I reached into my pocket, "let me see. It could be this one here." And I held up three shells for the rifle.

Just as I thought: they couldn't see me as well as they would have liked at 150 yards, so they didn't know if I was holding a key or a widget.

They smiled and formed ranks again, and I started toward them, still holding my rifle tightly to my left side. I counted as I walked—ten paces, thirty yards. They looked at one another as if they had just won the lottery. I dropped to my knee and raised my rifle, now at 120 yards. This was going to be like shooting fish in a barrel.

They stopped laughing and pointed their pistols at me. I let the skinny one have it in the knee, as I figured him for the fast one of the bunch. Was I ever wrong. That fat boy could run like a linebacker for Notre Dame. He was running for the concrete wall extension that kept the dirt off the entrance to the hangar door, so I just waited for a while. Thought I would see if he had enough air to make it that far.

"If you clip him just beneath the ear, boy, he will hide in his hole but be dead as a squirrel for sure."

"Tex, where've you been? I thought for sure you'd left me."

"I did but knew it was time to come out of hiding, as these guys are really bad. Their pistols are Russian made and can be made into a rifle. If you look closely at the guy on the ground, he has his almost put together now."

"So, I better not kill them with Bud here and all and the boss on his way."

I pulled one off and shot the fat one in the ass. He hit the ground so hard I thought he would have knocked himself out. I turned to the other one just as he squeezed one off at me.

"Damn, that was close to me, boy, just over my fat ass. You'd better hug the ground a little closer."

"Yes, I'd better."

I let another fly, popping out my clip and loading in the other from my pocket. Those three-round hunting clips were good for hunting, but that's about all they were good for.

"Good shooting, boy. Put that one down his barrel just like when you were a kid shooting ground squirrels with me. Always had to think of some game with you, or you would just plain outshoot me every time."

"Well, I don't want to kill them. Just want to keep them at bay until the boss gets here."

"Hell, the boss isn't coming. He set you up like he did in Colombia. You'd better finish this now."

"You're wrong, Tex. He didn't set us up, ever. He's my buddy, my friend. He knows Bud and Connie are with me."

"Bet you they got more guys coming, as well as the dang air force, to help take care of you. And they got your kid now and Connie."

"Go check for me now, will you? I'll shoot these two while you're gone, OK?"

"You guys ready to give up, or will I need to separate you just a little more from your body parts?"

The fat one was trying to crawl behind the wall, so I let him enjoy a Texas two-step. I let him have one in the left foot that would make him dance. He sure could yell. I knew those soft-lead hollow points didn't go very deep, as they were made to mushroom out on impact.

"Well, boys, what do you say? Had enough play for one day?"

"Hell no," the skinny one yelled back at me. "We've got reinforcements coming anytime. You better give up now."

"Well, in any event, if you do have some coming, they won't be able to help you."

"Duke?"

"Yes, Tex."

"Get it done. Look, I see dust flying like there must be a dozen of them coming. Bud will get it for sure!"

I turned my head and shoulders to look at Tex just as one shell whistled by my ear and clipped the shoulder plate of my rifle.

"Sure is a lot of dust, Tex, sure is. Dang, did you see where that one shot came from?"

"Yes, he's on top the hangar. Sorry, didn't see the third guy. I should have scouted a little better."

"Guess you should have. Put some marker up so I can see this guy. Never mind. I got him, Tex. His scope is reflecting in the sun. Let's see if the old saying from World War II is true: shoot him in the eye as he looks at it coming."

"Now, boy, oh boy, that's what I call a good shot. Didn't kill him, but he has a scope in a thousand pieces now."

"Yes, for sure. I'm finished here playing these simple-minded games."

Bang!

I let another one out and shot the guy on the roof as he lay on his side, rubbing his eyes. Fat boy was still over there two-stepping it, so I laid him to rest for eternity. Only skinny mouth was left.

"Well, sir, looks like just you and me now, and it will be thirty minutes before the gang's all here. You give up?"

"No, sir. A ranger never says die."

"A ranger, are you?"

So I let him have it in his right shoulder. I didn't want to hit his heart. I jumped up, ran over to him, gave his broken weapon a kick, and unlocked the door. I got the radio on and told Connie to drive the hell out of here.

"Stay on the path. It's a good road. I've kept it up for you. It just doesn't look like it at first. Go home, and wait for me to call you there. You remember the drill, baby?"

"Doc?"

"Yes, love?"

"They got Bud. He's OK, just a graze along his neck. He was standing on the camper watching you."

"You sure he's OK? I'll kill every last one of those effing bastards if he isn't. I will peel them like grapes just to see them squirm."

"Yes, he's OK. I'm out of here. I know the drill. We've practiced it from when we were first married up to the last time I was here. Thought you were going overboard on this stuff but not anymore. Love you, my man, and yes, Bud is OK. The bleeding has stopped, and for God's sake, be careful until Jim gets here."

Connie was a good gal, and I could see she wasn't sparing the horses as she tore down the hidden road I'd graded a week after the last heavy rain with an old tractor I'd borrowed from my Basque buddy. I hoped he hadn't wandered in when all this shit was coming down. Connie knew the path because we had built it. And for sure she was a good shot in her own right. God help anyone who tried to get between her and her kid. On a day like today, I was glad Connie had done all the training here with me. We had built long-range tanks into the pickup, and that old Chevrolet pickup had a nice seven-liter engine with five hundred horses under the hood. And that old pickup wasn't sparing one of them, as her engine faded from my hearing in short order.

I poured a bucket of water on Skinny's head and looked him in the eye.

"Who sent you here to die?"

"*Tex, they got Bud. Did you see?*"

"*Not until Connie said something. Looks like he's going to have a hell of a scar, but he will be OK. She's a good girl. Remember Mexico? She fixed us all up.*"

"Don't know for sure. They just call him boss something or other."

"Not good enough."

I pulled my custom, homemade 1911 forty-five auto from my shoulder harness and let one go into his hand.

"Tex, how close do you say they are now?"

"Quarter mile."

"OK."

I reached inside the door of the hangar and armed the laser mines to go off when the beam was broken, knowing that Connie was safe now. I clicked on a switch to arm her escape road, just in case people were thinking of following her.

I looked into his eyes again as he held his hands tightly together.

"Tell me now. I don't have much patience left in me, asshole."

"Bosses—yes, bosses," he stammers in pain. "Boss Jim."

Hell no!

I looked at Tex, and he gave me a shrug, saying that the only thing that talks in this world was money.

I was mad then—really mad, for the first time since Nam. I wanted to skin this guy alive and play with his mind until I found out everything he knew. But I didn't have time, so I shot him in the throat. If he survived, he wouldn't talk for some time.

I was brought back to reality when I heard the first vehicle set the beam off. Now they were all set, ready for some explosions. It was last car first and then up the line. I figured when I first set that trap up that the last one was usually the head guy, and I'd wanted him to suffer the longest.

The explosives were just enough to tip a car or truck over, not destroy it. I went into the trailer, locked the door, picked up the Murphy bed, and latched it to the wall. I opened the double doors under the bed that looked like closets and went down through them. The next set of doors was securely locked, and the first set automatically shut. If someone made it that far, each chamber was set with gas to knock that person out. The first lock was a fingerprint pad and the next a combination lock. Both looked the same, except the last one was booby-trapped to sense if a finger touched it. If that happened, it would let the first door shut and lock and then fill both small spaces with gas.

A hidden key was the only way to get through the second door—the combination was just a ploy. When I'd built it, I'd taken the idea from a 007 movie. I grabbed Old Betsy from her resting place, told her, "Sorry, old gal. Time for work again," and then went down the long old mine tunnel and out another set of doors. Looking at the whole area, I could see the boys had stopped to help their boss out of the Humvee that was now lying on its side. The spotting scope didn't show me anyone I knew, past or present.

"Tex, do we know any of them? What? CIA? Yes, I see their shoes. Yes, all the same, so you're right, they're CIA. Must be scared of something I know or did. Why me? Sure a lot of firepower for one guy."

Looking over the compound now on my right, I saw that all was intact. I screwed the muzzle blaster off and put on the silencer. It was only good for thirty or forty shots with this caliber, but I was too close. I would be heard but maybe not seen at least. I sure didn't like the odds, and I knew I needed to change that.

POP!

The Humvees were all armor plated. They must have been out of the Fallon branch.

"What do you think? Should we hit two at the same time because they're back to back? Might scare them back inside their Hummers. What? You see a flaw?"

"Just under the front glass is a slight piece of metal, no armor."

"OK, let's take two out. That will leave only ten, if we count the boss. OK, good, good shot, old girl."

The two dropped like old dead flies from a glass window as the steel bullet passed through them both and ricocheted off the open door, slamming it shut.

I grabbed my cell phone from my inside coat pocket and dialed Connie's number. I never used speed dial or caller ID, so if the cell phone were ever taken, they'd have to work at the number to see whom I'd called.

"Hello, dear. Yes, all is OK. Change of plan. Jim and I will be gone for at least a month or more. Go to our old make-out place and stay until you hear from me. If I don't make it, never go back to Winnemucca. Take all the money we have out of all our accounts and live a good life down at our place in Mexico. Gotta go. Love you. Tell Bud I'm sorry he got shot. I love him so much. Tell him that, and then explain about our work and how work comes first and that I'm doing this to protect you both. I swear this is my last job ever, so that's why it will be a little longer. Love you both. Never worry. Only the good guy dies young."

"Tex, OK, they're all loaded up. Watch them for me for a moment. I need to load up the spare clips that are in the ammo box. Tex, tell me, what did I do? Something so wrong that even Jim couldn't talk to me about it. I swear on my dad's grave all these bastards are going to die. Jim will die as well. He should have known me well enough to know that when it comes to my family, hands off. But instead, he let the paid assassins inside our show and ordered my family dead as well as me. Why, Jim? Why, you fucker? I will get you if it's the last thing I ever do."

Tex didn't know why either. Didn't know what could have happened or what had gone through their minds to turn on us that way. We had always been good soldiers.

"Tex, watch this!"

A series of mines went off, starting at about fifty yards behind them and working their way toward them. That pushed them up the road toward me.

"OK, let's see if you're right, Tex. Let's make the one on the driver's side in the front Hummer hum a hymn. My God, you're good, old man. Wish Mike had come back. He helped me set up the zones so I would never have to figure, just look and click. Did I hear someone call my name? Oh, Mike, you're here! Thought I'd seen the last of you."

"OK, now, down two clicks to ten, right four."

"They're on the mark now. First Hummer is hurt, about ready to pass out. He's veering off the road. They're all bailing. Going to run behind the second one. That's two down, Mike, Tex. Two to go. They haven't figured it out yet. They don't know where to shoot or what to shoot at. OK, guys, let's move to some white rounds and see if their run-flat tires can endure that much heat. OK, guys, look. They're spraying their own guys that I propped up by the hangar. They think they're the ones doing the shooting. If they only knew.

"OK, Mike, I'm so glad you're here. Did you hear that these guys were sent to kill us by Jim? Mike, when this is all over, we will go get Jim, that Commie bastard, for sure. Bet we should hurry. Knowing Jim, he'll have the air force 'accidently' drop some napalm on here, a few tunnel bombs. OK, let's pick up this hatch and pull some water out of that K-ration stash. My mouth is dry from all this shit. Here we go. Let's finish this thing off and get out of here.

"OK, white is doing an excellent job. The Hummer can't take the heat. Poor Hummer—it's smoking, and its tires are on fire. Let's put a white one inside the last two Hummers. With them both having Willy Petes inside, they won't last long now. OK, Mike, what're my clicks, up, down, side, what?"

"Maybe a half down now."

"Well, what is it?"

"Yes, a half down, no side clicks. You're good, Duke."

"Yes, it is. Good job, Mike. Look, it went through the same spot Tex had seen. Good eyes, old man, good eyes. Well, now let's pop them off as they run for cover. That's it.

"All gone. Looks like boss man is too scared to come out. Think he will burn up in there.

"OK, let's hide Old Betsy in the dugout. It might survive here if they plan a party for me like I think they will."

"OK, boss man, come out of there. You fool, you trying to shoot me with that peashooter of yours while I stand behind your own bulletproof glass door? What a fool. Oh, look, your pants are all wet. How did that happen? Doesn't smell like you spilled coffee on yourself. I won't kill you. Just slide out of there and take your jacket off first. Looks good. Now, let's walk to the hangar. Who sent you?"

"Boss Jim."

"Well, he should have known better than to send you here to try to take me in my own home. OK, walk up to your dead guy there, and sit down on him. I said sit. Now, tell me how you talked these stupid guys to come up here by themselves."

"Well, see, we're all Black Ops and get a million if we get you on our own."

"Is that a million each or a split?"

"Each."

"You guys sure know how to waste money, don't you? Well, now, thinking about it, it's a sure bet the head cheese wouldn't have to pay it off, so why me? Why did Boss Jim want me out? Why didn't he just ask for me to come in?"

"We were called in by the National Guard to look at the shooting in Idaho when their helicopter was shot down. We talked to a farmer who said he rented a barn to a guy for his small plane. When we asked your name, he said it was Ben Franklin. You need to change that line, D. Moore. Jim said it had to be you: it was your MO, it was your dad's homeplace, and no one could shoot like that anymore. Had to be you, so he said for us to go here, and we would find you and get you when you came out the door, thinking it was him. Guess we were too early."

"Good thing, as my kid was with me. Or was that part of the plan?"

"Yes, terminating your wife and kid was part of the plan. There are people at your home by now."

"Hello, Connie? Where are you? On your way with the new car? Listen, this is worse than I figured, so go to plan C. I will call you in a day to check on you. These guys want all of us, not just me. Yes, I'm OK. Got a scratch, no blood. I have it all under control. Ditch the cell phone, and don't turn one on until I am scheduled to call. Now, stop and run over it, and then go. You know the map and directions are in the middle bundle of money, yes? Yes. Love you too! Bye.

"OK, guy, what's your name? No, don't tell me. Dumb ass, correct? If you don't want to die, let me have a few things from you. Your cell phone first, then your cuffs. And grab the cuffs of the guy you're sitting on. That's right, be a good guy, and maybe you will live to tell your grandkids about when you almost got the Duke. Now, cuff your left hand to his right, and I will do the same to your right and his left. Now, I know you got Boss Jim on speed dial. What's his number?"

"One zero zero seven."

"Does he think he is 007? What a laugh!

"Hello, Jim? Yes, you got that right. Here with your guys all handcuffed together, enjoying some nice lemonade. Yes, we can wait for you. How long do you think it will be? Two hours? It will be dark if you don't hurry. Yes, the generator set works. I will have the coffee ready and this place lit up like the Fourth of July. OK, see you in two hours. But if I know my old pal, it will be like three or four. You've never been on time a day in your life."

"OK, Tex, Mike, we have one hour to get the hell out of here. This guy? He won't run off now. OK, Tex, you're right. I do need to make sure."

Boom! I shot him in the foot.

"You're OK. Jim's on his way for you. What? He's going to level this place? Well, so sad to hear it, but I'm gone."

He ain't my bro, he—he was my bro,
Gotta get out of this place, go run and hide till the day be mine.
If it's the last thing I ever do, I will see them die.

Damn you, Jim. It will be the last thing you ever do, going after my Connie and my Bud. Now you've pissed me off.

I opened the hangar doors and pushed the plane half out the door to make it look like it was ready to take off down the runway. I put all the gas cans outside, under the wings, so it would be sure to burn like a wildfire. But I was still wondering what could have made Jim turn on me, let alone my family. I looked into the plane as I set the last jerrican down under her wing, grabbed her tail section, kissed it, and turned my face so she couldn't see me cry.

You've been a real good girl, my lady, but you won't feel any pain. I will miss you every day of my life from this moment on. You're the most faithful girl I have ever flown, and you don't deserve to die this way. But so is fate, my love, so is fate.

I yelled at Tex and Mike in a voice raspy from crying as I pushed my homemade dune buggy out from under the tarp. I had hidden it so that if ever I had company, they wouldn't ask what I was building there.

"Let's go, guys."

It was a neat machine, and I was very proud of it. I'd always thought it would be a hit if anyone ever took the time to manufacture it from my prototype. I'd made the frame from seamless, heavy-wall tubular stainless steel two by four. I'd used a Goldwing Honda power plant as it had a shaft drive, hooked it up to a Jag rear end that I had narrowed as much as I could and still keep the independent suspension working. It had inside stock disc brakes, housed now just for protection mostly. It was great fun to run it inside those old tunnels. It was long, and you sat down low, with air-lift shocks that could lift you up over boulders and then set you back down. It had a low center of gravity, so low that you could make the skid plate drag on the ground. It was nearly impossible to see it, tarp covered behind the sagebrush.

The radiator on the roof was at an angle so that when the automatic electric fans turned on, the radiator sucked cool air by the driver. An electric air machine made from a home breathing apparatus converted to DC pumped air into the left half of the roll-cage tubing so that the driver could be on oxygen the entire time. It was behind the driver with a long hose hooked to a helmet that was a lot like a jet fighter's helmet. The air machine kept a bottle-like affair full of oxygen so that the driver could breathe for an hour or more. In the event the air machine died for any reason, I had installed a carbon filter behind the regular air filter attached to the roll cage to help keep the air pure. The same tubing housed the machine's air filter so that neither the machine nor my lungs were ever exposed to dust or water. When the frame tubes and bottle had been filled by the autoregulator, it automatically switched to a part of the frame that I had hooked into the air intake. Because of that, it was able to drive underwater for a short time.

I extended the skid plate to secure the engine oil pan on both sides of me. The seat was held in place with a full five-part safety harness that was bolted to the armor plating that protected the driver from land mines and such. Two large tubes, watertight, ran on both sides of the driver's legs. One had my M60 so it would be closest to my right side. On my left, the other tube held my hand-built AR47. There was also a place for Old Betsy 3, if I wanted her next to the M60, and I always took her everywhere. This left one tube empty, and that is where I put my deer rifle. The tubes acted like part of the roll cage, set far enough forward that I could sit in the seat and pull one of the rifles out with ease. On the slope tin behind the roll cage, between the motor and the roll cage, were two lockable boxes for all my ammo.

Air was fed automatically from an electric sensor regulator. The top half of the tubing was for the engine; the back half behind me was for me. The bottom mainframe tubing was for cooling—part for oil and part for engine water. Tubing filled with fluid was ten times stronger when it came to bending it or trying to punch a hole in it, as fluid could move and absorb shock.

The other half of the tube behind me wrapped around the engine was for fuel. Under the seat, a small piece of armor plating was welded to the metal of the skid plate, extending from the front of my feet to the back of the seat. This, I hoped, was strong enough to allow me to survive a small land mine.

I was set, ready to go like a bat out of hell under the sagebrush I had set up on a drip system to make it grow large for just this kind of occasion. The tunnel I had found went to the lake—White Horse Lake, it was called, named after the ranch that had built it. The lake was not too deep but covered around eight acres, making it a nice watering hole for the ranch's livestock. The water hid the entrance to the tunnel well.

I knew the tunnel entrance was all right, as I had just checked it out six months earlier. At that time, I had also checked on all my listening devices and cameras. The entrance was made up of two double doors. I had done all the work on the tunnel myself during my time off and had always kept its existence to myself. Of course, Tex, Mike, and Connie knew about it, but I could trust them never to reveal it to anyone. We were too close to have any secrets among us.

The tunnel shaft was about ten miles long and on a slow incline. The old miners had left their rail tracks and ore cars, so I was able to make it all run again. I used it to haul cement up and down the shaft.

Before the tunnel hit the lake, around fifty yards above the high-water line, I had another camera outside the doors. The shaft was full of cameras as well, all tied to a computer just inside the first set of doors where I entered the tunnel. It allowed me to check everything before going in.

I left the machine just outside the first door and went inside to check it all out. Hurry was what got a lot of good men killed, so I took it slow and easy, checking every footprint. All was clear: the batteries were full, the air tanks were full, and the tunnel was clean. I set the computer to turn itself off in sixty minutes. If anything went wrong before then, it would signal my mobile phone with a special code that was accessible only inside the tunnel.

"Yes, Tex, what is it?"

"Mike just said he could feel the Hummer coming down the hill like an earthquake starting up. We'd better get inside and sit for a while so we can't be picked up by heat sensors."

"That, Tex, is why we left skinny out there. I'm hoping they'll think it's me, waiting for mister traitor, Jim. But, yes, Mike, let's go. Tex is right. We need some depth between us and the surface."

So off we went. The machine was heavy when it was fully loaded, and it was always full and ready for a fight. I'd never got the time to put a fold-down armor plate in front, but I hoped that would turn out all right.

Oh, baby, you know that I like those fireballs from heaven.
Hum, hummmm, la-la-la…
Yes, baby, fireballs from heaven,
A good lay, a wiggle from you on top,
Sweet dreams of you, sweet memories of you,
How I wish I could watch you burn…

"What did you say, Tex? I'm a bad singer, and I never get the words right? Let's hear you sing a good one, then."

I'm the meanest old man in the meanest old world,
Baddest as they come. I love to shoot the world is my joy.

Second verse, same as the first.

I am the meanest old man in the meanest old world,
Baddest as they come. I like to shoot the world is my joy.
Did you ever see a night so long
That tracers seem to just crawl along under the moon,
Even if the moon goes behind a cloud to hide?
Please let me cry?

"OK, you guys can stop any time now. Neither one of you can carry a tune in a bucket, so let's just sit down here and see if we can hear what's happening."

So we did that. The batteries were good, pumping air at full capacity from my homemade air machine, and we were coasting nicely with the motor off. I could have made her electric, but then she couldn't have gone underwater very deeply.

"There they are, guys, the last set of doors. Now, we check the outside one more time. Go underwater about five feet for around twenty yards, and pop up like a breaching whale. Mike, check the snorkel while I look outside. Damn it all to hell, the door won't open! Tex, what was the new code? Won't matter if it's clear or not if the door lock is jammed. Yes, got it—your RA number, one eight eight six zero six two seven. Still no good! Hell, I must be losing it. Look here, Mike. I took the batteries out so they wouldn't rust and put them right there by the computer. Losing it! You're riding with a crazy guy."

"So, what's new?"

"I'll tell you what's new. You can just stay here, Mike, and swim out on your own. You laughed at me when I rigged that impeller to work off the back of the rear end. You thought I had lost it then, but now we'll see who gets the last laugh. OK, now she's opening. Let's go one hundred more yards, and we'll be out of here, gliding on down. Air pressure is up to snuff. Close and lock the door, and put your masks on. OK, firing up the tank. Let's go for it. Snorkel is good. Exhaust is up to snuff."

I switched to a P-trap snorkel. The exhaust was all good. The air in the mask was at full pressure, the electric air pump was off, and the intake was closed. Into the water we went.

FOURTEEN

Being Team Leader

"D. Moore? Captain wants to see you. Better head up now. He's waiting for you!"

"Now? I thought we were flying back to the base now."

"Yes, sir, I understand that you want me to memorize these pictures so I won't get lost or shoot the wrong guy, but I already did that, sir, while we were talking about each one."

"Step over here, and tell me what you see, then."

"Yes, sir. Three guys by a car. From right to left: first guy is six feet tall with black slacks…"

"OK, Captain. I think we see that you're correct. Lieutenant Moore is very good."

"Yes, Mr. Director. Is that it?"

"Captain, let me talk to Lieutenant Moore with no interruption. I want his insight firsthand. Duke, I am the director of the CIA."

"Yes, sir."

"Just Mr. B will work—I'm not in the army. So your captain thinks you're ready to be a team leader. What do you say? Can you handle the pressure? Besides having a photographic memory, what can you do? You seemed arrogant when you were brought in here, so tell me your story. What's up with you and your team leader, Sam?"

"Sir—I mean, Mr. B—the truth is I guess I am just a mite cocky, as you say. Me, well, I look at it with the knowledge that I'm able to do my job and do it well, very well, sir. You see, I am second lieutenant, but I've been in the army for only just over a year. I went to every school and passed them all in the top five. When I first started the schooling, I was told I would achieve another rank if I were in the top ten. Well, here I am: three schools down but still at second Louie, so I just put in for warrant officer training. I was told I need two years in before I could go for that training unless I had some letters of accommodation. So I have one, and I need some more, sir.

"But I do love this army life. That I joined up you know, but what you don't know is that I joined because my dad was very abusive to me. He beat me up a lot, so I joined, and to answer your question about whether I can handle the stress of being a leader, I think I can. Ask my teammates. They will tell you that I lead those most of the time anyway, like the mission we just came back from. Can I tell you about it, or will I be in trouble?"

"Hell, Duke, I was the one who ordered the mission. Tell me what happened. I saw your letter, but I'd like to hear it firsthand."

"Yes, Mr. B," I said as my captain nodded to me. "Well, sir, I know I can handle the pressure because when we went over the border to our target area, I was to be the backup shooter, and Sam, the team leader, was to be the main shooter. Mike spotted for us both. When we were finally in position, Sam told me to take the guy on the right and that he would take all of them on the left. My position was in front of the door, so Sam said to close the door. That means that if anyone else came out, I was to drop them. He gave me the sign to start, and all was good. The other team members were giving the go sign, and I waited for Sam to shoot. But he was frozen. So I popped mine and then his. When he saw his guy go down, he crawled over to me and said his guy was a white guy. I told Sam he was the one in the picture, so no big deal. I only shoot. I'm not here to make the decision of whom to shoot or not shoot. I just follow orders. Well, Sam was mad and wanted to have my hide.

"So I said, 'Sam, listen. He was the one in the picture, and so was mine. Mine was white also. So let's go.' Our silence had been compromised, so I started laying down shot after shot to pile them up, Mr. B, and there were too many of them. When my sniper rifle was empty, and I didn't have any more reloads, I crawled off.

"The team and I were shocked about Sam. He was in here, the Special Forces, for a long time. But he was really pissed at me for taking the shot. Well, it took us some time to get back. We missed the boat and had to change routes many times. We sat down after an hour of running, and everyone looked at me. Sam was just out of it. He wanted to fight me, not the enemy. So Mike, my spotter, said to Sam that if we were going to get out of there, he voted they go with me, and everyone was in agreement. They knew Sam was team leader, but Sam and I are the same rank, so they knew it wasn't a mutiny or anything like that. Just two officers having a little spat.

"But Sam, he was losing it, as far as I could tell. So out of respect for him, I asked the group what they wanted me to do. They said they wanted me to lead them home. We needed to make tracks, so I said we should circle around the stash, if you get my drift."

"Yes, I know your stash. So go ahead, Duke."

"So we did. We needed the water and ammo, but I thought if they'd found it, they would wait there to ambush us. I for one was not up to another fight. So with Sam being so mad, I made a deal with Mike to take Sam's ammo from him as I held him. That's why Sam said I'd hit him. I didn't hit him, sir, Mr. B, just pushed him to the ground and told him that when and if we got back, we could go finish it anytime he liked. We all knew he was a real scrapper from Jersey, but I wasn't as scared to get my ass kicked as much as I was scared of being shot. So we left. Made a wide berth around the way we came in. It was dark by then, and I was glad of it. I took point, as I always do after dark, as I can see better than most people in the dark. I told Mike to watch our backs, as I was sure Sam would shoot me if he thought he could get away with it.

"Nothing came out in the debriefing about any of the discord, and when Sam looked at me, I thought, 'Well, he is covering his ass, but I don't care. If he is silent, so will I be.' We need to be a better team out there. Each of us, at one point, will need help if we get scared. And anyone who doesn't ever get scared, I guess, is either high or crazy or both, sir. So, that's why we went to the gym and fought a week ago. I told Sam I wasn't mad at him. He was still team leader, and we didn't need to do this. He called me a so-and-so and then hit me before we ever got to the gym, so I went. He wanted bare knuckles, and I agreed.

"Mike was in my corner and told me that Sam was a good street fighter. Mike had seen him fight before. Told me Sam liked to fake a hit and then kick first thing out of the box, and he did just that. So when he went to punch, I didn't return his jab like he was used to. I stepped back, and he was already in motion to kick. I sidestepped him and let him have a left hand as hard as I could. Guess one punch sure did mess him up. Broke his nose, split his lip so bad he needed stitches, and he was out like a light. We left him there with his friend, some guy I didn't know. The guy yelled at me, 'Lucky punch, you sick SOB,' so I turned around, went back, and kicked him in the nuts. As he went down, I told him I used to play football and that I'd bet that one had been a field goal for sure. No luck to it. I'm just a mean bastard.' So you see, sir, that's why I think I can lead. My men respect me, and they know I won't freeze up. Might puke after it's all done, but not until I'm home safe with everyone still standing."

"Well, Duke, we knew the story, but we wanted to hear it from you. Sam did tell us he had been unsure of the targets and never fired a shot the entire mission."

"No, Mr. B, I don't think he did ever fire his weapon, not even when we were in the heavy firefight. And then I took all his shells. My mission was to shoot the targets that had been given to me, and that's that in my book. I don't ever second-guess my commander; I just do it. Never want to die for you out there, let me say that. Love my country, God, the whole ball of wax, and I'd lay my life down for you here and now, if it came to that. But out there, that's me, sir. I know how to survive out there. I see no need to die for it in the jungles of Nam. 'Win the war, lose a battle, but live to fight another day' is what they said in jump school and survival training. You think I'm wrong, Mr. B?"

"No, Duke, not at all. That's why I wanted to talk to you directly. 'Live to fight another day'—that's a line we all need to remember, so you're good out there. Sharp, remember the faces...but the maps. What about that?"

"Well, sir, the maps are easy to read, and then I think about where we are at all times. When I go in, I find my spot on the map."

"You do what? Find your spot? You're not to take anything in there, like a map or photos."

"Sir, the map in my head."

"Oh, the map in your head. Go on."

"The place is easy to locate. They show me a map, like you did today, and there is always writing on it—places of interest, like where we are now. Look at it, and I'll show you from here. See the mark in a light-blue dot? That's us now."

Mr. B and the captain looked at each other with an expression of disbelief on their faces.

"You've seen a map like this before?"

"No, sir, I've never seen a map of this area. But the army maps are all the same, so I know without doubt where we are right now without having to look at that map again. And if I walk to the town north, it will be ten klicks. And then there's a town to the east and a town to the west. What direction do you choose to go?"

"East."

"Mr. B, east it is. So going east...let me think. There was a hill around two klicks from us now, but a bit more to the north and east, there was a red dot. The red dot is an ammo dump of some kind. I can be there before dark, scout it out, and we can resupply ourselves there. And now where to, sir?"

"Let's go to headquarters in Nuremburg. How far is that?"

"Well, we went the wrong way, so let me see. It's around fifty klicks, so let's go south up over this hill and then some west, and there is a town there where we can catch a ride. Of course, we won't ask permission—we will just use it and then get it back before they miss it, if you like. I would say we should be there in three hours tops if we ride, tomorrow morning if we walk. Because we don't want to be seen, we'll take Route 22 on the air force map if we drive. If we walk, we'll have to stay close to the roads, because there are a lot of fences out there. Fences mean livestock, livestock means dogs, and the dogs won't speak English. So we would either have a lot of noise or a lot of necks to break."

"What the effing hell?"

"Sir, Mr. B, what is it?"

"I am looking at this map and can see your every step as you tell it to me. I just never met a guy before with such a talent as this. So here's the deal. When the general gets here, he will give you another rank. That's what you want, isn't it? And I will give you a letter, so when you have your two years in the army, you can go to warrant officer school."

"What's the kicker, sir?"

"The kicker? Haven't heard that one in a long time. The kicker is this: you have to be team leader. We will rotate Sam back stateside, and you can be the one in charge. We have a mission I will tell you about after dinner. We on?"

"Well, sir, Mr. B, I couldn't do that to Sam. He's been through a lot for you guys, and he has only one year left before this enlistment is up. And he is a lifer, sir. It would kill him."

"OK, so the answer is no. You will follow Sam, then?"

"Well, sir, can I just build a new team? Have a new team, except for Mike? Mike has been my spotter since sniper school."

"Yes, I think that would work. Hell yes, another team here. That could work. I will present it to General Pat Wright and see what he says. Go get some dinner, and see us back here at 19:00 hours. And no talking about this to anyone."

"What should I say?"

"Tell them that the brass said Sam's story was a little different than yours and that you will be notified after dinner what the brass is going to do for you, to you. How's that, Duke?"

"OK, sir, sounds good."

So I formed a new team with Mike and some guys who were fresh out of school and eager to win the war. I'm sad they never did. What a shame; what a waste: John, Allen, and Tom.

The mission was to go into Russia and locate some guys we were to snatch. We never did find them but almost got snatched ourselves when we were behind the iron curtain. We never had any markings on us, so if we had been caught, we would have just been traitors who went AWOL. And that wouldn't have been good for anyone. I built a good team. We had three or four missions after the first into Russia before our big last wahoo. John and Allen stayed in Nam; Tom, well, he went a different path. Can't tell you where he is.

If you're right, you're left,
Ain't no sense in looking back, Jodie's got your Cadillac,
Ain't no sense in looking down, ain't no discharge on the ground,
If you're right, you're left—left—left—left—

"OK, Mike, Tex, let's go back to sleep. This buggy is needing to dry out, and the fireball from the sky is now gone. We are safe. Yes!"

Humming sweet dreams of you,
As I lay me down to sleep
I pray the Lord not to let me wake, but if I do,
Protect us from the slob that sent us here until we can cut his tongue out.
For sweet dreams of you, oh, how I yearn for you, sweet dreams of you...

"Hello, Connie. Good morning, my love. How are you? What? You're scared? Just calm down, now. We have rehearsed this a lot. I am out, and they're looking for us, so just be calm. You know the routine. I will see you there in a few months. I need to go talk to Jim and see if he can help us in any way."

That was the first time in fifteen years I told Connie a lie. In my mind, I did it to help protect her and Bud. I didn't want her to have that sick, tied-up feeling in her gut that I had, thinking that our closest friend was wanting to kill her, Bud, and me. Well, I could understand about me. I was a rotten bastard—been that way all my life. But after so many hours of talking to Jim, telling him that the only thing in this world that mattered to me was my son and my wife and how I would do anything to protect them, how I would kill anyone who came close to hurting one hair on their heads, why was he doing this? Why did he want to kill an innocent boy?

"So, Mike, let's go up on the ridge, get out Old Betsy 3, and see if she is OK. We will need her to talk to old Jimbo. Yes, that's exactly right. I plan on killing him. You say you vote for a shot in the spine but not a kill shot? What do you say, Tex? Wake up here, old man. Yes, you. What do you think? Should we kill or cripple old Jimbo? OK, Mike, you heard him. Cripple it is, Tex votes. Mike, you guys win the vote for a cripple shot. OK, got ya. A cripple is long lasting. Remembers his screw-up the rest of his life. So guess I vote that way as well. A cripple he will be.

"It was a good idea you had, Tex, to make this strongbox up here to hide Old Betsy 3. She is as good as new. Load some ammo in the space, and off we go. Jim knows about the old Basque guy, so we'll need a new route. What do you say we go to the old ranch, see if we can buy us a pickup for a few days, and swap this buggy out for it as well?"

The ride was long, even on pressured air. It made me tired, having all the dirt thrown up on my body. But my mind was on Jim, and I was going over every detail of his place in my mind. I'd been there a thousand times. It was just out of Kingman, Arizona, up on a hill for safety, he said. No one to look down on him unless that person could shoot from a mile-plus away. Well, that was what I planned on doing. I'd never done it since school, but if I missed crippling him and killed him instead, I guess I just missed.

"Look there, Tex, an old Oldsmobile like yours. What do you think? Shall we see if we could make a trade?"

"Hello, in the house! Anyone home? Sorry, miss, I didn't mean to scare you. My dune buggy is quite home built, so I can hunt from it. I was wondering it that old bucket of bolts still runs, and if you would like to trade it for this nice buggy? It's like the car my old grandpa used to have, and if I brought it home, he would just about have a heart attack seeing it. It would be like walking back in time for him."

"It runs, but it's out of gas, and it needs a battery."

"Well, I have an extra battery here in the buggy so that I would never be caught with a dead one. Where is your guy?"

"He's out hunting as well."

"OK. If I can get her started, I'll give you fifty bucks to boot. Your guy will love you tonight when he sees this buggy you just bought. It's the best ever built."

"Tex, what do you say?"

"Sounds good to me."

"I'll give her the fifty and load the trunk up."

"OK, miss. Running fine. I just put enough gas in her to get her started, so is there a place I can buy some gas for her? OK, got ya, over at the hay farm I use your name, Bridgett. OK, thanks, and here's your fifty."

"Man, oh man, let's see if we can get some tunes on the old radio. Here's a dumb song: 'She really likes my tractor.' Stupid rednecks. A tractor really turns her on. What will they sing next? Now there is a song. 'Sweet Caroline, you're so sweet horseflies keep hanging around your face, front teeth missing but just fine for kissing, makes me feel like the only rooster in the hen house, guess it shows.'"

"Look, mister, all I know is that I bought this car from Bridgett, and she said you would sell me a tank of gas so I could make it to town. Call her if you like, but I have the cash right here. I'll pay you a dollar a gallon, and that's twice what you paid for it. Correct? So we have a deal?"

"OK, Tex, now listen to this old Detroit iron purr. They don't make them like this anymore."

Hello, there, Max.
My right fist is made of steel, and the other is made of iron.
If the left one don't get ya, the other one will. Hummmmmmm…

"See, Mike, these are real tunes, real tunes. These redneck stations know their music. Now that we have some real wheels, I say we take the long way around—I mean the really long way around. Let's take I-40 to Lakeview, then hit the three ninety-five and follow it to Donner Pass. There, we'll take the old road to Lake Tahoe and follow the old road around the lake to Zephyr Cove. Rest up and stock up on things in that little old town. Should make it in a day and a half. When we are rested a day or so, we'll drive on down the back way to Minden. We miss all the checkpoints that way and so won't be stopped by someone who wants to look into our trunk. At Minden, we'll stay on three ninety-five until we get to Bishop. There, we'll spend a short night in some flea-bitten place and get ready for the last leg. The last leg will be slow going. We will stay on three ninety-five to the old truck junction of fifty-eight, head east, and at Barstow pick up the I-40. We'll stay on that until we get to Needles, then switch to ninety-five, and at Laughlin, we'll take the sixty-eight to come into Golden Valley. That, my friends, is only a mile from the north end of Kingman and a few hundred yards to the trail that leads to the hill that is right across from old Jimbo's place. We'll set up camp and shoot that SOB when he comes out to go to the office.

"It will be perfect. We'll go back a bit until we can get up behind him, putting the morning sun to our backs and in his face. Mike, you take some readings. I have it at well over four thousand feet, elevation

almost to five. You read the same? Man, that's thin air, and the distance of two thousand eight hundred and fifteen yards is a far piece. Don't think we've ever done this distance since we were in school. With a drop of eight hundred feet, that's going to be one hell of a shot. OK, dew point and, luck has it, no wind. Let's make a lean-to and get ready for him to come out for work. Night to you guys. It's been a good day. Nice tunes and a joy to drive good old iron like that again. A great day. I've set the alarm in my head for five, and we'll see what's cooking in the morning. Wake me if you guys hear anything. I'm bushed."

Big, bad Duke.
Stood six feet two, a mountain of a man,
Heard said he killed a man at almost two miles away
with one simple bullet from his big Old Betsy girl…

FIFTEEN

OLD SCORE

"Good morning, team. How are you this nice sunny, or almost sunny, morning? Yes, I'm hungry as well. I could eat the ass off a wild bear on a dead run. So looking at all the settings and doing a visual scan, everything seems the same. Yes, Tex, I see that sneaky bastard made himself a tunnel and a nice garage. But the stupid bugger made it fifty yards from the new elevator door. Seems he got himself an armored SUV. Looks like an old president, which means a lot of armor.

"Mike, damn, this will be a shot for the books. Two thousand eight hundred and fifteen yards—that's eight thousand five hundred and twenty feet and well over a mile."

"But it's downhill."

"OK, Mike, I see that. I'm adjusting my clicks. I forget, is it up for downhill or down for downhill? I'm not worried. I know you have that all figured into the angle of the dangle and all. But the best I can figure, it will be a shot just to scare the hell out of him anyway.

"OK, got it, Tex. You agree, Mike? I'll just shoot at it at the added range, and the projectile will drop in on target. Well, let's hope so. Yes, I see them. Looks like his kids are loading up to go to school. If I know old Jimbo, bet they're in a private one someplace. Well, the guard *is in now, and look, there is the little weasel. OK, that's it. Let's try an armor-piercing shell to see if these new titanium ones are as good as the boys claim they are. Look, right through the hood. Bet the motor is dead as hell now. The kids are going for the elevator, back up to Mommy. That's it, shut the door. And now a Willy Pete round to seal it, a nice glancing blow to kick the door handle off and make it hard to run. Look at that stupid bastard of a guard, hiding behind the door. Bet he's going to have some white on white in just about two seconds. Changed my mind. Let's shell this place with the whites: some on the door, some on the car. Let's just scare the hell out of him and my good old buddy Jimbo."*

"Hello, there, Jimmy, old buddy. Yes, it's me shooting you from the heavens. Nice thing you did to me. But to my kid and my lady who have never been a part of it? So, yes. You cannot run from me. The sky is raining white on you.

"What would it take to make me stop and leave your kids and old lady out of it? Nothing. You're all dead, just like you tried to do to me and mine. Burned to a crisp. Remember how we laughed at that gook you shot with the old Willy Pete? White hellfire, as you called it, and he had to just cut body parts off to stop the fire from burning up the rest of him. Well, now I am going to see you in hell, old buddy. See you in hell."

Bang! Bang! Bang!

I lit the place up for my old buddy and watched them jerk as the stuff ate them up. The guard was in bad shape. A lot had landed on him because he'd been hiding behind a worthless old car door. He was screaming so loudly that I could hear him clear up at the top of the hill. Old Jim, he dived into the back seat. Didn't want to play. He looked up once and saw the stuff eating the flesh off the guard's arms, neck—everywhere it had touched. Even a speck could eat a hole clean through a person.

"Mike, did you see that the guy just stood out in the open and was firing all over the place with his toy gun and then discharging the last

one into his own head? Now, that guy had more guts than a government mule. Don't know of many who have the guts to shoot himself under fire, do you, Mike?"

Tears came to my eyes as I looked at the top of his head. "Damn you, Mike. You really fucked up this time," I muttered as tears clouded my vision and the shell left.

Jim needed to feel that pain, so I loaded up some armor again and hit the windshield. It took four shots to shatter it into a million pieces. Then three whites into the SUV, against the back window, in the side door—just let it splash all over the place. He had his hell then. I wanted to see if he had as many balls as his guard. Not so sure the desk jockey could help himself to a bullet the way his guard had. I wasn't sure that weasel had it in him at all. I let off one last shot very high to let those in the house know they were mine if I wanted them. The large plate-glass window looking south shattered, and I could hear voices coming from their hiding spot.

There was only one way out now, and that was down the staircase toward me. I knew I wouldn't bring them into this, but I wanted to let everyone know not to ever think about my family again, or those kids were mine next time. I didn't care who, what, or where: Jim's wife and kids would be toast.

Singing my song as we packed up and left,
We got to get out of here; they're coming at last,
Thing is they never do, we ever do,
He's not my bro. he's never been my brother.
On and on we will wait, to the end, yes, the end.
For he's heavy now, he's still not my brother anymore.

SIXTEEN

GOOD TIMES OVER

We all thought the next guy in charge was bad for business, but then, well, he was OK but not good. Not good for the Black Ops team, as far as we were concerned. Hell, he made a mess of getting the hostages out of a bad fix. He used straight army. Should have sent us in; we would have gotten them out on our first try. Would there have been death? Sure as hell. They were in our embassy. Then our buddy R, he had us doing stuff all over the globe to fight the "war on drugs." Well, we were already doing that shit. "It paid the bills" is all I can say about that.

The old guard changed some after that. I thought it would be better having Mr. X as president—you know who I'm talking about—but it was worse. We were having to hide more. Everything we did was under investigation. That was when Jim came into the picture. As a supervisor, I knew him from the Special Forces. His team and mine even did a few missions together. So he and I were preparing for the worst—him in Kingman and me in the Denio area. Well, I did my job, but there was a lot less work than before. Younger guys were coming up who could really shoot, and, well, they were a problem in my book. I thought the sniper code was being pushed out the door. The young guys were getting out after four years, more or less, and then writing a bloomin' book. And then there were some tell-all former high rank-and-file guys who wanted to do the same. I didn't have a problem popping any of those guys. It was a job, not a church social, you know. Connie and I were very happy, and the only thing that was good about the war on drugs was that it kept me from working that old tire shop that I hated so much.

First to Venezuela. I recall I had a three-man job there. It took me over a year of living in that jungle. It was so bad—bugs and living off the land. How much fish or croc can one person stand to eat anyway?

Then there was the Nicaragua job. I took Connie with me on that one. She was great. We blended right in, and it was very nice to have everyone think we were Italian rather than Latino. We would write down the information we heard, and then we would code every word before we sent it on. That was what kept us from getting killed, for sure. When people think you don't understand their language, they say all sorts of things they wouldn't otherwise say.

There was one job from which we both thought we would never make it back alive, but there we were. Connie never went to the hills with me. She stayed behind, and we used our satellite phones so we couldn't be traced. By them anyway. Old Ron would do anything to make himself look good, including selling us out. "Negotiations," we were told, but we figured out who the leak was. Yes, old R, you know who I'm talking about. Maybe I don't know that as a fact. Just talking, you know.

We sent her home in the middle of a job—PG, you know. She was a tough girl, but PG was taking its toll along with the not-so-good food. After she left, I made a nice, safe spot for me to hide and watch the drug factory. You know, I had to wait until all the big guys had assembled, take the picture, and send it in by satellite phone. At night, when I knew everyone had gone, I would sneak down there to the drug hideaway and plant stuff for me to shoot, stuff that would make a hell of an explosion. One day when we—yes, we as in Mike, Tex, and I—were sitting around, drinking our cold coffee and eating some kind of chicken thing—boy, did I lose weight on that job. Anyway, they all showed up around midnight. They all went inside. I had the place bugged, so I could tell they were looking for something. Finally, the bigwigs were in their little office inside the dugout factory. Mike recalculated for the night air. I screwed a fire suppressant into my silencer, as I knew it was so dark that the flash would give me away. We didn't have the modern night-vision stuff, but the old stuff worked well for me. The sound bugs were humming, and thanks to Connie, I was listening and understanding every word. Because I knew what they were saying, I knew this was the first time in more than a year that I'd been watching that the big boys were all there in the same place. I got the go-ahead from the head office to "eliminate."

I had buried explosives at every angle leading away from the escape hatch, and I zeroed in on the one buried under the front of the only door. I had located one other escape hatch, and its exit was close to me. I had buried all sorts of stuff along that escape route, as I didn't know for sure how many would be inside. Lots of their own drugs were hidden inside the place, so they were used to it. When I let the first round off, I hit the bomb buried at the door dead center. It went off better than I had hoped. I lit up the hideout and then worked on the guys as they moved out the main escape hatch, hitting the others with the explosives so they had to use just the one close. What I remembered as I pulled the trigger was that they were coming to me like fish in a barrel. I had to move quickly from one to another. I think all in all there were maybe twenty guys. I didn't count. The hideout was a dugout sort of thing, so the eye in the sky couldn't see it, but it was burning better than I thought it would, thanks to my bomb placement and old white-nosed Willy Pete.

Willy Petes. You know, all the shells were different colors, so you never had to guess what you were using. I liked the tracer red ones, but they left a trail back to you, and at only a quarter mile away, it was too easy to do that tracking. I had a nice, neat plan, and it worked. I made it look like a drug-manufacturing venture had gone wrong. My outpost had lots of drugs in it, along with local food wrappers and smokes. I brought them into the outpost and scattered them around so that it looked like a guard post for the drug-dealing compound. That way, when the army came, they wouldn't look long for anything, as the place looked like a guard post with their stuff, not mine. I was careful to take out what I used. I had picked up all the brass shells that had missed the attached recovery sack. I had a very good count of it. Now the fat one was coming out of the tunnel very close to my position. I knew he was the head guy, the one everyone wanted me to eliminate. The others were a big bonus for me and for the war on drugs.

He stayed low, looking around the area. I thought I was in a good place to watch and wait. I was guessing there were four district bosses who had gone in but hadn't come out yet. I decided I would use my AK, as it had a new silencer and was well suited for the close-range shooting. My AK held a lot of shells, as I had the large clip, and I could pop them very nicely at 350 yards. Behind the head guy came another three. They didn't come out quite as I thought they would, so I lit the place up. Closed the door, you might say. I had a bomb planted right under the door, some C-4 that would blow down rather than up. Then I turned my attention to the four on the ground. There was a lot of brush where they were hiding, so I had to work at it now to make sure they were all taken care of. I lit up some cans on the trail. As the cans went off, they would just jump up to run without thinking, and I could see them and pick them off. *Pop*, and they were down, just down. Not a sound. As their friends looked on, they didn't know what to do. So they would jump up and start to run as well. Down they went.

The last one, the big boss, the fat one, wasn't brave, just smart. He was behind a tree that was as big as he was—a nice dead tree. I'd known all along it would be a problem. I lit every can around it that I had left, and now they were all gone, but he wasn't coming out. I pulled up the big girl, put in one of those new titanium shells, and took a shot through the tree. Still nothing. I was getting nervous that my time was running out, so I took another couple of shots through the tree. Still no guy.

I looked back at the camp, and there was still no life or movement there, so I turned my attention back to the tree. After the sixth round had gone through it, it was showing signs of falling over. I knew that if I didn't do something, the army would find it and know it had been shot to shit. With five whites, I worked the trunk over below the point I had pulverized it, and that worked. It started to burn, and then it burned more and more. I started feeling good way down deep inside me. Around twenty dead drug dealers lay between me and the camp, so I was whistling a tune, singing my song. The boys chimed in, and it was so much fun I could hardly stand it.

Look over yonder and what do you see?
Nothing but a fire from a dead old tree.

I hummed along, picking up my brass and putting them in my sack of junk. I picked up my AK and, for the first time, shot up a lot of tracers. If there was someone out there and someplace he could hide, I wanted some return fire. Everything was ablaze, lit up so nicely that the eye in the sky could see it all the way back to Jersey. Still no guy popped up, so I picked up big Old Betsy girl and slipped her over my shoulder, over the top of my backpack. I had been at the camp way to long, and I needed to move. I dropped some extra clips for the AK into my jacket pocket, zipped up my jacket, and crawled out from my cover, the guard post. I for sure wasn't sad to leave that stink hole. I lit the fuse to the incendiary bombs so the whole thing would burn nicely.

I slid down the hill, keeping the old dead tree in front of me. I thought I must have killed him with some sharp metal or that he had a new tunnel I hadn't known about, but I stayed quiet as a church mouse. I was crawling toward the tree when suddenly I smelled him. He was vomiting all over himself. I was about twenty-five yards from the tree, and I could hear him. It sounded like he was praying. All of a sudden, he jumped up and looked up the hill, scaring the piss clean out of me, and he fired over the top of me toward the burning enclosure. Then he stopped, out of shells in his forty-five auto, and dropped back down to the ground, grabbing his knee. It was all bloody, so he wasn't going to walk far on that. He still didn't see me, and I began to wonder. I whistled at him, and he jumped up. I could see the fear in his eyes, his white teeth smeared with blood and coke—he had self-medicated for his pain.

I knelt in place, and he began to look for his gun. I pointed to it about three yards to his right, my left, and shook my rifle at him. I spoke to him in Spanish. "No, it's empty anyway. For all the mothers in the world who have cried over their sons because of your white dust of false hope, you die now."

He pointed to his coat and pulled out a wad of money. I motioned for him to toss it to me, and he did that, saying as he took his money belt off that there was more. It was as big as an ammo belt, and it was stuffed full. He told me there was more in the car, lots more, that this was just pocket money. Then he grinned at me. I told him it was a shame it had all burned up, just like he was going to be. He was struggling to understand my Spanish, so I switched to English. I told him his car and money had all burned up and that he was going to be as well. He was still looking at me with those questioning eyes. Tex told me to hit him in the kneecap, because he wanted to see it explode. Tex thought that should lead to some nice singing on the fat guy's part. As I pushed the lever to full auto, I told him again in English that he was going to burn for all the mothers in this world and their sons. Whether those sons were good, bad, or indifferent, it was still going to be good to see him burn for his sins.

In English, he told me I didn't know what I was doing. He said he was a general in the army, and the army would never let me get away with this. He said they would hunt for me until the end of time. I pulled the trigger, and the tracer rounds came out so fast he didn't have time to move before the last rounds were in him and he was on fire. He looked at me, smiled, and pulled his shirt off so I could see his vest. I thought I didn't have time to reload, but in a matter of seconds, I had two more in him—and not in his vest but in his hand that pointed to the vest and then his legs, his arms—all that wasn't covered. He screamed that his vest was on fire. I loaded some white shells into my empty AK clip, popped his eye, and watched the fire burn his brain and then his ear. I shot his testicles. The smell was not what I remembered a human burning smell to be.

I picked up all the shells, looked around to see if there was anything that I might not have remembered to pick up, and off we went.

Tex said, "I like the eye thing better than the knee thing by far. We should use it more often."

We walked down the backside of the hill. It would be daylight soon; the sun was popping over the mountaintop. We could still see the smoke rising in the dark and could smell the drugs burning with the flesh—a smell you never forget. The entire hill looked like it was on fire. The smell that drifted our way was bad, very bad. Choppers were coming in but luckily not over me. I reached my old pickup by noon, stashed my goods, and drove off. I slept like a baby that night after I crossed over into Colombia. It seemed like home, I had been there so many times working.

It was a long month. I drove to Panama. Thank you, Jimmy Carter, for giving that place away. I hopped a small fishing boat and headed home to Mexico. Man, could those fishermen cook fish tacos. Best I have ever eaten, but if Connie ever got wind of that, I would deny I ever said it.

So, I got my $500,000-per-person kill money for the big guys. The head brass wasn't going to pay for the others. Not in the deal, so they were saying. The army said their four top generals and the generals' aides had died in a big gunfight with a drug lord and that soon the army would have them all rounded up. They could say whatever they needed to say as long as I got paid. As far as the money the fat guy tried to give me, I counted it in front of the fishermen and gave it all to them—$50,000 in all. When I left them a few miles from my place, they all had big smiles on their faces. So I tossed them the keys to my old pickup and told them they were my best friends. They said they had been glad to help me and to come look them up anytime. I said I would and got their addresses.

I liked my work. I really did. I would have done it forever, but things just never work out the way you think they should. Take Jim, for example. He helped me get the place and fix it up. He used government money and workers to do my place and his place. And I helped him build his place. He designed it, and I just helped with the nailing of boards. He always said he wanted to have an elevator put in some day. So while the place was under construction, he must have drilled the shaft that I hadn't known about. His wife and Connie became good friends. He was my son's godfather, and I was godfather to his kids. I had only one child, but I loved mine as much as any man could love. Connie and I decided to have just the one, as Connie had a hard time with the birth and had to have some surgery. And that was all OK by me. I love her more every day. The long times away from home were bad. I got a few jobs taking care of some rich dudes and their kids. Their kids were a joke. In their eyes, I was their enemy: wouldn't let them go anyplace I hadn't checked out first. That job was a bust in a hurry. The years went by, and my dad became sick. Mom was gone, and he was alone. My dad didn't know me when I went to see him, but if I would call, he talked to me like we were long-lost friends.

"Hi, there, Dad. How you doing?"

"Just fine, boy, just fine. Why haven't you called me for a long time, maybe going on a year now?"

"Called last week and told you I would call today. And here I am."

"If you had called, I would know about it. I'm the only one here now. Rented some of my property to a trailer-building guy, and he seems to be doing OK. Think I will have him move into the old trailer on the place. His wife is a nurse. Said they would take care of me until

I die. Heard from your mother. She's off down in Mexico. I heard she was shacking up with some old bum down there. You know, none of you kids are mine. Raised you like you were, but you ain't."

"Well, now, Dad, look at your dad's picture and my picture. Line all our pictures up and look. We all look the same, and then you go and tell me that."

"For sure you're not mine."

"Well, whatever, Dad. Need to go off to another job."

"You working where, now?"

"Still the government, doing contract work. Headed to the Philippines now. Should be back in around eight to ten months if all goes well."

"Why don't you have your kid come stay with me and take your wife with you?"

"Don't think she would like that. She gets mighty homesick for the little guy. Got to go. Will call you from over there and reverse the charges if you like."

"That's OK. Call when you can steal a moment from one of those government phones. They have a lot more money than me."

So those people came in, stole from him, got him to give them everything in his will, and said he was OK when we all knew he wasn't, or he wouldn't have given them anything. I got the brass to give me the OK to shoot them. And I did it. End of that.

"Tex, why is my dad the way he is?"

"Because he sees things in only black and white, is all."

"Well, one day I might get that. But for now, are you and Mike ready to do a job down in the Falklands? Seems we need to go help the Brits out some down there."

"Sure, why not? I heard we get paid double for this one. Am I right?"

"You've been told correctly. Seems like we only have to paint this time around."

"Hello, there in the house! Is anyone home to welcome a strange man home from the hunt? My God, woman, you're prettier every time I see you. And look at that boy of yours, walking already! He is as pretty a kid as I ever saw. Takes after his mom, for sure. Better get you a big stick, as every girl in the country will be after him."

I loved my home life. I was just caught in the trap the brass made for me, and I couldn't get out. It wasn't the right timing, they would say. I reupped twice, and then, after being hurt in Germany coming home from a mission into the Russian side of the Berlin Wall, it took two years to heal that one up. Then, when I was ready, they put me in with Mr. B's team full time. From there, I did a lot of traveling. Saw a lot of guys get popped and some from me as well. Guess I just got to liking it too much. Didn't ask to get out. Then Connie got pregnant, and my world started to turn. Made some friends, like that asshole Jim, who sold me out for a few bucks when he had more than he or I could ever spend. Never could figure that one out. If it hadn't been for Connie, I would have popped his old lady for him right in front of his eyes. Would have hired some gangbangers to work her over at the market and then send her home to him. But I knew she liked Connie so I didn't. But I got him, and he knew it was me. No one ever shot from that distance before, and he thought he was safe.

◆   ◆   ◆

"What did you just say, Doc? How can he be alive?"

"The paramedics saved him, rushed him into surgery. The surgeon had to take most of one arm off, just below his shoulder, and a leg just above the knee. A lot of his skin looks like he's been in a fire, but he's the one pushing for your innocence. He says that you were the one ambushed."

"Well, I'm at a loss for words. So he didn't sell me out?"

"Oh, he did. He's saying he thinks you did what any guy would do in your spot and asked me to tell you when the time was right that he thanks you for not coming over and shooting him point blank and for not hurting his kids and his wife. He knew it was you. He said you called him just before the white rain from heaven came. Don't know what he meant by that. But anyway, he is thankful you spared his wife and kids. He says most wouldn't have. Everyone knew it was you all along. They are just wondering why you turned yourself in."

"Well, Doc, I can't answer that for you. I've just seen too much and had too much in my head. But Jim alive! Get me a picture, if you can."

"He said you would ask, so here in your file is a picture of the place as you left it, of Jim, his wife, his kids, and the dead bodyguard. I never knew about the Willy Petes until I spoke to him. He said you really liked to use it. Said it made you happy thinking about a person having to cut himself up to save himself from it. Bad stuff."

"Man, old Jim sure does look like he's been in a napalm drop zone, for sure. Guess he won't be playing any more ball now, unless he does it from behind a desk. So anyway, I told you all about myself, so I guess I should go back to my bunk and get ready for the shot of junk you told me about. If you have any more questions, can I ask that they wait until tomorrow?"

"Yes, they can. It's Friday anyway, so let me listen to the tapes again, and we will talk on Monday."

"Whatever you say, Doc. I'm not going anywhere this weekend anyway."

"What's that song you're humming?"

"Oh hell, Doc. I'm trying to teach these guys a new song or two. They're driving me crazy with the old ones."

"Who are you talking about? Tex? Mike? Are they here now?"

"Sure, they're always with me. I told you about them."

"Yes, but I thought they died."

"They did, but now they live inside of me. We're a trio."

"You know that, and you know that for a fact, Duke?"

"Hell yes, Doc. Where else do they have to live? Anyway, see you Monday."

Thank God and the army he is gone,
That big Betsy rifle is shooting my song.
If you're left, you're right, it's a mean old world I live in,
and I am the meanest old man in the meanest old world.

◆   ◆   ◆

"Well, good morning, Doc. How was your weekend?"
"Good. Thank you for asking. I have been listening to your tapes, and I'm not clear on a few points. So tell me a list of your jobs in order. Can you do that?"

"No, I don't think so. Why? Why does it matter? I try to put most of them out of my head anyway."

"What? What?"

"Is Mike talking to you?"

"Yes, and Tex."

"What did they say?"

"Well, I don't think you want to know really, do you?"

"Yes, for sure. I want to know more about them."

"They say you're crazy, and for you to want me to relive any more than I already have is crazy. They say you're crazy for asking and should go get yourself checked in someplace. That's what they said."

"You know it's not really them, don't you? Just your mind talking to you as if they're really alive."

"Oh, yes, well, here we go. Whatever you think, Doc. But who spotted for me? Who woke me up when some danger was near? Who looked after me, warned me when someone got behind me or whatever? What the hell do you think, Doc? These guys have been here with me all along. Mike knows he died from my gun. He asked me to, but that was before he went to live inside of me, looking out for me, the eyes in the back of my head. Hell's bells, Doc, do you really think I could do all that stuff on my own, pop so many bad guys, without getting caught or even hurt? Hellfire, Doc, I told you the story. You think

I could always see those things they say, scout the places out on my own? Fuck you, Doc, and the horse you rode in on! So you think you can fix me—that it's all in my head? Well, fuck you! You don't know shit. That's all I've got to say about that. Yes, and Tex said we told you how he stood guard as I slept, and then Mike to make sure, and how they could run around and make sure the coast was clear. Better get a grip, Doc, as they are as real as you are, and they have more common sense in their little fingers than you got in your entire body. So go admit yourself, Doc, and just leave us alone. We will do OK on our own."

"Well, now, Duke—"

"Don't call me that. It's Mr. Moore to you, asshole. You got any trouble with that, AH? If you do, come take these cuffs off me, and let's see how you can handle yourself. You know I am as strong as three men, so just get me back to my bunk, AH."

"AH? What's AH?"

"Asshole, you stupid jerk."

"OK, OK, let's just take a break. I didn't mean to piss you off."

"Well, you got a funny way to show it, AH."

"Don't call me that, please. I respect you, and I'm sorry for this mishap, so let's talk about something else for just a little while."

"Like what? Sorry, Doc. You just hit a sore spot. I've been told many times that I was crazy, but understand this: I would have been killed many times if these two weren't looking out for me. In summary, they said for me to tell you that you're an old bushwhacker and that I should just tell you where to go and how to get there."

"Now we are out of here, boy. Let's go."

"They said, Doc, to also tell you to put it where it never shines and dance on it for a while. I won't tell you that, but I will tell you this: when I was younger…I might be repeating myself, so stop me if I tell you the same story twice."

"Go ahead. It's OK. I might have missed a spot or two along the way."

"Spot or two, my ass. He missed the whole damn train."

"You see, Doc, my dad hated me deeply and tried to kill me twice that I can remember. Anyway, once when I was four…yes, four…I think back when my kid was four and how innocent he was—just wanted to be with me all the time. He went to the compound, and I taught him to shoot, as Tex did me. We both did. Hell, I mean all three of us took care of that kid, and with their help, he turned out OK. He could outshoot me, but I won't let him touch more than a hunting rifle. If he shoots it, he has to eat it. That's our code. So, anyway, when I was four, Tex kept my dad from killing me. My dad had already broken my eardrums, and that's why I stutter and can't hear worth a shit. But damn it all to hell, Doc, if you ever say a word against Tex or Mike again, cuffs or no cuffs, we all three of us will kill you dead, and I won't have to move from this chair. Got it?"

"Yes, I do understand that what you think is the truth is a strong belief inside you."

"When I was eleven, Doc, my dad lost it. The old man lost his temper with me again. Guess I better be more up front with you so you can follow along, being the slow one that you are. Hell's bells, Doc, my old man gave me a whipping in front of all the relatives on my eleventh birthday—just to show he could still do that, you know. Anyway, I hated him for it, and from then on, Tex was always there for me. Later that year, my dad hit me over the head with a plate so hard I went to my knees. The plate broke on the next hit. It was a melamine plate."

"Don't think he's old enough to know what that is, boy."

"Those plates were supposed to be unbreakable. I couldn't stand, so I crawled downstairs to my room. I should have died then, but I didn't, and from then on, Tex has been my savior. I moved into my granddad's house next door, but all the same, my dad never tried that again. One day while I was at school, Tex came to me and told me his body couldn't take it anymore. He said he wanted me to know that if I chose to have him with me, he would be inside me until my death. So he moved in like I had with him. When I got home, Mom told me my granddad had died that day. I asked her where his body was at—the hospital or the morgue. She didn't answer me, so I told her I would change my clothes and do my chores. Mom said that I had to stay there with her and Dad from then on. I looked at her with a man's eye, the meanest look I could give her."

◆　◆　◆

"Why? I'm not moving back here! Grandma needs me. And that's the end of this conversation."

"Think so?"

"Yes, I know it is. Between the two of us anyway."

OK. Well, I was fifteen at the time. I told her that Grandma needed me, so I would do my chores and then go home to Grandma. My mom and I had some words, and she said I was a no-good kid who should have a little respect. She said my dad had just lost his dad and would need some time to get over it. I told her again, in the most polite way I could, that I would do all the chores—even Dad's—and then go to my house, as Grandma needed me more than Dad ever would.

Dad was even meaner to me after that—for no good reason that Grandpa and I could see. When I was seventeen, Dad began to follow me around. He would sneak into my room at night, and Tex would wake me up to save me from a beating. When I was twenty-three, just out of the hospital from my injury, I went home. I hadn't been home for a long time. The time of year was in the third cutting of hay. I began dating the local judge's daughter, and she was a wild girl. We got caught doing the wild thing in the park, and my dad told me he wasn't going to let me see her anymore. I told him I was twenty-three and that he had no say in this part of my life. He told me that I would do what he said. He said that as long as he was alive, he would be boss of this family, and he had a good notion to just kick my ass, and it had been too long coming. He said I sure as hell needed it.

Mike and Tex were in me then, and as I was them, I was a super-strong guy. Tex said, "Don't hit your dad. Let's just go," so I told my so-called father that I was going to finish loading the hay and then I would just get out of there, never to return. He slammed on the brakes of the tractor and jumped off. I was sitting on the side of the hay wagon, and he said, "OK, I am going to kick your ass."

Tex said, "He's a lefty. Move to his right and don't let him grab you." Mike said he would get the pistol out from under the seat of our pickup, so I did as Tex said. I moved to his right and told him he had better knock me out with one punch, as I would let him hit me only once for free. I told him I would let him have the first punch, and then all bets were off—I would treat him like any other aggressor. I would just have to kill him. He stopped short and asked me if I would really do that. "Yes," I told him. "No one has kicked my ass since I was a kid, and I ain't no kid no more." I felt Mike put the pistol into my back pocket. Dad just stood there, and I kept moving, not stopping. He looked at me, shook his head, and said I had way more guts than he did.

"Boy, way more."

"What do you mean by that, sir?"

"You just do. I told you when you were young never to let anyone get the first punch in, as it could be your last. But here we are. If I hit you, you will kill me. And how will that happen? I'm not that old, and you have been sick way too long. So how do you think that would ever happen? More guts than me, as I would never let you hit me first."

I reached into my back pocket and pulled out my pistol, clicked the safety off, and shot a round into the bank behind and to the side of him.

"Like I said, old man, if you hit me, you better knock me out, or I will kill you for sure."

"Listen, Dwight, I was mad, that's all. You don't have to shoot your old pa, now, do you?"

"Don't ever call me Dwight again. That's just for my friends, not you. You call me Mr. Moore."

"OK. Let's go finish this load of hay before you go."

"No, sir. I am walking back to my pickup and leaving. See ya around sometime."

"It's a half mile back to the house. Are you going to say good-bye to your mom, or don't you love her either?"

"No, sir, on all counts. Tell her whatever you like, but I'm out of here."

◆　◆　◆

"See, Doc? Don't tell me they're just in my head. You know, when Mike screwed up, we were in an ambush, and he was there every inch of the fight. Hell, if it hadn't been for him, I would still be back there in the jungle. Tell me again, Doc, how this shit is all in my head, and I will tell you time and again how Mike and Tex saved me. I went out drinking after that. Tex and I really tied one on, and at the bar were some girls who wanted to take me home. But they didn't want to take the friend from school I was with. I had met him at the bar. We were sitting at the curb in his car. He was too drunk to drive, so I said I would get him home. Then two bouncers came out and said they were going to kick my ass along with the friend I was with. I asked why, and they said they'd just heard I was a tough guy and wanted to check me out. I said tomorrow would be soon enough, as we had drunk too much beer for a fight. My friend said not to worry about those two, that we should just leave. The bigger one of the two stepped to the side of the curb and moved to hit me. Mike caught his hand, put my hand on his, and then pulled me up. Mind you, I was drunk, and so was Tex. Mike was on call that night, so he didn't drink but one beer. He had me behind that guy, pulling his arm up so high he was screaming for his mommy. I looked at the second guy and told him if he wanted some of that to come on now or get back in the bar. He went inside. Remember I told you Mike was six foot something and was so strong he could carry a VW a mile by himself? As soon as the other guy was inside, Mike had this guy pressed so hard face first on the brick wall of the building that his nose started to bleed, and he was still crying. I asked the guy if he liked to pick on drunks and if he was in school someplace. He said he was a linebacker on the local university's football team. I told him his career was over as I heard Mike give his arm a big yank. You could hear the bone breaking, and he passed out. I could hardly stand, let alone walk. The girls came out about then and started to scream. I told them they should go back inside and call for help.

"See, Doc? Should I go on about how it's not all in my head? Remember, I told you that Tex told me Jim was going out a door at the base of the hill. I would have had to move positions to see that. And when we were in the firefight at camp, my camp, I told you how those two risked their lives to save mine from the guys who were hiding. Hell, Doc, I could tell you many stories, if you like."

"Sure do, Duke. Can I call you that again, or are we still upset about yesterday?"

"No, the guys and I had a long talk into the night. Sorry we were so hard on you. Yes, call me Duke. You didn't know, so, yes, I will explain it some more.

"See, most think I just have dumb luck. But me, I know where my luck comes from, and now you do too. So when you put the last shot into my veins, well, you will be laying to rest three of us at once. Granddad has been with me all my life, in person until he took up residence with me. And Mike, well, he's the best friend I ever had. We learned to shoot a lot better than anyone else. They write books about the longest shots, the best recorded kills, but we just shoot. Most of our kills were secret missions, so we didn't go home and write a book to become famous. We couldn't care less about that. We just did our duty, God and country and all. I was a consultant for a brief time at the Special Forces sniper school but left for a new job and never looked back. I think most of those guys were in it for the glory, not God and country, like we were. Later, in the other jobs, I did get paid well. It was my retirement, you see. I had no other, and I wanted my kid and wife to have something from me. So she has all the money in secret accounts.

Who cares? I do, and Mike and Tex do. We love them both. That's why when Jim went after them, I went after him. The code of honor is gone now, it seems to me. We were sworn never to tell, ever—not then, not now. The debriefing shit that you had us go through was just that— shit. But anyway, back to Mike and Tex.

"Yes, we are buddies. Hard-hitting, no-bullshit kind of guys. It's hard for me to sit here and tell you all the stuff I did and saw, as it was a job. We did it, and that's that. Can you tell me your first job, detail by detail? Well, I can find anything, everything, in my mind, but who wants to remember?

"Oh, yeah—Tex just told me to tell you about when we were in the small town in Bolivia. Mike saved my life then, along with Tex."

"What town in Bolivia? I don't know anything about this."

"The town was La Santisima Trinidad…I'm sure of it. Yes, Tex just confirmed that was the town. Anyway, I was intent on talking to my contact. She was very pretty. Mike was outside, casing the place, and Tex was wandering around inside. They both came to me very fast, out of nowhere, saying we had to go outside and take a piss. I could tell by the way they were talking that they were more than just excited. I excused myself to the lady, saying I had to go to the outhouse. Once outside, they hurried me across the street and behind a brick wall. In a matter of seconds, the place blew up. All was lost, and Mike said we lost her too. The story was in the local paper. A gas leak had destroyed the place, and all eighteen inside were dead. The owner escaped because he had just left to go to the storehouse to get more beer, or so the paper told the story.

"Mike had cased the place well, followed some guys, and so we knew where our stakeout would be. We holed up in a dirty hole-in-the-wall place just on the outside of town. We could see the place very well, and we watched them for a couple of weeks. We knew all the guys so well that we gave them all names. If it were just in my head, Doc, tell me how Tex could go out and buy us food and water to keep us alive? Now, after a time, we were sure the one we called

Boss actually was the boss. We decided to follow this guy next time he left what we called the office. Mike went back and carried all our guns and explosives to us. He hid the car in plain sight, as everyone was sure we were dead. Because of that, they left the car alone and let their guard down. We learned a lot from being dead. And I would have been dead, Doc, if it weren't for my two guys. It wasn't just dumb luck, Doc, not at all.

"So, they went out searching side streets for me and keeping an eye out. Tex came back and said there was a guy he didn't like walking along the same alley we were on. We could see him cross the alleys and knew we were on to the right guy. We didn't think he was the big boss, so when he got to the place he was going, another guy we had never seen before came around the corner. I could have grabbed his leg he was so close to me, and we were just sitting in our hiding spot. We could tell he was a watchdog for the boss because he smelled like a smoke factory. First thing you learn in sniper school is to know your targets and to realize that time is usually on your side. And don't eat or drink smelly foods or liquid, and for fuck's sake, don't smoke—I can smell you five hundred yards away and can see you light up a thousand yards away in the dark.

"Anyway, Mike said he would go find out what was up, and if the guy went someplace, Mike would hide in the trunk of the car. A moment after Mike went out, here came a car, and we could see that the trunk lid was ajar. Mike waved to us, and we sneaked back to the far end of the room. Luckily, we had water and snacks, because Mike was gone for three days. When he came back, he said there was a big drug-manufacturing plant this guy took him to, and sure as hell, the main office was there. He said the boss wasn't the big boss—he was just the boss for distribution.

"Mike stayed for a day and a night and then walked back to where we were. He said it felt good to stretch his legs after all the long sitting around we had been doing. We made a plan to go and watch the plant, and when it was full of everyone we knew to be part of their organization, we would call in the strike and paint it hot for the flyboys. And that's what we did. We made some good money on that job, but when you calculate it by the hour, not so good, I guess. We were in that country for three months, so the hours we spent plus food, lodging, and car, all the stuff we did, came out to around a hundred and fifty dollars per hour. It was OK, I guess. At this time, we were doing it because we thought we were helping out the war on drugs. Little did we know that all we were doing was helping eliminate the competition.

"See, Doc, there was lots to having these guys looking after me. They said I was doing the right thing, coming in after all this, but now we wonder. So from now on, Doc, when you ask me to tell you, don't say it's all in my head. If it was, how did I do what I did? Like, Mike—he found the plant, and it was nearly twenty miles up in the bush. Even the guys themselves walked the last two miles or rode a horse. How did I do it all by myself? Ask Jim—I was a loner. They never understood how a one-man team could survive and get the jobs done, but I did, time after time. Ask Jim, and he will tell you that I was alone after my last team guy was killed. It was too scary to predict how someone would handle the firefights or handle the days before, when you're lying around, waiting for the correct time to strike.

"Doc, I see you have my medical records. Is there something in there you want to ask me about? Or talk about?"

"Yes. It says here you have symptoms of Agent Orange exposure and that you have been operated on many times. Care to tell me about those—in part or anything at all?"

"Well, Doc, the first time I got hurt, we had this new guy who was assigned to me. We were coming back from a job there in Germany. Our day job was to train other countries' soldiers to be better killing machines. On the way back, the fog rolled in, and we hit a truck head on. Killed the new guy. He had been driving. And as for me, the thing that saved me was Mike. The doors on the car were locked, so no one could get inside to get us out of the car. They were trying to kick the window in to get us out. Tex and I were knocked out. They said that when I was humped up on the floor, a hand came from me—not mine but a hand—and unlocked the door. So, thank you, Mike, again."

"Duke, I understand how Tex and you buddied up, but how did you and Mike buddy up?"

"Doc, Doc, Doc, I told you about it, but let me slow down and go over it in detail for you."

SEVENTEEN

DEMONS, MY DEMONS...OR FRIENDS

The team was sent to Nam on another mission. Not sure of the exact date—early seventies is what sticks in my mind. Mike and I were in the lead. As usual, he was slightly behind me to my right side. I was moving slowly. We knew by the signs that we were close to something. It was an old French plantation, we found out later. Mike found this dumb land mine. We did everything we could to try to disarm it. The only thing was, it was too old, and the plunger-lock device wouldn't fit. So we tried to get Mike off the mine, but we couldn't do it. I sent the rest of the group ahead to hide and be ready for an ambush. We didn't know what to do. Mike wanted me to kill him, but I couldn't. He was my best friend. We had been together since I'd joined the Special Forces. A five-man team gets mixed up with new guys now and again but not Mike and me. We were always together. This was to be his first time as main shooter, and we were to be close enough to use the 308s. But anyway, I took everything from him. He gave me his backpack. We couldn't hear a timer, so we thought it would only go off if the trigger was released. If it did, our cover would be blown, so he stayed on it. He just stayed lying down and asked me to shoot him. I cried for him, wept right there in front of him, and started to walk off.

"Don't leave me to die here alone, Duke. I wouldn't do that to you."

He didn't know at the time that Tex was a real person. Mike thought of him as my talking buddy, I guess. With tears in my eyes, I had to walk off. I told him I wouldn't leave him there. Told him I would come back for him but that I had to take care of the guys first. Then I'd come back, after taking care of the misfits. I whistled the all clear to him, and he whistled the all clear back. I went back to the bank of the little stream, and I could look over the top and see him lying there, looking around, watching, and listening for anything to come. I took aim, swearing at him, hurting more inside than I ever had in my life or any time since. He was my true brother. Tex was mostly there for soft talk, not out and about all the time like he and Mike are now. But as I was taking aim, he asked, *"Boy, what are you doing?"*

"Tex, he wants me to. He's dead, one way or another. What would you do?"

"Just what you're doing, but let me go get him and bring him to us as one, as I am one with you. What do you think? Give me ten or fifteen seconds. I will do it if he's for it, and I know this kid—he will go for it. Then pop the body out there. That's just what it will be, a body. Mike and I, we will be you, and you will be us. Understand? Remember when I came to you at your school?"

"Yes, Tex, for sure. Let's do it."

I wiped my tears, took aim, and saw Tex squatting down, talking to Mike. He stood up, and both of them had smiles on their faces. I popped the body, and we all left. When the firefight started after we ran to get clear, I was with Tom. I called him Mike, and when he corrected me, I knew I had to speak to them from then on with my mind, never out loud, like I used to do with just Tex. Mike and Tex took point and pushed guys around to save Tom and me. Tom and I, we did the buddy crawl out of there, and sure enough, we were safe. We went to a place the scout didn't know. We hid, and Mike and Tex saved my life.

◆　◆　◆

"From then on, Doc, it was they who did the figuring out how to get out, not me. Don't you see they are my family, my granddad, my brother? They keep me safe. That's how I do what I do. Not alone but as a three-man team. That's us. Do you think I couldn't get out of here now if I chose to?"

"Well, Duke, you're cuffed, and there are locked doors to go through. It's a hospital for—"

"Doc, this place is a cardboard box. If I wanted out, the guys and I could leave at any time. As for the cuffs here, you hold on to them. Tex picked the pocket of the only guard on duty last night. He's still wondering where he laid the keys down. Doc, you OK?"

"Yes, I was looking at the cuffs. They're the newest thing. How did you do that?"

"Look, here's the key ring. What do you think? If you want to make sure no one ever gets away from now on, do what we do: get the biggest snap ties you can get, and use them for cuffs. OK, Doc?"

"OK, I believe you, so put the cuffs back on. Give me the keys before the guard comes and we're both in trouble."

"Will it make you feel safer, Doc? OK, but know that I am a team, no bullshit. And if we wanted to kill you, we would have a long time ago. Mike has been to your home. He said you have three kids, all nice. He said the oldest two are girls and are nice looking like their mom. And your son is about two years old. You live in a nice home up on the hill about a fifteen-minute drive from here. What was the name of the street? Oh, yes...Mike said it's twenty-three fifty Camel Back Drive, off Harrison and Pinecone. Is that the correct info? Do you believe me now? If you want more info, Mike can tell you more. Doc, are you OK? There now, take a sip of water. It's OK. We would never hurt your family or you. We just needed for you to know that we are what we say we are. OK?"

"Yes, I'm OK. And yes, your information is correct. I believe you. I also don't want you to hurt me or have my family hurt. I know you think everything is the truth and nothing but the truth, but you could find all this information in the hospital faculty directory. So, yes, I do believe you believe that all you tell me is a fact. I still don't know that I fully understand it—not just yet anyway. Back to the topic at hand: Did you know your wife, Connie, sent me a letter?"

"No, why would she? Connie knows what the procedures are. And why would she break silence? Let me see the letter."

Tex, Mike, go check on her and Bud.

"No, I can't do that. She wanted me to tell you she is pleading for you, but she doesn't want her letter read by you."

"We will see about that, Doc. I am very upset now, and I want to go back to my room. OK by you? I need to think about some stuff."

"OK, I'll see you tomorrow."

"What day is it now? I lost all track, not that it matters."

"It's Wednesday."

"OK, Doc, let's just hold off until Monday. Is that OK by you?"

"Yes, that will work. I have plenty to digest now anyway."

"Doc, did I make you think that there just might be a paranormal existence out there and that you're looking at one now? I'm tired. I'm going to lie down now. See you on Monday."

"OK, see you then. Is there anything I can do for you now?"

"No, Doc, the boys are on it. They are going to see about this letter writing, and I'm going to take a nap. You OK with this stuff? Are you still thinking I am crazy or something?"

"No, not at all. We'll talk on Monday."

"Good morning, Doc. How was your weekend?"

"Good but disturbing."

"How so?"

"Well, my papers were being strewn around, and every time I went out, the papers were out of order when I came back."

"Yes, I know. Mike was having fun with you. Looks like you've been doing some homework. The papers you're reading are not very flattering to me. This so called research that a bunch of jokers wrote really says to me that they don't understand a dang thing about any of the veteran mental problems they are struggling with. Give me a break, Doc. Is that really what you think? It says in the editorial you're reading that we veterans with mental problems are of low intelligence. Well, I think you should tell those so-called experts that they have the low intelligence. They keep their minds so closed to the reality of any aspect different than theirs that maybe they're the ones with the schizotypal personalities. I read all the research Mike brought me from your office twice this weekend. And let me tell you, Doc, those experts are so far from knowing what is real and what is make-believe in their so-called research that they should be here locked up, not me. Every one of those authors is hurting more people with that nonsense than I ever thought of. They take normal vets who have a few problems and lock us up because they think they understand what's going on in our heads. They have no clue, and they are putting forward pure falsehood. This illness is not derived from low intelligence. It comes from one thing, Doc, pure and simple: their effing war. Hell, Doc, give them a call and let me have an hour in this room with any two of your choosing. I guarantee that when they leave, they will want to put the straitjackets onto themselves. Their words *ignorance*, *deprivation*, or *deficiency* —what a crock of shit. Tell me, Doc, have any of those experts seen a day in combat?

"So, you think I am a little off, do you? Well, I opened up to you, but I think that from now on when you ask a question, I will answer it, but no more of this telling you my life-story bullshit. You have my medical records, and you know I am way above you when it comes to having some smarts. I stutter, and I'm hard of hearing, but beyond that, how dare you think such a thing of me? Now, hand me your cell phone. I want to call my wife. Now, I said! Sit back down, and hand me your cell phone, or I will take it from you.

"Thanks, Doc. I told you we didn't want to hurt you, but you're pushing the mark hard here. I also told you the three of us were in no way going to let anyone ever hurt our kid or wife. You got that, Doc? Answer me. Don't just sit there. And, no, don't turn on the recorder from here on out. In fact, hand it to me.

"Thank you very much, Doc."

I dropped it on the floor and crushed it under my chair leg. I played with his cell phone, dialing, hanging up, and he watched me with fear in his eyes.

"You should have listened to me, Doc, when I said the things I did. I told you I have no conscience, especially when it comes to saving my bacon or a loved one. Now, I think that you are not trying to help cure me; you're here to vindicate the upper brass. Well, that's OK, I guess. Anyway, Doc, I don't know how to take you really. When I came here, I was told you really work for the vets. Now I'm not so sure.

"Hello, Connie, my love. Yes, I'm OK. Are you? What's this bullshit about you writing a letter telling the Doc I'm a nice guy and all that? Hell's bells, my love, we talked. You knew when I left that I would never be coming back. No, no, listen, this has to be a short talk. Go to the house, and dump all the bank accounts, just leaving a few hundred in each one. Drive down to the fishermen. You know the plan. Just do it. I will be OK if you and Bud are OK. Get rid of that cell phone, and activate the next one, but never call this one again. It's the Doc's. When the word gets to you about me, that's when you must do the plan. Set it in motion for you and Bud. Yes, we all love you very much. In a year or so, when you're ready, you find my kid a good dad, and live happy. Love you. Bye."

I took the back off the cell phone, pulled the SIM card out, and took the cell phone apart. I moved over to the wash sink, let the water get very hot, and then put all the pieces in to soak.

"What are you doing to my cell?"

"I'm making sure you never find that number again. I thought I could trust you, but it looks like I was stupid. I should never, never have believed that you care about us veterans at all. You don't understand. You never served in combat for even a minute—never even got close to it. Now, Doc, what do you think? Where do we go from here? What do you want to see us do? Got someone you need to have popped?"

"No, not at all. I never would. That's not my way of doing things or dealing with any of my problems."

"No, it's just that you're too uptight about it all to say it. What if I told you that at this moment, Tex and Mike are sitting in your wife's car coming home from the hairdresser? And when they get her home, they will have their way with her and then with your daughters when they get home from school. And for some reason, you will get a call from the day care saying your son was never picked up by your wife, but not to worry, your brother, which we all know you don't have, was there to pick up the boy. And your 'brother' asked them to call you and say they would see you at home for dinner. And don't be late, because we're having veal tonight—fresh cut, very tender. Bet then you would unleash the beast in you, wouldn't you?"

"Why—why my family?"

"Not your family, *my* family, Doc. See, I want to make sure you know how sicko I am. They did it to me, so put me down, and see where the guys end up. You couldn't catch them, so that's my insurance. I want you to know that if my family is ever touched, it will be on your head, or is it blood on your hands? Here, Doc. To prove a point, use this cell phone that I borrowed from the orderly. I told him you said it was OK and that you personally would give it back to him. So call the day care, and ask if your 'brother' has been there to pick your son up, as your wife went home sick."

"Hello? Yes, it's OK. Yes, I know. My cell phone broke today, so I had to use this one. No, it's OK. Yes, my brother. Yes, thanks. Yes, you too. Bye.

"If anything happens to my family—"

"You will do what? I told you, Doc, I am just proving a point. Nothing is going to happen. Your wife and kids got a call and were told that Dad was off early, was picking up the boy at day care, and would see them at home. See, I just wanted you to know that I don't make idle threats. I do a job and do it well, and yes, I work alone. Check me out, and for now, I will see you on Wednesday. I haven't been sleeping much, and I need some rest. See, now I know you will check me out. Find out from Jim who to call. I don't lie to you or to anyone. It is what it is. See you, Doc. Oh, by the way, your boy is in the back seat of your car, sleeping like a baby. And, no, we didn't give him a thing—he just fell asleep. Now, go do your homework, and let me rest. Oh, Doc, don't forget the cell phone. Give it to the orderly, OK?"

Oh, when the saints come marching in,
Oh, when the saints come marching in the...
Oh, when the saints come marching in...

Damn, I knew it was a good song. Wish I could remember it.

When I was just a little bitty boy, my mommy used to rock me
in the cradle
In them old rocky fields back home.
Use a yellow ribbon to tie up your hair,
If you still want me in those old rocky fields back home,
And they never came to see me here,
Where is my mommy and poppa and my old girl Sally?
She's a fine old girl in those old rocky fields back home,
as I ain't no senator's son.
It's a mean old world, and I am a mean old guy,
Love to shoot you every chance I get, just to hear you cry,
In those old rocky fields back home.
As they lay me down beneath the rocks of home,
Yes, they all come to see me
In them old rocky fields back home.

EIGHTEEN

LAST SHOT

"OK, boys, here is the scoop. We are going to go out tonight and march three days to this point here on the map. Then, when the sun is up on the third day, we should be here, in place to watch for these two guys. Mike, you're lead shooter on this one. D. Moore, you're his backup and the spotter. Also, you're to take point. John and Allen will finish our team. I will be in the middle to watch both front and rear. Any questions? If not, I will tell you that these are very dangerous guys. They've been selling arms and who knows what. All the top brass want them gone. 'Pop them, or don't return' are our orders. OK, men, let's go. Choppers in thirty. If you're ready now, then let's go. From the choppers, there'll be a ship ride of about four hours, so take plenty of what you need. No stashes on our way this time. We carry it all in and all out. D. Moore, let's just take the 308s on this hike; no need for the big girl."

"Well, sir, that's not Mike and my MO. We don't mind carrying the extra stuff. It's no trouble, sir, and she can come in mighty handy if we don't get close enough to take them out."

"OK, but just you and Mike are to do it. Don't want to lug down the rest with your extra stuff."

"Yes, sir, we don't need any help, do we, Mike?"

"No, sir, we don't. This isn't our first rodeo. No, sir, we can take care of the old girl, no trouble."

"So, Mike, what's this about, do you think? You're lead shooter, and not the big girl to take along just for the ride? I think you're up for some more rank after this. Hell, we'll make it—we always make it. But listen, if they make you a top shooter rather than just a spotter, that's great. To tell you the truth, I don't like splitting us up, rank or no rank. Let's be on our toes. This is not a good feeling."

"Yes, Captain Marks knows what he's doing, and with your memory, we won't need to worry. It's just that we need to be quiet, and those two new guys want to be cowboys, as if they're from Texas or someplace, rather than being city boys. John and Allen, they couldn't keep from talking for three seconds, let alone three days. Shall we teach them the signs?"

"Hell no. I don't want anyone but us knowing those codes. They'll be like two old hens, whistling all the time. Hand signals will be enough. OK, looks like they're loading up on the C rations. What do you think?"

"No, not me. Those things give me the shits. Besides, we need to take all the smokes out. They know the rules, all of them. Just plain old raw oatmeal and tons of water is good for me. You?"

"Got you there, my friend, got you there. Captain, we're ready."

"Good, D. Moore, but this is Mike's team. This time, we move with his command."

"Yes, sir, was just going to say…but Mike can."

"Yes, Mike, what is it?"

"You know, sir, D. Moore and I…uh, I…sir, I don't allow any smoking while we are on a mission. Not a good idea. Can we make sure all the guys—and you too, sir—throw them all away, sir? Please."

"OK, men, you heard the boss. Open up the C rations, and unload all your smokes and lighters as well. We go by Mike's book on this mission. New leader; same old rules."

"Thanks, sir. I will, or Duke will, buy you all a cigar and some new smokes when we come back."

"Mike?"

"Yes, Duke, my rules: you will buy."

◆　◆　◆

"Can you see anything, Allen?"

"No."

"If you guys don't be quiet, I will ask the captain to let me shoot you now."

"Let's see if in these last few hours we can walk like we're really trying to sneak up on the enemy instead of telling the whole damn world we're coming. Got it, you two motormouths?"

"Yes, sir, Cap."

I crouched, raising my hand for all to follow my lead.

"Mike, go tell the captain we are close. I can smell their cook fires. They're low, charcoal I think—not sure. But I can still smell them. Can you smell them?"

"No, but I believe you."

Mike waved for the group to take cover, to hide in the brush, and he went back to the captain.

"Captain Marks, Duke said we are close. He can smell their fires up ahead. We want to leave you all here. Dig in, make a retreat point, and unload your gear. Be ready. It looks like one and a half hours, maybe two, to sunup. Water up, eat some grub, be very quiet, and we will be back for you. Code word *Yankees*; return is *New York*. OK?"

Mike and I belly-crawled for what seemed like a mile, and then, sure enough, there we were right on top of them. About five hundred and fifty yards away must have been about three hundred of them in that big place plus two choppers and a ton of hardware.

"Duke, what're you thinking?"

"Just a moment. Still looking over the place."

"Yes, Tex, what do you think? Yes, me too. Our guys have gone AWOL and giving it all away to the enemy for money."

"OK, Mike. What do you think? You're our leader on this one."

"I think the captain should leave those two in the rear to keep the back door safe. You've been seeing what I've been seeing with that spotting scope?"

"Yes, sure have. They're our guys, Mike."

"Here's what I think, Duke. The captain and I could have good cover over there in those rocks, and you could go by yourself over to those dead logs. Take the big girl and all the ammo you want. When it's right—your decision—you take her and plug those turbines on the choppers first with a few holes that will make them unusable. Then we will look for the head guys to start coming out, and if they do, we will pop them. The ones on the left are yours, if they come out together or wherever they come from. I will start from the right side and meet you in the middle. The captain can take as many as he can, working from close to far. If you feel like making a lot of turmoil, then keep her going and see if you can hit targets. The farther off they are, the better; make them think they're surrounded. Looks like the gas and ammo are close to the far side of the hill under that tent. If you can make that go up after the choppers are disabled, then I would say do all you can. You and me and Cap are the only ones who are on silent, so if we hear any pops from the rear, we know it's time to leave, as the back door has been compromised. We will let you go first, even if the targets are moving out. When the commotion gets bad, we will drop on them with as much as we can from our spot. Remember to make the fires only on the far side so our escape will be easier. We don't need to wipe out the entire village. What you think?"

"Yes, you're right. I will keep on silent the entire time and first take out the choppers, then the fuel, and then the ammo dump on the far side of my left side. By then, I can work on the fools who are running for the jeeps and the deuce and halves. I would like to think that when I'm finished with Old Betsy, nothing will be running. If you don't mind,

I will let you do all the popping of the brass and work on the autos and any other vehicle that comes into sight. But first, I say you're the boss, so we do it your way. Just saying, is all. But I think you should hit the targets as soon as both come out. You may not get another chance. What do you think, boss?"

"Sounds good to me. You move into your spot, and I will go get the captain and secure the boys in a good spot for our back-door closer and have them watch for some patrols, if there are any. I'll give you a birdcall when I am set and ready. Ten four?"

"Ten four."

The birdcall was good. Mike was getting a lot better at it. I just hoped the boys wouldn't panic and start shooting at every little sound that came their way. That would make a real mess of the hide-and-seek plan we had going. They should be OK, but one never knew about a guy when the fight starts. Even veterans like Mike and me have lost it before. Sometimes a guy just snaps.

The first chopper was armored. I watched and heard my bullet just bounce off into space, leaving hardly a mark. I changed to armor-piercing black tips, but it was still no good. I couldn't figure out what the hell they had on those birds. I made a mental note to check it out when I got back. I made a dent, but hell, the birds were turned sideways to me, so I didn't have a choice. I guessed the fuel tank was about where the paint was different some, and I wondered if I could... Holy hell, that was the spot, all right. I didn't think it would go up like that. Now for the other one. It was hard to see with the smoke. When I looked at Mike, he was really frowning at me. The first shot, a ricochet, could be heard for a mile and a half. So now the perfectly placed shot made them go up in a hell of a blast. He was never satisfied. He would make a good commander, for sure: never satisfied. OK, now, there it is. *Pop*, and another one bit the dust. I thought I had better quickly get to the jeeps. Guys were running all over the place now. There were guns mounted on some trucks, so I thought I had better do those first. White rounds, here we went—one down, two down. I decided to wait to see what was happening. They weren't moving as fast as they had been. They were trying to hide now, and if I hit the breach on those mounted up with some white rounds, it would disable them all. It looked like there were ten in all mounted, no big deal, and ten more trucks and jeeps lined up like fish in a barrel. There they went. Now, Mike popped a few of the guys, and I hoped they were ones we had done this all for.

How does it feel to know you're the one?
Yes, how does it feel to love someone?

I spotted an underground hangar, and an old P38 fighter was being pushed out. I guessed there were more in there. Some white in the middle of the spinner would be nice shooting from my spot. I couldn't figure out why the hell I hadn't seen that camouflaged door. Thought I must be going blind.

Mike looked at me and gave me a signal to look at the plane. It had its motor running by then. I see it, and I'm on it, my boss friend. With the damn engine running, he could decide to turn the guns on us. I shot at the front of the motor, but I missed the spinner. The Willy Pete must have done something as the smoke was boiling out the front of the engine housing. I must have gotten some old Willy Pete on the pilot as well. He floored the throttle, and he had the trigger of the guns pressed full open. He was shooting all over the place and had the plane in a tailspin. I bet he would go back inside before the guns ran dry. Looked as if the white must have passed by the engine enough to burn a hole in his balls, poor bastard. I needed to see if I could find some fuel in there or something to light it up inside. No telling how big that place was. Those little gooks could dig better than a backhoe, and that was no lie. They'd tunneled halfway across Vietnam before the war was over. There were a couple of wild shots, maybe his, but I took the credit, and the place was on fire. Then I turned back to the rest of the motor pool. I had one last jeep and a few trucks. Looked

like the mechanics had done their jobs and kept them full of fuel at all times. The books said they never exploded, but they didn't know about old Willy Pete, did they, now, when they thought that one up in World War I.

◆ ◆ ◆

"Duke, sorry to interrupt your story, but did you take the pills that I sent you this morning?"

"Yes, Doc. Why?"

"Well, they're to make you sleepy, so when the doctor gets here we can finish the treatment. You agreed. Wanted to end this as soon as possible, Duke. Go on with your story."

◆ ◆ ◆

I saw Mike pointing at some guys who were making their way up the ridge away from us. I couldn't understand his sign language. What was he saying? OK, take it slow with the sign language.

"Two on the left; they are the ones out of my range."

"OK. How far are they?"

"I guess eight hundred to one thousand, when they're level with me."

"Yes, nine hundred seventy-three when level with you. The one in the lead is number one. The next is number two, and number three is the big cheese."

"OK, got you, boss. You're not making much sense with the sign language, but good as done. To your credit, team leader."

I went back to regular rounds. When number three became number two, I started a fire. But I saw that Mike was coming over to me, leaving the captain by himself.

"What the hell, Mike? You talked to me in sign, and now you're here. What the fuck are you doing? You could give us away with the movement and all!"

"Duke, the guys in the lead are not the ones, after all. They keep dropping a guy between them to confuse us. Look at number four and number six. Watch when they get to the switchback. They kneel, let one or two pass by, and then fall in like nothing ever happened. I'll watch the lead, and you watch the last one. We have time before they reach the top, so let's take the last one first and then the lead."

"Oh, hell, Mike, let's have some fun. Let's take the first. They'll all stop and kneel and wonder where the shot came from. They have to know it's from here someplace, and then, as they watch him roll down the hill like a sack of taters, I will work my way up the line. What do you say? I know, just the bad guys, but I have two mags, five each, and two left in this one plus the one in the chamber. Let me have some fun. We'll say we were just making sure, OK, spotter boss? What's your call?"

"OK, take them all in any order you like. If one breaks out running, then we know he's one of the leaders, for sure. So, yes, use all the thirteen rounds you have out there, and let's see if you can do it at a fast pace. No hopping around, OK?"

"Yep, OK. Let's go top to bottom until we have the ammo done in. Spotter, what's the clicks? Yes, OK, got it. Now windage. Yes, OK. Here we go, changing the clips. Use the last three for reserve, OK."

Pop! Pop! Pop-pop-pop-pop! Pop! Pop-pop-pop-pop!

"Hold up, boss. You see that one was hiding behind another? In fact, two were hiding behind them. Three in one shot—that's a record, is it not? Glad we did this. We could have missed them, for sure. I want to finish this."

"No, let's go. I'll go get the captain and meet you back there at the back door. But be careful. Those two have been alone a long time."

"Yup, see you there."

◆　◆　◆

"Duke? Duke?"
"Yes, what is it now?"

"The doctor is here. He will be ready in a few minutes. Are you sleepy yet?"

"Hell no, Doc. I'm trying to get out of this spot without getting killed."

◆ ◆ ◆

"Mike, I should shoot this dumb bastard. Look, he shot me in the top of my left shoulder. Missed everything, not bleeding much. Can I, Captain? Can I pop him here and now?"

"No, let me look, Duke. Sure is a good thing you wore your vest. Just a scratch. No need to shoot him."

"A scratch, you say, Captain? I can feel it's broken in there. A scratch for you—you're not the one shot. Dumb bastard, gave him the code word, and he returned it. When I sat up, he shot me anyway. What the hell, John? What the hell did you do that for?"

"Well, Duke, sir, my finger was frozen on the trigger. I knew it was one of you, but when I saw you, I went to let go of the trigger, and it just went off."

"Damn. Good thing you had the selector on single, not auto. Good thing for you, or I would have killed you for sure. Mike, what the hell do you want now? Yes, you can pack my shit. Thanks. Now, let's put some stuff on this so-called scratch, as it's bleeding again. Cap, we should leave him here to walk in our footprints and scoop up all the blood, so we won't be tracked by any of them. Just pick up every last drop, and put it in your helmet liner. Got that? What do you say, Cap, Mike?"

"Yes, John, do that. You know how to do that, don't you?"

"Yes, sir. Mike, he took my rifle. Duke took my rifle."

"Duke, his rifle."

"Not until he's in front of me can he have it back. OK by all of you, as I am now not in any trading mood, if you get my drift."

"What if he—"

"Allen, shut the fuck up. Who asked you? If any one comes up on us from behind, he better get it in gear and not get caught with his pants down. Thanks, Cap, that feels better. What do you think?"

"Bullet went clean through. Broke something in there. Tuck your arm inside your shirt, and let's get the hell out of here. We've been way too long now. If we don't saddle it up now, we won't make rendezvous point when we're supposed to be there."

"I can take lead for now, until the pain gets to me. By then, we should be clean, and we will make it, for sure. We can take a shortcut by the waterway and make good time."

◆ ◆ ◆

"Sir, wake up. Wake up, sir."

"What is it, orderly?"

"You were talking about being shot in your sleep. We could hear you swearing from down the hall."

"Sorry, mate. What time is it anyway?"

"It's somewhere almost three. You OK?"

"Yes, thanks. I'm OK."

We're having a great time in the old town tonight,
Yes, a great time in the old town tonight.

"If you don't go back to sleep, I will knock your ass out here and now."

"Doc, I am not the least bit sleepy, but go ahead and put the IV in anyway."

"Hoooweee! Testy, are we?"

"Sure as hell, Mike. Sure as hell."

◆ ◆ ◆

"Mike, this here shower is sure nice. How are you doing over there? Mike, what's wrong? What are you swearing at me for? We are safe now."

"Duke, you know. Doesn't it bother you? Shooting those guys and watching them suffer? Well, it does me. I hate it. I don't know why it

makes you so happy to do it. I see the smile on your face. How do you live with yourself?"

"Mike, I smile because I know that I just did a horrendous shot, and it makes me smile to think that I am pretty good at this shit. And if it weren't me, it would be someone else. And maybe they would be better at it, but I don't know that. Mike, we just follow orders. We don't make the war or the rules, but it's my job to bring you all back safe. And Mike, it was your job on this one to bring us all back safe, the pressure of it all. We are the best on the team, of any team, and we work well together, and that is why we are given these tough jobs. So just put that shit out of your head, and remember they want the best for the tough jobs, or they would let the SEALs do it, or some other team. We work well together. You're the best spotter in the army, and with that, you make me the best shot. Hell, Mike, I couldn't do it without you. I would never get the yardage right; I'd always be off—but not with you. You give me the edge. You are so exact with everything. So, Mike, please don't break up the team. Say we are a team forever."

"We are a team forever, and I won't be the one to break us up. But, Duke, you have to be honest with me, OK?"

"OK, Mike. What is it?"

"Tell me about this Tex guy you speak to, and for God's sake, please give up the singing. You're bad at it, and it just makes us all think we are following a crazy guy to hell. You always get us home, that's a given, but for God's sake, please don't do it. It makes the guys talk too much. To tell you the truth, it scares the hell out of them—and me some. But the captain is sure to have that shrink Ford lock you up. Then you will be the one to break the team up. That's all, Duke. Feel some remorse, if not for them, then for us, the team, to make us believe that you really are human inside, for sure. Is that too much to ask?"

"I hear you loud and clear there, Mike, loud and clear. But Tex, well, he is just my guy inside me whom I talk to, like my guardian angel. It's hard to explain very much about him here and now, but some day, when we are out of it for a long time, we will sit down and have that talk, if you still want that. I am bad, but are you any better? And I think most of the time I just sing to myself, not out loud, but you say all you guys can hear me. That is really disturbing to me—something for me to ponder. That makes me think that I am thinking out loud way too much. And for a sure bet, you guys think I am going crazy. With that said, I will do my darnedest to change all that, for sure. I ask you, my friend, that if I do start doing it without being aware, you use a code word, like mom to stop me. Is that fair with you? The last thing I want to do is have Cap send me to the funny house. You good with all that? And I really am not happy about the killing any more than you, but I do take great pride in the fact that, hell, I might just be the best shot the army has. That is why I sing and look happy, like back in sniper school, making the longest shot when no one else came close. And it's not just me—it's us, my friend, it's us. Mike, are we good now? Are you good?"

"Duke, yes, I'm OK now. It's just that all the killing, seeing a person up close, not like it was before with the long sniper shots and all. The sound, the look, as they gasp for that last second of life. It was a horrible thing, Duke. Well, anyway, I like being a spotter with you. And I guess I don't really—not far down, really—care about all this shit. Just that as my brother, I think it hurts too much to think that you really like to hurt people, that you take their last breath and breathe it for yourself. Guess that's what I don't stomach. Can't get my head around it. I just can't walk past that, brother—just can't do it. Not if you're happy with the pain and hurt. I know we didn't make the orders or have the rules bent. We just shoot who they tell us to. There is something to that, but still, brother, you don't have to sing and like it. Don't do it, Duke. Don't become their killing machine. It will eat us up. It just will—both of us."

"Yes, I know, Mike. I really don't like it, but what I do like is to think, 'Damn, that was a hell of a shot, and no one cares.' In my mind, I don't look at it like I shot a person. It's just an enemy, another target. I'm not trying to set any records. We took a stand, swore an oath, but that's not a story for us to tell. Let the guy out front get the glory. We, well, we, my brother, are here to help save lives. If we didn't do it, who would? It would get done, sure it would, but at what cost? For now, it's just another red, bloodstained rage in our minds, that's all. We will survive this, as we do all missions. So, Mike, you OK? Ready for some chow? Let's go, what do you say?"

So we went on leave as soon as we got back and had gone through our final debriefing. Things got good for Mike. He was soon back to his old self, but in my mind's eye, Tex and I could see there was a change. So one night over some cognac, we started talking. He had been with some ladies of the street and was feeling fine, and my wallet was feeling very thin.

"Mike, my brother, are you feeling good now? Well, good for you, my friend. So, if you want, I will now answer all your questions on how the last mission went down. The truth of the matter, not the cock and bull the brass hears, but just you and me, never to leave our lips again after we leave here. What do you say? Do you want the answers, or are you good with me now, as it is this moment? You know, when we get back, we have to go to the Philippines and train with their elite marines. That will be another three months of our lives living in the jungle. Are you ready for some more of that kind of stuff?"

"Yes, Duke, I'm ready, and I feel ashamed of the way I was on board the ship. Forgive me. You don't need to tell me anything you don't want to. I am fine, brother. Don't worry, it won't happen again!"

"Good, Mike. You scared me. Thought I was going to see you whisked off in one of those funny white jackets. It's not the way to get out of the army, for sure. You know that, brother. Not good at all. Not good. But one thing I must tell you: I do have—and you swear not to laugh at this or ever tell a soul, will you? OK, then—I really do have a guardian angel I can talk to. He tells me shit, like where the snipers are in the trees, the command center, the SEALs being there, dug in and ready for a good fight, and that Colonel Charlie was a snake. So I shot him in the ass. It didn't kill him, so he ran to his buddies, but he couldn't talk, so they—like John said—just shot the hell out of him.

Then a guy stood up and popped him in the head—his eye, it looked like—so I popped that guy with one of the last white rounds I had. I think it was someone who knew him, and I think he thought Charlie was a double. That's why they were being ambushed. The guys you met up with were the ones waiting for us at our stash. Colonel Charlie never thought about us not going back to get our food, water, and ammo. He was at a loss. So, yes, my angel talks to me and I to him. I know it sounds funny, but think back since you knew me, and all will be clear. The correct distance at sniper school, everything. My angel is Tex. He's my grandpa. That's right. He hears you and sometimes your thoughts, so don't weird out on me. OK?"

◆　◆　◆

"Dang, Doc, you said when you and the doctor put this stuff in my neck vein, it wouldn't hurt. Said I wouldn't feel a thing. You guys are bad at this."

◆　◆　◆

Well, we were very close after that. Mike never gave me any shit. He knew I was correct. He never heard Tex talk, but he knew that when I had that far-off look, I was talking to him. And Mike would say, "OK? Is the boss good with everything, Duke?" And I would say, "Hunky dory."

I don't remember how many more missions we were on. We were on the go so much of the time that it was like a nonstop parade between missions. We were in constant training, never with the same guys, but once in a while, we were all back together again. That was when I came to realize the mission was of the greatest importance anyway. So here we were, ready to go back and see the SEAL team again and do another nasty, as Mike would say, for the brass—and always with another Charlie. We began to think the only guys the brass wanted popped were our Colonel Charlies. They are the ones who knew too much, so the brass would let us go pop them. That's when Mike and I became a trio with Tex, on that last mission. We had more to do, but I told the brass I couldn't do it anymore. I had put too much of myself into every mission, was what I said, and there wasn't any more of me to give. Then the war was over, thank God. Then there was just a cold war to fight and, oh yes, the war on drugs. Seeing how I was already there, I was able to move to a private contractor.

I am the meanest old man in the meanest old world.
It's a mean old world, and I am the meanest old man.
I like to shoot you just to hear you cry.

◆　◆　◆

"Then, after all those years, we just ended up here. They just outgrew me, Doc. That was the whole of the matter—they just outgrew me. God dang it, Doc, this shit is stinging me like hell. My whole body is hur—"

EPILOGUE

"Hi, there. I'm here to speak with your bouncer. My name is Katie Wright."

"Yes, Katie. Well, now, there he is—under the stairway, sitting at his table."

"Hello, there. Did I hear you say Katie Wright? Are you a Pat Wright's, General Pat Wright's daughter?"

"Yes."

"How is the old man?"

"Good. Thank you for asking. He sent me here to fetch a bouncer. He said you knew him from the war days. And your name is?"

"Sorry, Katie. Didn't intend to be rude. My name is Tex."

AUTHOR BIOGRAPHY

Hank Dace was born and raised in the rural Northwest amid cowboys and country humor. After serving in the army, he returned home to attend college and start his own business. A longtime lover of knowledge, Dace enjoys creating stories from real-life observations and experiences. His favorite tales involve themes of love, loss, courage, and the human connection.

Made in the USA
Las Vegas, NV
04 November 2021

33698279R00128